Ms. McClelland's gritty and endearing heroine takes you for a wild ride through the Montana countryside filled with murder and intrigue.

—Sam Morton,
Winner of the Wyoming State Historical Society
Award for Historical Fiction

JIM CREEK HILL

A Marley Dearcorn Novel

JESSICA McCLELLAND

COLD RIVER STUDIO
NASHVILLE, TENNESSEE

Published by Cold River Studio, Nashville, Tennessee

No part of this publication may be reproduced, stored in retrieval system, or transmitted in any form or by any means, electronic, mechanical, photocopying, recording, or otherwise, without written permission of the publisher. www.coldriverstudio.com

First Edition: 2015

Printed in the United States of America
ISBN 978-0-9904986-3-6

For Michelle,
who is just as surprised as me that we made it this far.

JIM CREEK HILL

CHAPTER 1

I could tell she had been dead for hours. A slick sheen of dew coated her face, making her ghost-white skin gleam under the pale light of early sunrise. I knelt down next to her body in the dry ditch grass beside the bent highway reflector post and flicked aside her torn jacket to get a look at the damage. There was hardly any blood, but the little I could see told the story pretty plainly. Red trickled from both nostrils, stained her upper lip, and a small trace of spray from a single dying cough had spattered her chin.

From the way her left arm lay beside her, bent backwards and broken, it wasn't difficult to see that she'd been hit by a car. The fact that her legs looked like they were shattered only reinforced that conclusion. Her right leg in particular looked mangled from the impact. It was curled up next to her thigh in a way that would have been impossible had the bones been intact.

I scanned the ground, kneeling carefully on a clump of grass and doing what I could to avoid scuffing the tire marks in the dirt. I assumed the impressions were tire marks, or what was left of them anyway. The ground was damp now, but last night the soil had been dry and packed hard from many windblown days without rain. It didn't look to me like there were any recognizable tire impressions left. This morning's slight drizzle had produced just enough moisture to erase them.

The young woman was no stranger to me. In Killdeer, nobody was truly a stranger to anyone else. Secrets didn't keep in our tiny Montana town, and it wasn't a surprise to me that I knew this person lying dead on the side of the road.

Her name was Phoebe. She was twenty-three years old.

Aside from the few years I'd lived in Helena, working for the Fish and Wildlife branch office, all of my life had been spent watching the locals of my hometown go through their daily lives, struggle to make ends meet in a community that floundered economically, and generally do what they could to survive. I was about to celebrate my thirty-sixth birthday but I felt decades older than that. I'd known Phoebe all her life. I'd watched her grow into one of the most beautiful young women in Killdeer Valley. Like the other denizens of my small community, whenever I'd caught sight of her dashing from the grocery store, or hurrying to the post office, I pondered what it was that kept Phoebe chained to home. Her talents were generous. She wasn't simply a pretty girl. She was quick with a joke and her smile warmed a person to their toes. She was clever and her future was brimming with possibilities.

Well, it had been, before she'd been run down and left shattered beside the road, lying in the ditch weeds like some discarded rubbish thrown from the back of a pickup.

But her face was still perfect. Aside from the little bit of blood marring her delicate features, she looked as beautiful as always. Her long black hair blanketed the ground beside her cheek. Both eyes were open wide, looking like two sapphires set in alabaster. She stared up at the sky with a permanent expression of utter shock. It wasn't hard to guess that the last thing Phoebe Robinson had seen before dying was a pair of headlights.

I stood up and peered through the mist in both directions. We didn't usually get much fog in Killdeer, but when we did it was so thick even the field mice were left groping. U.S. Highway 89 out of Killdeer was totally deserted, and the lonely fall morning's lack of traffic was doing nothing for my sense of well-being. Living in cattle country taught you that daylight hours were precious, and 7:30 a.m. was typically considered a late start, even for October. There should have been someone out moving around, besides me, but straining my eyes in each direction didn't conjure up any telltale pinpricks of light signaling that another vehicle was coming. Somewhere beyond the fog sunrise was glowing through the misty air. In a matter of hours all the water vapor would burn off and our local sheriff would be able to see the whole scene clearly.

I reflexively reached back to gather up my strawberry blonde hair and loop it in a loose ponytail, and when my hand encountered the short crop instead, for the hundredth time I scolded myself for my forgetfulness. I'd cut my hair back to a style I hadn't worn since third grade. It was far too short now for ponytails. But it was easy. The last three weeks had brought me a deep desire for things that were easy.

I turned my back on Phoebe and opened the door of my black SUV. Inside the glove compartment was a cell phone. Down in the valley, cell phones were as useless as wearing high heels working on a hay wagon. But here, up on the hill leading north out of Killdeer and heading towards the closest town of consequence, the signal would be strong.

I flipped open the phone and pushed the power button until it chirped to life in my hand. When the screen winked that it was ready, I punched in numbers for the Killdeer sheriff station and held the phone to my ear.

He answered on the fourth ring.

"Shucraft."

I felt a flood of relief. "Loy, it's Marley."

"Marley?" he sounded surprised. "When did you get a cell phone?"

"Listen. I'm up on Jim Creek Hill. When's the soonest you can get here?"

The sheriff of Killdeer heaved a sigh and I could almost see his bloodshot eyes squeeze shut. As far as I knew, he still hadn't hired a new deputy and sleep was not something he got much of these days.

"Did you slide off the road? I told you not to drive so darn fast. That hill is dangerous, Hun."

"I didn't slide off the road. It's too warm to snow yet."

He slurped something beside the receiver. Probably coffee. Loy had been without a deputy sheriff for almost three months now. He kept himself jacked up on caffeine and sugar, and had lost ten pounds from handling midnight calls as well as the daily squabbles a typical small town sheriff had to contend with.

"Last week Steven Kimble rolled a trailer with two cutting horses in it up there," he said. "Damn I hated to shoot that mare."

"Loy, listen. This isn't a car wreck. Not exactly."

"Oh Christ, what now?" he said.

"It's Phoebe Robinson," I said.

My tone forced him into silence. After a long pause I reluctantly explained what I'd found. "It looks like she got blindsided while she was walking."

"Do we need an ambulance?" he asked quickly.

I grimaced. "We need the coroner."

"Dammit. Are you sure it's her?"

"I'm sure. I'll stay with the body until you get here. There's no need for sirens."

Loy and I had known each other since grade school, had dated briefly back in high school, and we shared a long and tattered history. Most of the time our friendship consisted of me getting into trouble and Loy trying to keep me from it. Sometimes he was successful. Usually he wasn't.

He hung up and for a moment I lingered with my ear pressed to the phone, listening to the drone of the dial tone.

When I punched the button to end the call I felt alone. More than that, I felt adrift.

Absently, I slid the cell phone inside my coat pocket instead of putting it back in the glove box. I was so unaccustomed to having a cell phone it was a nuisance to carry the thing. Since the signal in the valley was almost nonexistent, I just kept it in the car for road trips.

Not that I'd traveled anywhere further than the front porch of my house for the last three weeks. Going anywhere, socializing or seeing other people had been too much for me to deal with. The only reason I was standing on the side of the road at the moment was because I had to be out on this day. In two hours I would be sitting in an office listening to an attorney, and since I couldn't get out of the appointment, here I was, staring down at a dead girl.

My feet seemed to wander back to Phoebe's body of their own accord. As awful as it had been to see a person lying in the ditch beside the road, I was mostly numb to shock. Not numb, exactly. More like saturated.

My husband, Leif Gable, had been killed in a plane crash three weeks ago, and I still hadn't been able to accept that he was gone. We had been married in August, and by the end of September I had become a widow. It was a little too much for me to process.

Our romance had proceeded at a blinding pace. Just as suddenly as I'd become the happiest woman in the world, all that joy had been snatched from me and I'd found myself waking up in an empty bed every morning, shivering from nightmares.

As short-lived as our marriage had been, the sudden void left after Leif had been killed was worse than any pain I'd ever experienced before. I'd always considered myself a strong woman, but dragging myself out of bed that morning to drive to my appointment with Leif's attorney in Billings had taken all my strength. I'd cried so much over the last few weeks it felt like my eyes were broken.

And now, stretched out on the cold ground, another young woman had been cut down on the cusp of a life full of promise. It was true that sorrows came not as singles, but in packs.

I chastised myself for being selfish. At least I was still alive.

"What happened to you, Phoebe?" I squatted down, my lace-up Ropers pressing into the damp soil, so I could get another good look at the ground beside her body.

The weeds were dead and brown, crusty from the heat of a dusty fall. Two rows of compressed rough bristle grass clearly showed where the wheels of a vehicle had plowed off the road and left their mark. I stood up again and peered through the mist in both directions. The fog was too thick to see very far, so I walked down the side of the road in the direction the car or truck that had plowed into Phoebe had come from. After a few yards I stopped and searched the weeds for anything helpful.

Being a librarian didn't qualify me to assist in an investigation, not by any standard. But in my recent past I'd been caught up in situations that had forced me to get involved with homicides and unsolved crimes, and since I'd been close to Sheriff Shucraft and I still was, I knew he wouldn't twist off at the seams if I looked around and offered my opinion.

The first thing I noticed was the reflector post. It was bent at a ninety-degree angle, and had been flattened to the ground with incredible force. The next post was in the same condition. Since the reflector posts were set in the ground at least ten feet from the pavement, it was obvious whoever had been driving the vehicle that killed Phoebe had swerved from the road. Either that or they had fallen asleep at the wheel. Or been too drunk to know what they were doing.

I jogged the next hundred feet and was a little surprised to see that the next post was flattened as well. Three reflector posts run down? Even a drunk or a sleepy driver would have managed to pull the vehicle back onto the highway after hitting three posts in a row. Unless that driver had completely passed out, which I had to consider a possibility.

I turned to look back at where Phoebe's body was in relation to where I stood, and although I couldn't see that far through the roiling mist, I could see the glow from the headlights of my SUV.

"Last night it was clear," I said, talking to myself. "The fog came in early this morning. She would have been visible from here."

I walked further down the road, but the fourth post away from the body was still standing, so the driver had swerved off of the pavement just after it. I headed back towards the first downed reflector and scanned the ground carefully until I saw the sign of a tire mark leaving the pavement and flattening the dead grass.

Two wide streaks marred the vegetation where the driver had turned the wheel sharply and driven down the shoulder onto the dirt. If they had tried that maneuver anywhere else on this stretch of highway between Killdeer and the next town, they would have rolled their vehicle and probably not walked away from the crash. But up here, up on Jim Creek Hill, the ditch was shallow and smooth. It was a product of the steep climb. We called it Hamburger Hill sometimes, because it was the deadliest hill in

Killdeer County. The abrupt climb up, coupled with the steep drop on the other side, created the perfect limited-sight roadway that was responsible for more accidents and head-on collisions than any other paved surface in Killdeer.

But Phoebe was at the top, not over the rise in the blind spot on the other side, and so it was a safe guess whoever hit her had been able to see her shape outlined in his headlights.

This was looking less and less like an accident to me.

I headed back towards my SUV trying to picture it in my mind. This was not the first time my path had crossed that of a victim of violence. As usual, questions I couldn't answer swirled inside my head.

Where was her car? Had she been walking on the side of the road due to a flat tire or some other mechanical trouble? Or had she been in a car with someone else and gotten out?

Either way, Killdeer was a long walk from Jim Creek. I certainly wouldn't want to be alone on this road at night. Whatever circumstances had led her to be here, they could not have been good.

By the time I reached my SUV I spotted a pair of headlights easing off the highway.

Loy parked his sheriff's truck behind my vehicle and through the mist I could see him key the mike on his radio.

I shut off the engine to my SUV, not needing the headlights anymore, and waited for him.

He climbed out of his truck with weariness. His face looked heavy.

"Are you alright?"

His question covered a lot of territory. Loy had been the one who'd delivered the news of my husband's death. It was an understatement to say that the sheriff and I had been through a lot together.

I shrugged. "As good as can be expected."

"Where is she?"

I took him to Phoebe, nodded at the ground. "There's three reflector posts down, and a clear tire track leaving the pavement back down the slope."

Loy examined the area carefully. "Someone swerved to hit her *on purpose?*"

"Maybe," I said, not wanting to influence him in either direction. "Probably."

"Why probably?" He squinted at me.

"There aren't any swerve marks just before the body," I said, pointing down. "At least, not that I can tell. The driver didn't seem too inclined to try and miss."

Loy made a sound deep in his throat like a growl. He studied her body the same way that I had, flipping aside her jacket and examining the unnatural angle of her limbs.

He rested his forehead in his palm for a moment. "Or they were too drunk to realize they weren't on the pavement."

Like many residents of Killdeer, Phoebe wore old, worn-out clothing that had come either from a secondhand store or a farm and ranch supply warehouse. Her sneakers were still mostly new, but starting to show signs of wear. Her jacket was heavy, made of canvas and had probably once been brown but was now more tan from multiple washes. The tops of her thighs looked more white than blue, the jeans were so threadbare. The only jewelry I could see was a tiny pair of Black Hills gold earrings shaped like miniature leaves. They were probably the most expensive things she owned.

"That smell can't be her already." Loy wrinkled his nose and looked from side to side with irritation.

I smelled it too and glanced around, searching for the source of the stench of old death. "There. Just at the base of the fence."

He followed my gaze and nodded when he saw the carcass of a long-dead deer, crumpled at the foot of a wooden fence post a few yards from us. It was more skeleton than animal, probably dead at least a month, and most likely hit by a truck. Bits of flesh still hung from the head, mummified. It looked eerie, staring back at us through the fog.

"Marley, I wouldn't dare tell anyone else this, since I'm elected, but sometimes I really hate this job."

"I'm sorry, Loy. She had such a good life ahead of her."

The sheriff stood beside me and draped a heavy paw over my shoulder, giving me a supportive hug. "Phoebe? Honestly, I'm surprised she made it this long."

I gave him a shocked look, but he ignored it and pulled me away from the body before I could ask him what he meant. "Hun, there isn't anything you can do here. You should just go on home."

"I need to be in Billings in an hour and forty minutes," I told him.

"You going to see Leif's attorney again?" he asked.

"Yes. This is the last time. I think the will and his son's trust are all settled at last. There is just one more thing I have to finish up."

"When are you going back to work?" he asked tentatively.

I grumbled. "In a couple weeks, I guess. I'm not ready yet."

"Maybe this isn't a good idea, but why don't you come to dinner with me and Wendy tonight? I don't like it that all you do is sit at home by yourself. You need to be around people again."

My mouth refused to smile, even though I knew he was being kind. "I'll think about it, Loy. Thanks."

We stood in silence on the side of the empty roadway for a moment. The wind rustled what was left of the pale grass, making a sound like a waterfall made of sand. I shook my head once and toed the tired asphalt with my boot. It crumbled a bit, worn out from too many years without proper maintenance.

"What did you mean?" I asked abruptly. "You didn't think she would make it this long?"

The sheriff shook his head. "Nothing. Forget it, Marley. It's not like you put in an application to be my deputy."

"What if I did?" I asked.

He stared at me without even a hint of a smile. "I wouldn't hire you. Not in a million years. Hun, you've seen enough death to last two lifetimes."

My eyes blurred with sudden tears. I managed to keep them from spilling over, but only with effort.

"For once, I'm not going to argue with you, Loy."

He turned to the gruesome task of mapping the scene and I left him to it.

I drove away, leaving him to pick up the pieces of another shattered life, and as my headlights peered through the mist all I could think about was the expression of complete shock on Phoebe's face. Her pretty mouth was forever frozen in an *Oh* of surprise, almost like she couldn't believe what had just happened.

I selfishly believed I knew exactly how she had felt.

CHAPTER 2

"Would you prefer to be alone?" Mr. Toomey asked.

I stared at the tape player on the table and suddenly wished I'd brought my best friend, Irene Baker, along with me.

Or my father. Or anyone for that matter.

Facing this task alone wouldn't be as easy as I'd originally believed.

My husband had been an international businessman, and living in tiny Killdeer, Montana, population 901, had not been easy for him. He was required to travel often, and simply out of necessity he had become an accomplished pilot and purchased a twin-engine six-seat airplane so he could travel when necessary. Leif had been IFR rated, which meant he could fly at night, using only instruments. It was not something he was necessarily proud of. Being a skilled pilot simply made his busy life easier. In more ways than I could count, my husband had been an extraordinary man. One of the things that made him so extraordinary was the fact that he didn't think of himself as anything other than a regular person.

A box of tissues sat at my elbow. I glanced up at the sharp, unwavering blue gaze of Mr. Toomey and managed to shake my head. "No, I'm alright."

13

"As you know," he said with a cautious tone, "under normal circumstances this recording would not be in my possession. This is a copy of the radio communication between Mr. Gable and the air traffic controller in Denver. I was able to get this from the NTSB 'go team' investigating the plane crash. It is highly irregular."

Mr. Toomey arched an eyebrow. He was warning me in lawyer-speak not to talk about this to anyone else. I had no idea how he had managed to get ahold of the recording, since the NTSB representative had specifically told me on the telephone a few days ago that the report on Leif's plane crash would take six weeks to complete.

"I can allow you to listen to this recording," he said. "But it cannot leave this room. I hope you can understand."

"I do."

Under different circumstances, I would have liked Mr. Toomey. He was young. Too young to be the lead attorney for an international businessman of Leif's caliber, in my opinion. Leif had always referred to him as Eric. One glance at him and it would be easy to mistake him for a capable Harvard graduate student, not a junior partner in a cutting-edge law firm. But Leif had trusted him implicitly. After three weeks of watching him in action, I was beginning to understand why Leif had relied on Mr. Toomey.

His red hair was trimmed neatly. He wore a suit two years ahead of local fashion. It was slate gray with a perfect cut, and his pale blue silk tie was knotted expertly. He had a habit of uttering phrases in Latin occasionally.

Leif hadn't hired Eric Toomey to be his local attorney in Montana because the kid looked good in a suit and quoted Cicero. Mr. Toomey got things done. He was short on words and long on results, and my thinking of him as a kid simply because he was a decade younger than me was perhaps a bit condescending.

Not long after Leif and I had been married, he'd instructed me to sign a stack of documents taller than a three-finger shot of whiskey. I hadn't read them at the time, since trusting Leif with all things financial and legal had been easier than trying to decipher the stuff myself. Now I was wishing I'd gone through every page with my husband, because now it was too late. I was still in the process of navigating the labyrinth of all my new responsibilities, and Mr. Toomey was my only guide.

The week after the plane crash, Mr. Toomey had walked me through the process of dealing with Leif's will, and the trust fund for his son, step by ponderous step, explaining to me that I was now responsible for managing the money in the trust. Scott wasn't Leif's biological son, but he was his boy in all other ways. If Scott had one weakness, it was his mother, Leif's firebrand ex-wife, Virginia. Scott was more of a parent to his mother than she had ever been to him, and he found it very difficult to say no to her whenever she asked him for money. When he had been alive, Leif had managed Scott's finances by paying for specific things, like school, instead of simply handing over cash to his son. Now that he was gone, Scott would have access to a large sum of cash for the first time in his life. Leif had handled that issue by appointing me to handle Scott's allowance. His son would be taken care of financially, and in such a way that his mother wouldn't be able to bilk the cash with a tear and a whimper, like she had done in the past.

Feelings were tender on that issue. Virginia had been furious after the contents of Leif's will had been made public. She had thrown a fit after hearing of the arrangement, that Scott's trust would be managed by me, and the office secretary had told me she'd seen Mr. Toomey sitting at his desk, holding the receiver away from his head to avoid the worst of the diatribe, a look of intense disapproval set firmly on his face.

It was probably for the best that Virginia lived in Chicago. On the day she was told about the financial arrangements I could have sworn I'd heard the shouting all the way back in Killdeer. She wouldn't be receiving a dime from Leif's estate.

And Leif's estate, as it turned out, had been considerable.

On my fourteenth birthday, my father had surprised me by giving me a new midnight-blue blouse with a proper stand-up collar and still possessing all its original buttons. I'd been thrilled. The next day I'd discovered the Goodwill price tag still tucked inside the sleeve. He'd somehow forgotten to take it out. The beautiful shirt had cost a total of $2.99, secondhand, and I'd experienced a flash of shame that we were so poor even a small thing like a new shirt was out of reach.

But it wasn't as if anyone else in Killdeer had money to throw around. I'd grown up poor, but so had everyone else around me. We were nothing special.

To say that I was ill-equipped to deal with this sudden windfall was an understatement. The only reason I was keeping it together was because of Mr. Toomey and his calm instruction. By anyone's standards I was now a wealthy woman.

I would have traded it all for just one more day with my husband.

The thought brought my gaze back to the tape recorder sitting on the desk. I cleared my throat with more conviction than I actually felt.

"Play it."

He dutifully pressed the button, and walked out of the room quietly. I'd insisted to him that I was fine, but obviously he knew better and preferred to let me have privacy.

The door closed softly behind me and I stared out the window, letting my eyes lose focus. A sudden squawk of radio static erupted from the recorder, making me jump, and I heard Leif's voice.

I thought my heart would shatter from it, but I kept listening because I needed to know what had really happened.

"This is Baron 545 November Foxtrot, to Denver Center now on 125.35 checking in at 17,000 feet, 010 on the heading."

A second voice responded, and I realized I was hearing Leif contact the Denver control center and a female air traffic controller was responding. The woman's voice was smooth and deep, so relaxed she almost sounded bored.

"545 November Foxtrot, we have you loud and clear."

545 November Foxtrot had been the tail number for Leif's airplane, a twin-engine Baron Beechcraft. Several minutes passed by with no sound at all. Then the radio chirped to life again.

"Center, this is 545 November Foxtrot. I'm having a problem with my right engine. Fuel pressure is acting up and I seem to be losing power."

"545 November Foxtrot, I understand you are experiencing engine problems with your right engine. Please confirm, and advise of your intentions."

"Center, affirmative on the right engine problem. Now seeing traces of what appears to be smoke coming from right engine. I need to get this airplane on the ground."

"545 November Foxtrot do you wish to declare an emergency? Please advise."

"Affirmative. I am declaring an emergency. I show my nearest airport at r / 9 o'clock and 12 miles. Telluride. Can you confirm?"

"545, Roger Telluride as your closest airport. Suggest heading of 270 directly to the airport."

"Roger Center, 270 on the heading, descending now through 16,000 feet

for right downwind to runway 9 Telluride. Showing flames now trailing out of my right engine."

"545 November Foxtrot I show you on track for the right downwind approach to runway 9, Telluride descending now through 14,000 feet and 7 miles out, suggest you try to maintain 11,000 feet until established on the downwind. I have alerted emergency crews to stand by at Telluride. Suggest you broadcast your approach on CTAF 123.0. Winds at Telluride on my last report from 040 at 30 miles per hour, gusting to 40."

"Center I am entering an extended right downwind for 9, will jump to CTAF now and then report back."

"Roger 545."

The radio chirped once and I could hear a click as Leif switched frequencies.

"Telluride traffic, this is Baron 545 November Foxtrot, 5 miles out on high right downwind to 9, descending now through 12,000 feet on an emergency descent on one engine, any traffic in the area please allow me direct access to runway. Switching back to Center."

Another click told me he had switched back to the Denver controller.

"Center I am back with you now at 10,000 feet, and starting my right base for 9. Gear down and locked. Lots of flames coming from that right engine now. Prop feathered."

"We have you 545."

"Center, I'm right base for final now for runway 9. Gear down and showing three green."

"545 your track looks good but altitude is low. Suggest you maintain altitude."

"Center I'm advising Telluride."

"545 maintain your altitude!"

"Telluride traffic, this is Baron 545 November Foxtrot. I'm on final on one engine for runway 9, all traffic stand clear. Center I am back with you, now on short final for 9. Lots of gusts. Now on full power to maintain altitude. Showing 9,000 feet."

"545 you are too low. I show you one-half mile out."

"It's going to be dicey, Center. I can't get any more altitude."

A loud squawk erupted from the player and the woman's voice, frantic now, broke into the static.

"This is Denver Center to Telluride tower. You have a twin-engine aircraft approaching runway 9. Do you have a visual?"

"Denver Center, this is Telluride. We cannot confirm visual yet. Stand by."

"545 what is your altitude? 545 November Foxtrot respond. What is your altitude?"

"Denver Center this is Telluride. There is no aircraft on the runway. We can confirm. There is no aircraft on runway 9."

"This is Denver Center. 545 respond. What is your altitude?"

"Denver Center, this is Telluride. Please advise."

"Telluride, this is Denver Center. Be advised I have lost transponder for 545 November Foxtrot. Repeat. Have lost transponder for 545. Do you have an aircraft on the runway?"

"Denver Center, we can confirm there is no aircraft on runway 9. We have visual on 9 and . . . there's nobody out there."

The recording ended in static. My hand touched the player of its own accord and pressed the rewind button. I played the tape again, listening without breathing.

It felt like I was sitting in the cockpit with him. Every muscle in my body was clenched with the effort of willing the plane to climb up over the wall of rock at the base of the runway and land safely.

But that's not what had happened. Leif's plane had hit the rock wall below the runway in Telluride, Colorado, and exploded on impact. The NTSB investigators, according to my friend Sheriff Shucraft, had stated it bluntly. They had told Loy to relay to Leif's widow that it had happened very quickly, and he probably didn't have time to feel a thing.

As if that was supposed to comfort me.

I played the tape a third time. When it stopped, I felt a hand rest on top of my shoulder and Mr. Toomey set a slender glass of water next to me.

I hadn't realized tears were streaming down my face. The top of my blouse was damp. I dabbed my neck and cheeks with a tissue, stemming the tide.

Mr. Toomey resumed his seat across the table and rubbed his forehead with one hand.

A jagged pain in my chest reminded me of the here and now and I managed to slide the recorder across the table. "Thank you for this. I know it probably wasn't easy to get."

"Mr. Gable was not simply my client." He carefully stowed the recorder inside an aged leather briefcase.

I managed to sip the water he'd given me. It was still not easy to breathe.

"Eventually the NTSB will allow you access to a copy of this after they have completed their investigation. I suggest you affect the emotion of surprise and sadness upon hearing it," he said.

"That won't be hard," I told him.

"Of course," he said. "I needn't tell you that."

"I don't suppose you know anything about the investigation?" I asked.

His glance was cautious. "They will report the cause of the crash that killed your husband was a massive mechanical failure, and not a result of pilot error, as so often is the case. His right engine literally disintegrated mid-flight. It wasn't his fault. Mr. Gable was an exceptional pilot."

"Mr. Gable was an exceptional everything," I said.

He was silent, watching me with those sharp blue eyes and an unreadable expression. "I will not utter some banal platitude in an attempt to offer you comfort. But might I say this? It is to my immense relief that you recognized, and appreciated, what a just, honorable and deserving person he was."

"Didn't everyone?" I had never met a person who hadn't loved Leif.

"Fortunately you were insulated from most of the undesirable characters he was forced to associate with. There were a select few, might I refer to them as *scumbags*, that Mr. Gable was not popular with."

I wiped a damp palm on my slacks. "I know he worked as a forensic accountant for the government sometimes. He warned me that a few of the corporate criminals he helped to catch were not very nice people."

Mr. Toomey blinked. "I'm not referring to them. For the most part they were chump change in the scumbag department. I'm talking about the men from Wall Street. You will never find a bigger contingent of wretched thieves."

I managed a half smile. "That's what Leif always said."

We both stared at the vast oak tabletop. I absently spun the wedding ring on my left hand, letting my fingers play over the row of diamonds. Sometimes the ring Leif had given me felt like the only real thing left in my whole life.

"I must say, Ms. Dearcorn, you are managing to cope with this situation quite well," Mr. Toomey remarked.

I hadn't taken Leif's last name, something I sorely regretted at the moment. I was still Marley Dearcorn, and that fiercely independent part of me would always stay intact. But right now my humbler, sadder side was wishing I'd become Mrs. Gable instead.

"I'll fall apart in the car on the way home." I wiped the corners of my eyes slowly.

Mr. Toomey straightened in his chair. The expensive leather creaked. "I will maintain this copy of the recording between Mr. Gable and the Denver control tower in my personal files. If you feel the need to revisit the recording at any time, I will leave explicit instructions that you be allowed access to a conference room and the tape whenever you so wish. It may seem a bit graphic to some, but to me, I can fully understand the desire to maintain that connection with a loved one."

There was nothing else for me to say. "Thank you. That's very . . . considerate."

He stood up and extended his hand.

I shook it purely on reflex. Honestly, the past three weeks I'd hardly been aware there were other people on the planet at all. Mr. Toomey had seemed to recognize that, and this was the first physical contact we'd had since I'd met him.

"If you need anything at all, please do not hesitate to call me. I will continue to respond to the letters of condolence that we are still receiving from Mr. Gable's far-flung business associates. He was highly regarded in the international business community, and news of his death is still reaching the more remote areas where he was known. Also, I will continue to monitor any financial correspondence that we receive. Be reassured, there is precious little for you to concern yourself with. Mr. Gable was quite thorough, and you can rely on me to handle any situations that may crop up."

"I appreciate everything you have done for me, Mr. Toomey."

He placed a hand over his heart, a very chivalrous gesture. "Amicitias immortales esse opportet. Friendships should be immortal."

I managed a smile before leaving, and for some reason the thought of being stuck in an elevator was more than I could stand so I navigated the empty stairwell back out to the busy parking lot and climbed inside my vehicle with relief.

It must have been close to noon before I thought it was safe for me to drive again. Hearing Leif's voice had shaken me to the core. No more tears came. All I felt was a horrible, hollow shell where my heart had once been.

I shifted in the seat, feeling something pressing against my back with a sharp pressure. Reaching inside my jacket, I fumbled around until my hand closed over the cell phone I'd stashed there earlier.

The phone was silver, generic-looking and compact. It wasn't even mine. The person who had given it to me was also long gone. Shortly before I'd married Leif, I'd gone through a torrid, intense relationship with a man named Finn. He instigated our breakup, but after word had gotten out I was engaged, Finn hadn't taken it well. Which was another way to say that his head had practically exploded. When it came to Angus Finn, the only way I could think of to describe our past relationship was to call it confusing.

I traced a finger over the smooth surface of the phone, recalling the day Leif and I had been married. Finn had come to the wedding, a simple ceremony performed in the back yard. My new husband had shocked me by pulling Finn aside and insisting that the two of them have a private chat. At the time I had imagined Leif was warning Finn to keep his distance from me and let me go on, try to find some sort of happiness. But as I'd watched them from a distance, not able to hear what was being said, Leif had pulled out an envelope from inside his sport coat and handed it to Finn with determination. I remembered Finn's eyes were as wide as silver dollars, and he had tried to refuse the envelope. But Leif had persisted. Finally, Finn had accepted it and left the party, grim-faced and solemn.

My relationship with Finn had ended badly, but we had somehow managed a cautious friendship in spite of that fact. When I learned that Finn was quitting his job and leaving Killdeer for good only a few days after I'd married, I felt hurt, in spite of the celebration. I couldn't help but think some sort of bargain had been agreed to between my new husband and my old flame, but for the life of me I couldn't imagine what it was. What had been in that envelope?

I probably wouldn't ever know the answer to that question.

Finn had given me this cell phone the day he'd left Killdeer, and as usual, his last words to me had been cryptic and evasive. He'd told me repeatedly that he could not see me at all, but when he handed me the cell phone he'd spelled out, slowly, a single word. I-C-E.

I learned later that it stood for In Case of Emergency.

Out of curiosity I flipped open the little silver cell phone and scrolled to the contact list. Only one number was listed there. No name was associated with it.

I stared at it, not believing it was any sort of phone number I'd ever seen before. The first time I'd seen the number I'd thought it was a date. November 27th. But that didn't make any sense. It was too long to be a date. It began with 011, followed by the number 27 and then a series of seven digits. Had I been curious enough about it in the past I would have looked it up online to see what it really was, but at the moment I simply needed something to distract myself, so I studied it, thinking.

Was it his number? Finn was not American. He was originally from South Africa, and folks were always making the mistake of assuming he was British, since the accents sounded similar. Maybe it was nothing more than his phone number in South Africa. All this time I'd most likely been overthinking things, as usual.

I punched the dial button and held the phone to my ear. A series of beeps was followed by a click, and a woman's voice, perky and cheerful, answered.

"Cheers. Hiser."

I froze, staring out my windshield, trying to think of something to say. Someone had actually *answered*.

"Um, hello? Could I speak to Finn, please?"

The pause was legendary. "Finn. You mean Angus?"

I swallowed. "Yes. Sorry."

She coughed. "And which bird is this? You aren't Tracy, are you?"

"No. I'm Marley."

"Marley? That's a new one. Listen, Chopsticks, Finn's not in."

"I'm sorry. This was a mistake. So sorry to have bothered you."

"Wait—"

I slapped the phone shut as fast as I could. What a stupid thing to do.

This was not an emergency. And whoever the woman was, it was pretty clear Finn was her problem now.

I shut the power off and tossed the cell phone back inside the glove box where it belonged. One weak moment could always lead me into an embarrassing situation. Reaching out to friends had been so difficult since Leif had died. Most of the time, unless it was Irene or my father, I hated talking to people. They just stared at me with that infuriating look of pity on their faces. More than once I had to physically walk away to avoid punching someone in the nose. I hated that people felt sorry for me and were so awkward when they spoke to me. I had known for some time my grief was filling me with anger, so I kept myself to myself, to prevent any social mishaps.

"Too late now," I said, starting the engine of my car and heading back towards Killdeer.

CHAPTER 3

Just outside of Parkman, the closest town of consequence to Killdeer, I noticed my fuel light blink on.

Fortunately for me, the Gas N Dash was only five miles from Parkman and I could fill up there, and avoid the crush of ranchers and the high school lunch bunch crowd at the Sinclair station back inside the city limits.

I was a little surprised to see Loy's sheriff truck parked at the Gas N Dash, but this station was only about six miles from the crime scene where I'd last seen him, so he was probably interviewing locals to see if they had witnessed anything the previous night.

The gas pump had finally been upgraded to accept credit cards, so I could fuel up without going inside the store.

As the pump ticked away, laboring to separate me from as much money as possible, my eyes wandered the parking lot of the convenience store. A little red Volkswagen Golf caught my eye. The car was small, a two-door compact, and ancient. It had to be twenty years old, and maybe more. Rust had eaten holes in the wheel wells. One huge dent marred the driver's side door.

That wasn't why it caught my eye, though. It was surrounded by yellow crime scene tape. I frowned and stared at it, wondering.

"It's Phoebe's car."

Startled, I glanced behind the gas pump and saw a middle-aged woman hunched over the windshield wash bucket. She was watching me watching the car. I hadn't noticed her before. She'd been working, emptying out the buckets that hung on the side of the gas pump and held the squeegees used for the ever-necessary bug removal ritual all Montanans had to perform.

"The red Volkswagen?" I asked.

The woman stood up, her curled mass of thick blonde hair looking out of place atop her plump body. She looked like she had been overly familiar with cigarettes most of her adult life. Lines creased her face.

"Phoebe didn't have the cash to drive home last night," the woman said.

"She ran out of gas," I said with confusion, "at a gas station?"

Even as stingy as most folks around Killdeer tended to be, surely someone would have been nice enough to cough up two bucks to at least get a young woman home at night.

"She's worked graves for two summers, now," the woman said. "But it's never enough. Phoebe scrimped. But this wasn't the first time she had to walk home."

"She worked here at the Gas N Dash?" I asked. "And she worked last night?"

The woman nodded with a grave expression. She gave a half sob, jerking a coiled water hose fiercely to straighten it out. "Sheriff's in talking to the owner now. I didn't really need to come out here and clean these buckets, but I couldn't stand listening to it."

"Listening to them talk about Phoebe?" I asked.

"Listening to Adam badmouth the girl."

"Did you know Phoebe?" I asked.

The woman honked her nose into a stained tissue. She shoved

it back up her shirtsleeve. "She was a sweet girl. Makes me sick, what Adam had against her, and I didn't feel like I could just sit in there and listen to him tell the sheriff what a troublemaker she was. Phoebe was a hard worker."

"You said this wasn't the first time she ran out of gas and had to walk home. When was the last time that happened?" I asked.

The gas pump had clicked off and I dutifully removed the nozzle, trying not to spill any drops of gasoline on my shoes.

"Oh, couple weeks ago, I'd say," the woman said. "She could always get a ride with someone, even at six in the morning after her shift ended. Usually someone from the Big Bear would stop and give her a lift. But last night she clocked out at three. Marianne, she's the morning girl, well she told me Phoebe started walking about a quarter after, said she'd come get her car later. I guess she never caught a ride."

The Big Bear was a local coal mine at least an hour's drive from Killdeer. Some of the hardier residents of the valley commuted. But the shifts were probably not over at three a.m. and it was no surprise Phoebe hadn't been picked up by one of the miners.

Killdeer was at least fifteen miles from the Gas N Dash. I frowned, staring down the road, calculating the daunting distance. "That's a long way to hoof it."

The woman's name tag said *Betty* in bright red letters. Her eyes were so bloodshot they matched the name tag. "I told her she couldn't keep doing that. But her mom's a drunk, and I always thought it was probably safer for Phoebe to hitchhike than it was to call her mom to come get her."

I felt my jaw tighten. I knew Louise Robinson. She was a notorious alcoholic who had crashed her hulking Buick on more than one occasion. For me, drunk driving was intensely personal. My mother had been killed by a drunk driver when I was only seven. To me, it was the ultimate act of pure selfishness. I completely understood Phoebe's reluctance to telephone her mother for a ride, and the fact that she would take her chances hitching a ride home rather than rely on her mother told me a lot. Phoebe was intensely independent and stubborn, and her mother was a worthless parent.

Even though Phoebe was twenty-three years old and an adult, she'd obviously been forced to rely on her mother for cheap rent to survive. The two of them shared a dilapidated mobile home on the outskirts of Killdeer in a small trailer park we all affectionately called "The Burbs." There wasn't anything suburban about the trailer park. It was the last stop on the road of poverty, and once you parked your wagon there, you usually never made it out.

Life was not always kind, even to those who struggled and weren't quitters.

"Betty, what does Adam have against Phoebe?" I asked.

She shot a glance towards the door of the Gas N Dash. Nobody lingered there and she answered me without taking her eyes off the store. "Well, I shouldn't be saying this, but she wouldn't sleep with him."

I felt a blast of chill air from the north and shoved my hands inside my jacket pockets. "Did you tell that to Loy?"

She laughed. "You bet I did. I don't even care if Adam fires me. The sheriff should know when someone's telling him a string of lies because it's personal."

The early morning fog had cleared away and the long road was visible in both directions. The Gas N Dash was, literally, in the middle of nowhere. Parkman wasn't visible from here. And Killdeer was a twenty-minute drive to the southwest. It was the picture of isolation.

If Phoebe had been the target of a jealous boyfriend, or a jilted Romeo, she would have been an easy mark.

"What kind of a boss schedules a pretty young girl to work graveyards in a place like this?" I asked.

"The kind who knows a pretty young girl who is desperate enough to work it," Betty said.

"Do you know who the last person was she talked to before she started walking?" I asked.

Betty hung up the freshly rinsed soap buckets and filled them with water, not answering until the suds had reached the lip. "I have no idea. The same bunch of losers who always come wandering in during the graveyard."

"So the same people come in here every night?" I asked.

"Like they have been called by the Queen of the Dammed," she said.

My expression must have shifted to confused. Betty huffed with impatience. "You know. Vampires? The sort who only come out at night?"

"I get it. The living dead," I said.

"They aren't really vampires," Betty told me. "There's no such thing. The guys who come in here at night are just a bunch of freaks."

I folded my wallet back inside my jacket pocket and thanked Betty for her time. She was busy with an industrial push broom, clearing off the fueling area, obviously trying to find something to occupy her so she wouldn't be forced to go back inside and man the counter while Loy interviewed her boss.

It was none of my business, but I found myself wandering to the little red Volkswagen and peering inside.

The cracked interior of the car was black, smudged and worn. It was a stick shift, and the steering wheel was wrapped with an improvised cover that looked like nothing more than a piece of rawhide that had been duct-taped on by someone who wasn't very crafty. In Montana during a long hot summer, a black steering wheel would be a scorcher.

The floor of the car was littered with the usual suspects. Fast food wrappers, a soda can. The windshield was cracked.

The backseat held a sleeping bag, wadded up and stuffed behind the back of the passenger's side seat. A flat sofa cushion rested on top of it. It looked to me like Phoebe had spent more than one night inside the tiny car.

Even on my worst days I'd never been forced to sleep in my old Honda. It was becoming painfully clear to me that I'd known Phoebe Robinson, but only on a superficial level. Her hardships were a revelation.

"Marley, whatcha doin'?"

I straightened up and came face-to-face with Loy Shucraft.

I held a fist to my mouth and coughed. "Nothin', Sheriff."

"You see the tape on this car, right?" he asked stiffly.

"Yup."

"I thought you had to go see a man about a horse?" he asked.

Loy was steering me away from the Volkswagen with one big hand while he slid his brown baseball cap off his forehead with the other. Loy was the only Killdeer sheriff in living memory who had worn ball caps instead of cowboy hats. There were a few residents of my tiny hometown who flat refused to vote for him simply for that reason alone.

"I just left the attorney's office and needed to top off the tank," I said.

"Sheriff, just one more thing, if you don't mind?" said a female voice behind us.

I saw Loy close both eyes and he stopped, dropped his chin to his chest and turned around reluctantly. "Yes, Miss Bloom?"

"Did you say the victim was found at dawn or was she killed

at that time?"

I turned to see a reed-thin woman with severely straight black hair holding a memo pad. A large camera dangled from her neck.

"She was discovered at dawn," Loy said.

Miss Bloom jotted a note. "You didn't give me the name of the person who first found the body." It sounded like a reprimand.

"No, I didn't," he said.

I lifted my hand slightly. "I found her."

Loy reached over and shoved my hand back to my side. "This isn't important information."

The woman, obviously a reporter, fixed her slate gray eyes on me. "And could I have your full name? Spell it please."

"Amy, I don't want her name in the article," Loy said.

"Why not?"

"She's not an official witness, just a bystander," the sheriff said. His face was growing darker by the minute.

Amy Bloom lifted the camera and snapped my photograph. She lowered the camera and waited expectantly. "First name?"

Loy propped one hand on his gun belt, something he always did when he was upset, and raised one finger. "Amy——"

"It's alright, Loy. I'm Marley Dearcorn."

"Age?" Amy Bloom asked, scribbling.

"Thirty-six. Or, I will be in a few weeks."

"Marley, she doesn't need any personal information about you," Loy said.

"Are you a resident of Parkman?" she asked, ignoring Loy.

"I live in Killdeer."

"Can you describe what it was like when you first discovered the body?" she asked.

"Amy, that's enough," Loy said. "She doesn't have any comment."

"Did you know the victim?" she asked brusquely.

"Yes. I knew her," I replied, irritated.

"You were the first person to discover the body. Knowing her personally, it must have been a difficult ordeal. Can you tell me what that was like for you?"

Bile rose up in my throat and I had a sudden urge to slug her in the jaw. The injustice of it all was starting to eat a hole in my stomach, and here was this vulture feeding off the trauma.

I gave her a hard look. "What it was like for me?"

"I need to put a human face on the victim," Amy said. "Readers will identify with her more if I supply details."

"She already *has* a human face."

The sheriff snagged my arm. "You don't need to talk to her."

Amy Bloom charged on. "Can you speculate about the person who committed this crime?"

"I can tell you this much," I poked her shoulder with two fingers. "Whoever it is, they're going to get caught. You can *quote* me on that. If the son of a bitch thinks he can slaughter another human being and leave her on the side of the road like a piece of trash, he's got another thing coming."

Amy wrote the quote furiously in her notepad and Loy spun me around, giving me a solid shove towards my SUV. "She's got to go now, Amy. The interview's over."

I dug my keys from my slacks pocket and wearily climbed inside. As I fired up the engine and fastened my seat belt Loy rapped two knuckles on my window.

I rolled it down, managing to meet his grim eyes with difficulty.

He shook his head. "She's with the *Parkman Journal*. She gets carried away sometimes."

"Yeah? I know I need to keep better control of my temper. But does she have to be so goddamned pushy about it?"

Loy didn't reply, and my eyes drifted out of focus. All I could think about was finding Phoebe on the side of the road, abandoned and forgotten.

After Loy dropped his hand from the open window I managed to drag myself back to the present. "I appreciate the offer for dinner with you and Wendy, but I think I'll go over to my dad's tonight."

Loy grimaced, nodded and walked behind my SUV, giving it a couple raps with the flat of his hand as a way of saying *see you later*.

I left the Gas N Dash in my rearview mirror, catching a glimpse of Betty furiously washing the glass on the outside windows, doing what she could to avoid her boss.

Phoebe's death seemed to be stirring up a storm of feelings inside me.

I felt sick with the loss of my husband, sick with grief. The only thing that held back the pain was rage, and that seemed to well to the surface at unpredictable times. I even found myself feeling irritated with people I loved.

When I'd lost my mother to a drunk driver as a child, I'd felt abandoned and frightened. Grief was hitting me, as an adult, in a very different way. Losing my husband made me feel utterly helpless. And that, in turn, made me angry.

As I drove towards home I realized I was on the same path Phoebe's killer had driven less than twelve hours ago. I would be passing by the very spot where I'd found her body.

Maybe it was a mistake. Maybe it would be far better to leave it alone and not get involved. But the closer I got to Jim Creek Hill, the more I wanted to stop and examine the place where Phoebe had died, if for no other reason than to give my wounded psyche something else to focus on besides being angry at the world.

CHAPTER 4

My SUV seemed to slow down of its own volition. I parked a few yards away from the first downed reflector post and killed the engine. The sun was creeping across the October sky relentlessly, reminding us all that summer was over and soon it would be bitterly cold again.

The fog was just a memory now. The wide landscape was painted with clear sunlight and the pastel blue sky had traces of wispy clouds overhead. I let my eyes scan the slope up Jim Creek Hill until I spotted the place where she had been hit. I tried to imagine what it must have looked like from the driver's perspective, and my fingers tightened on the steering wheel at the thought.

Could the driver have seen her from here? I was fairly certain that even at night, with low beams, he could. Or she. I'd made the mistake in the past of assuming the gender of a killer, and these days I wasn't as quick to make that judgment.

I stepped out and my boots crunched in the loose asphalt. This stretch of highway was neglected. It always had been. The shoulder was uneven and pebbles had worked loose from the paved surface and littered the area beside the white highway line. Potholes were common. The highway between Killdeer and Parkman was notoriously underfunded and sometimes years would pass between repairs.

Now it looked positively forlorn.

Phoebe's body had obviously been retrieved by ambulance under supervision from the coroner. Whatever tire tracks or visible evidence there was had been documented, photographed, or picked up. The hillside was eerily still. Not even a sparrow chirped on the deserted summit. It was completely empty once more. Almost like her death hadn't even happened at all.

I walked slowly to the first reflector post and knelt down. It was bent to the ground at a ninety-degree angle. There wasn't a trace of paint, but a fleck of silver told me the vehicle that had hit the post probably had a chrome grille guard. And it had been moving at a high rate of speed. The post had a noticeable bend in the top from the impact.

I backed up and stared at the spot, scrutinizing it with an open mind, and crouched down again to see it at ground level. There were impressions in the wilted grass, but no definitive tracks to speak of. The soil had been too hard and dry at the time of the killing to leave anything resembling a clear impression. The light rain that had fallen shortly after hadn't helped matters. The only thing left to see was the flattened posts, and the impressions left in the dead vegetation.

From my angle I could see that the tire impressions straddled the first downed reflector post perfectly. The driver had bull's-eyed the post, hitting it squarely with the very center of the front bumper. The flattened impressions in the grass were evenly placed on each side of the post. I stood up and trotted to the next post and saw the same thing there. It had been straddled dead-center, and the impressions left by the right tires clearly showed the vehicle had hit the post exactly in the middle of the grille. It was about a hundred feet or so to the last downed reflector post, and when I got there I saw the same pattern.

All three posts were exactly the same, and when I stopped a mere three or four feet from where Phoebe had been lying, I could see that whoever had run her down hadn't been too concerned with avoiding the hazard of hitting a few highway markers.

The killer had lined her up from three hundred feet away, or so it seemed. Maybe I was jumping to conclusions that didn't have any real merit, but my instinct was telling me there was more to this than a simple accident.

"Why Phoebe?" I asked out loud.

Well, she was beautiful, and that could sometimes bring a girl unwanted attention. She was poor, but I couldn't for the life of me understand what that could have to do with it. She was an easy target, walking in the middle of nowhere alone at night. Maybe it had been a random, opportunistic murder?

Or was I seeing things that simply weren't there at all?

I shook my head and searched the area skeptically. This didn't seem random to me. It seemed deliberate. Brutal. Almost as if the person was bitterly angry.

A breeze tousled my short hair, making me sharply aware of the surroundings. Was there anything special about this particular spot? I intently studied the surroundings, looking for anything that seemed significant.

Not far from the road I noticed the deer ladder. The top of Jim Creek Hill was a wildlife crossing zone, and the long fence that ran parallel to the highway was broken up with a deer ladder, or a wildlife access gate. It was simply a steeply mounded and packed pile of dirt that led up to a gap in the fence allowing deer, antelope and the occasional elk to cross the fence without getting entangled in the wires. Cattle were not nearly nimble enough to climb it, but the deer and antelope were. It had been installed only a couple of years ago. It seemed to be successful because I hadn't noticed a deer carcass hung up in the barbed wire for months now.

Turning my attention back to the highway, I tried to picture the place at night. Was there anything remarkable about this stretch of highway? Not really. It looked like every other lonely mile of road between Killdeer and Parkman.

The only things different were the snow markers at the bottom of Jim Creek Hill. Which made sense. Winter usually brought howling winds and drifts of snow that piled up at the bottom of the hill in the depression, making it difficult for the snowplow drivers to see the highway. Sometimes the snow got so deep at the bottom of the hill, where it tended to drift the most, that the reflector posts were completely buried beneath a blanket of white. To solve that problem, the highway department had put in seven or eight double-decker reflector posts. They were twice as tall as the standard posts and had two of the bright reflective discs stacked on top of each other, and helped the snowplow drivers see the roadway when the drifts were severe.

That was the only thing different about this part of the highway, as far as I was able to see. In other words, a complete dead end.

I trudged back to my SUV and climbed in. I didn't feel like going home. The enormous house I'd found myself living in had a hollow feel lately. I'd never expected to be able to afford such a mansion, but Leif's standards for where he lived had been very high. Only the best would do. He was far too busy, and far too worn out, whenever he returned from a long business trip to suffer with a home that was anything less than utterly beautiful and comfortable. He'd always taken great pains to see that his home was a sanctuary. It sat at the end of the lane, not far from my father's ranch, and the tall pine trees surrounding the huge log house made the place private and secluded. It was majestic, but hadn't been my first choice of residence. We'd been forced into the home due to circumstance.

My life had been a string of disasters lately.

Just before Leif and I had moved into the huge home, our beautiful house that had stood at the very end of the valley, surrounded by secluded forest, had burned to the ground. We'd lost everything. The only things I'd managed to save from the fire had been Leif's laptop computer and my wedding ring. Leif had not contracted this new home to be built, but had purchased it only a few weeks after we had been married, and only then out of dire necessity due to the fire. Essentially, we'd started over with a new home only a few weeks ago, and hadn't had much time to accumulate any personal possessions.

It still didn't feel comfortable to me in the new place. Especially now that Leif was gone.

Now it was mine, but I felt like a houseguest more than an owner. The house was huge, with obscenely tall windows looking out into the surrounding forest, hand-carved wooden banister rungs lining the stairs leading to the bedrooms, and hardwood floors in every room. The kitchen was decorated with Italian tile. Even the furniture was ornate.

I'd grown up with a thirdhand bed given to me by my long-deceased grandmother. There had been days during my teenage years my father had apologized to me because all we had to eat was a freezer-burned round roast. But we'd managed. After my mother's death, my father and I had put our backs into scraping out an existence on the ranch, keeping it together with baling wire and spit. He was retired now, and to my utter delight, carrying on a happy relationship with my best friend, Irene Baker. She was older than me, and wiser. Since my father and Irene were the two people I loved the most in the world, it seemed only natural to me that they would be a couple.

I started the engine and headed back towards Killdeer with purpose. It was pushing three p.m. and the lunch rush at Irene's café would be long over. The dinner crowd wouldn't start showing up until closer to five, so I would most likely have Irene to myself for at least a little while. I just couldn't face the big empty house alone, and I'd lost almost ten pounds since Leif had died. Even I was alarmed at how loose my jeans were lately. Eating had become a chore. But the activity of searching the place Phoebe had been killed, putting my mind to the mystery of her death, had rekindled a tiny spark of life inside me. As miserable as I was, for the first time in nearly a month, chicken fried steak actually sounded good.

I pulled into the parking lot at Lil's and saw to my immense relief that it was practically deserted. Nobody knew why the café was named Lil's. It was simply one of those unofficial landmarks of Killdeer that endured no matter who owned the place. Irene had been the proprietor for many years now, and she had turned it into the best version of Lil's I'd ever seen.

I took my usual seat at the counter, sitting down on the center stool, and silently Irene set a cup of steaming, coal-black coffee before me. She scrutinized me with her sharp blue eyes and hatchet expression. Irene was the very definition of a tough old bird, even though she was only a little more than a decade my senior. She wore her blonde hair pageboy short, simply because she had far better things to worry about than messing around with makeup and curling irons. Her hands were always slightly red from endlessly handling hot plates and wiping down counters. Nothing got by her. Any piece of gossip, no matter how mundane or trivial, was instantly caught in her wide net.

"How much sleep did you get last night?" she asked, pulling her small stool out from beneath the counter and propping one butt cheek on it with practiced efficiency.

I took a sip of coffee and my eyes bulged with shock. "How long has this been reducing on the burner? It tastes like a cigar."

"Put some cream in it, missy. It'll be fine."

I poured enough cream into the cup to feed a week-old calf and took another cautious sip. "Better."

"Marley, just exactly what the hell were you doing up on Jim Creek Hill this morning poking around a dead body?"

I glanced up. "Is everyone in Killdeer talking about it already?"

She let her gaze slide down the counter until it rested on a man seated on the last bar stool.

I rolled my eyes to let her know I understood whom she meant.

Harvey Wilson, Killdeer's own version of CNN, squatted like a toad in front of the newspaper with his usual worn toothpick protruding from one side of his mouth and his fossilized John Deere ball cap pulled firmly down, shielding his piggy eyes. Harvey had sat in that same spot for at least thirty years, without fail, each and every day the café was open. His worn bib coveralls strained over the bulk of his stomach. Harvey leased out his acreage to a used car salesman from Parkman who planted it in alfalfa each spring and ran a string of prize quarter horses on the grassland. Harvey didn't do much farming himself these days and he'd taken on the physique of a landowner who'd delegated the heavy lifting to someone younger and more gullible.

"There's no living with him now that he got that new police scanner," Irene said.

"I heard that," Harvey called from the end of the counter. "Wasn't for me, you'd be getting all your info from the local paper, and everyone knows they are just a mouthpiece for the liberal wackos. I provide a public service."

Irene duplicated my eye roll and proceeded to ignore him.

"Order up," called her cook from the chef's window behind the counter.

Andy, Irene's flirty cook, shot me a wink when he noticed me looking at him. I gave him a tired smile.

"Phoebe Robinson, hit by a car," I said. "What did that pretty girl ever do to deserve that?"

Irene scooped up a plate of hash browns and bacon and eggs and held up one finger to me. "Be right back."

She was between waitresses at the moment, since Lil's was so slow this time of day she sometimes dismissed her floor staff.

Irene set the plate down at a table in the back of the café and I noticed Rebecca Winthrop, the pediatrician who lived in Killdeer, but had a thriving medical practice in Parkman, lift her eyes gratefully.

After Irene plunked a bottle of ketchup on the table and walked away, Rebecca's gaze drifted over to me and she simply stared. For a moment I thought she was looking directly at me, but then I realized she was not seeing anything at all, her eyes just happened to be pointed in my general direction. Since I'd been wearing that vacant, thousand-mile stare for nearly a month myself, I recognized it in others.

"What's wrong with Becca?" I asked, taking in the woman's blank expression.

Irene resumed her spot on her stool. "Cecilia had a stroke a few days ago. Rebecca's been going back and forth to the hospital in Parkman at all hours to keep track of her progress. It's not looking very good."

Cecilia was Rebecca's mother, a prim and stately woman with silver fox hair and finishing school manners. Rebecca doted on her.

"Poor Cecilia. That's got to be tough to manage for Rebecca

too. What about her practice?" I asked.

"She's shut her office down for the week until Cecilia's condition is better. Or worse," Irene said ominously.

I knew what that meant. Cecilia was probably not responding very well to treatment and the stroke must have been a bad one.

"Marley, I asked you a question," Irene said.

"What was I doing up on Jim Creek Hill, yes, I know."

She crossed her arms. "It had to have been pretty early in the morning."

"Mr. Toomey had one more thing he needed to go over with me," I said evasively. The last thing I wanted to do was relive the tape recording of Leif's last words by sharing them with Irene. And I wasn't supposed to talk about it, in any case. Mr. Toomey's offer to allow me to listen to the recording whenever I wanted had been a generous act, but I doubted I could take it again so soon. More than likely it would be months before I'd have the emotional strength to listen to it again.

"Can I get a chicken fried steak?" I asked abruptly.

Irene's eyes lit up like sparklers. "Andy! CFS on the hoof with a side of bullets and smothered fog."

Which was her way of saying chicken fried steak, rare, with a side of baked beans and mashed potatoes with white gravy.

"Thanks." I slipped the silverware out of the napkin and set it next to my coffee.

"I'm glad you came in because there is something I wanted to tell you," Irene began.

I watched her for signs of trouble, but she seemed less concerned and more matter-of-fact. With Irene, it was a good idea to proceed with caution. You never knew what she was going to say next.

"I'm taking a vacation."

"You? That hasn't happened since . . . since I don't know when."

"Hey, I took a week off in 2007 to go to Branson," she said defensively.

"Practically yesterday," I said.

"Smartass. Listen. I wanted to let you know about it, because it's a surprise for your father. I booked us a romantic getaway."

"I'm really happy to hear that, Irene. Where are you two going?"

She shoved her stool back underneath the counter. "It's a place up in Canada called Tofino. There are all these amazing hotels right on the coast, and this time of year the big recreational activity is to book a room right on the beach and watch the winter storms roll in."

"You are going to Canada to watch it rain?"

She sighed at me. "It's not as boring as that. The storms are really magnificent. All black clouds and huge waves. It's supposed to be spectacular."

"How long will you be gone? I suppose I'll need to go by the ranch house and make sure Dad didn't leave any water running anywhere."

She looked sheepish. "Well, it's sort of short notice. We are leaving the day after tomorrow and won't be back until the 26th."

"I'm not back working at the library yet, so it won't be any trouble for me to check on your place too, if you like," I said.

"No, you don't need to do that."

The bell rang behind her and Andy called out. My order was up already.

Irene's eyes gleamed. She plunked a heavy plate on the counter in front of me and slid a glass of ice water beside it. "It's good to see you eating again."

I gave her a grateful smile and tore into the food, feeling hungry for the first time in a number of days.

46

Irene disappeared to check on Rebecca, and to my consternation I noticed Harvey Wilson blatantly staring at me from the end of the long counter. After the fourth time I lifted my fork to my mouth and saw him follow the movement with his squint, I turned towards him, irritated.

"What? Is there a black widow on me or something?"

Harvey didn't smile. He fiddled two fingers around the tip of his worn toothpick, still watching me. "June Allen drove past you on the highway an hour ago. Said you was poking around that spot Phoebe got creamed."

I was on my feet and inches from his nose with a fist before I could stop myself. I shook my knuckles at him. "She was a person, Harvey. A human being. She didn't get creamed, she was murdered. Show some goddamned *respect*."

His hips crabbed backwards on the stool and he nearly slipped off.

I felt a hand on my shoulder and Irene was easing me away from Harvey with low, gentle words usually reserved for angry bulls and skittish colts.

"Marley, honey. Take a seat. I know, I know. He thinks he knows everything."

My heart hammered in my chest and my face was so hot with anger it felt sunburned.

I slumped back on my stool and rested my head in my hands for a moment.

When I finally looked up, Irene was back behind the counter and watching me with a hard look. "Better?"

I nodded, not entirely certain that I was. "Sorry."

"You should go talk to someone." Her tone was deeply suggestive.

"Like a counselor?" I asked.

"It might not be a bad idea, after everything you've been through. Marley, honey. These last two years have not been easy on you. Most people would have fallen apart by now."

"Irene, I don't know if you noticed or not," I said between clenched teeth. "But I did fall apart."

The plate of half-finished food had lost its appeal and I tossed a twenty-dollar bill on the counter. Irene didn't say a word as I got up to leave, knowing instinctively that I was not going to respond anyway.

The drive home through the tree-lined valley was a blur. I stumbled up the front porch stairs and barely got the door closed behind me before my legs simply gave out.

My back fell against the door and I slid to the floor as the tears came out like the Yellowstone River. Hugging my knees to my chest offered little comfort. Leif's voice echoed in my mind.

It's going to be dicey, Center. I can't get any more altitude.

It was nearly dark before I was able to rise again.

CHAPTER 5

The next morning a steady wind battered the tall ponderosa pines in the back yard relentlessly. Fall was on us with full force, and it would bring bouts of sleet and gusts of chilly wind at dawn, only to evaporate into seventy-five-degree heat waves late in the day that forced everyone to shed the layers of clothing they'd piled on to stave off the morning frost.

Hordes of starlings swarmed the cottonwood trees, making ready to abandon Montana for winter's duration.

I forced myself out of bed at 9. Irene was constantly pestering me about not getting enough sleep. Since my eyes were usually bloodshot, I could understand her concern. But my problem wasn't lack of sleep. Lately I'd gotten into the habit of falling into bed at 8:30 in the evening and not climbing out again until twelve hours later. If anything, I was getting too much rest.

Being unconscious was the only time I felt any relief from the intense grief, and being exhausted emotionally made it all too easy to drift off for half a day and not raise my head once, even to eat.

I made coffee and went out the back door in my pajamas and slippers. The chill wind shocked me into awareness and I forced myself to sit on the stairs instead of wandering back inside for a few hours of mindless television.

Birds squabbled for position in the trees, chittering noisily and comically, managing to force a smile from my tight lips. A few stalwart autumn leaves had managed to cling to the aspen trees, flashing gold smiles now and then, but were surrendering one by one and cartwheeling to the ground.

The birds angled for the top branch on the skeleton of a tall aspen, arguing relentlessly.

Their chirps ceased abruptly. Wind hummed low through the pine needles, but even with the breeze I could hear the sudden lack of birdcalls.

A fat red squirrel barked in warning overhead, and a snap of branches brought my attention to movement beyond the back yard.

I peered hard through the swaying branches and caught a glimpse of white/brown, furry movement just as a sharp squeal of a chipmunk pierced the air. I stood up in time to see two black eyes snap up through the trees and fix on me, unafraid and unconcerned. For a moment I couldn't quite make sense of the shape, but when the brown snout pointed towards me I clearly saw the sharp nose of a wolverine. The animal was watching me, unconcerned, from the forest.

The wolverine munched down the chipmunk heartily, completely indifferent to my presence. The chipmunk's long tail hung from the wolverine's mouth, dangling like a licorice chew, finally disappearing between the yellow teeth. He chewed a few times, sniffed the air with his eyes partially closed, and trundled off into the forest without a glance my way. I watched his hunched back and eager limbs lope off through the trees with fluid power. In a matter of moments he'd completely vanished.

I shivered and backed inside the house, not wanting to draw

attention to myself, and shut the door quietly behind me.

Normally something as remarkable as seeing a wolverine would have been a thrill for me, but today my mood was grim and dark. Not even the event of a rare sighting such as that was enough to snap me out of my lethargy.

I spent the day halfheartedly sorting through the few remaining items Leif had left in his office. Since we had literally just moved into this big house right before Leif's death, there was precious little in the way of personal belongings to attend to.

Leif's laptop computer, the one thing that he had guarded diligently, had been destroyed in the crash. The only clothing that was his fit neatly into two plastic grocery bags. They sat by the back door, ready for a trip to the Goodwill.

The office was furnished smartly with large leather chairs and a neatly organized oak desk. The desk was much smaller than his old desk had been back at our old house. A few files with financial information inside, far too complex for me to understand, were on the top of the leather blotter. I vowed to deliver them to Mr. Toomey at some point in the future.

As I rummaged inside the desk for a pen to write a note on the outside of the folder, my hand encountered a tiny envelope. I pulled it out, frowning. The small green cover opened with a bit of prying and a key dropped onto the desk. I knew instantly it was a safety deposit key for our local bank, and not Leif's corporate bank in Billings. The Killdeer bank always used green envelopes for its safe deposit boxes, and I knew that because my father had one just like it in an old coffee cup stashed up in the cupboard back at the ranch house.

A number was penciled on the tiny envelope. The lines were faint, but it clearly read box number 112. I slipped the key inside the envelope and put it back inside the desk. I'd get to it eventually.

More than likely the only thing Leif would have considered important enough to keep inside a safe deposit box at our little local bank, as opposed to his coporate bank in Billings, was something he would have wanted to get his hands on at short notice. Maybe it was a copy of his birth certificate or his passport.

Leif's remains had been cremated. Scott, Leif's son, had not been able to make a decision yet about where we should spread the ashes. He was in even worse shape than I was, and we had both come to the conclusion the week before that now was not a good time for us to make that choice. We had agreed to talk on the phone at the end of October. Maybe by then the two of us would be in a better place. Scott had taken his father's ashes home, in the meantime. It was a sad relief. If the steel urn had stayed with me, I would have been faced with a constant and ever present reminder of the loss of my husband. I felt guilty as hell, but I was almost glad that Scott had wanted to keep the urn with him.

I drifted through a shower and forced myself to wander into the kitchen for something to eat. As soon as I opened the refrigerator I could see immediately that my father had broken into my house at some point and left a selection of tempting foods. The freezer was full of Häagen-Dazs ice cream, White Castle microwavable cheeseburgers, Fudgsicles and a bag of sweet potato French fries.

I ate a plate of sweet potato fries, leaning against the counter, popping them one by one off a paper plate I'd heated in the microwave. No dishes to clean up.

A rattle from the front door startled me. Footsteps warned me someone was inside the house, but after listening to the firm sound of heavy boots for a moment, I quirked a half-smile and resumed eating, unconcerned.

Someone moved down the hallway towards the kitchen and I paused between bites.

"Hey, Dad."

He stopped by the kitchen table when he saw me. "You didn't lock your door."

"So I see."

He tossed a newspaper on the table and pointed at it. "It's not your best side."

I set the plate on the counter and lifted the newspaper, unfolding it with greasy fingers.

A photograph of my gaunt and angry face was plastered on the front page. The headline was cumbersome.

"*Local woman promises retribution for friend's death*? What is this?"

"That's what I'd like to know." He dropped into a chair and thumped a fist on the paper. "This article makes you sound like you are on some sort of personal vendetta."

"I didn't think she would actually print that." I eased into a chair across from my father and scanned the front page. "She says I have a reputation for solving cold cases?"

He folded his arms and leaned back. "Oh, it gets better. Keep reading."

I flipped the paper open and scanned the article. "Marley Dearcorn, Killdeer resident and recent widow, vowed that the killer of her dear friend would be brought to justice swiftly."

I was incredulous.

My father stared at me. "She goes on and on about how you were the one who figured out the person who killed your grandfather all those years ago. She says that the local sheriff is relying on you as an expert witness in the case."

I swallowed. "Loy's head is going to split in half when he reads this."

"Irene and I are leaving tomorrow. We will be gone for a whole week," he said.

I set the paper aside. "Well maybe you should be grateful."

"What I'm saying, Kiddo, is that we won't be here to look after you. What in hell are you doing getting some reporter all riled up and making her turn you into some kind of a local celebrity?"

"Dad, every village needs an idiot," I said.

He waved a hand. "You think this is funny? All sorts of weirdos will be reading about you in the paper."

My shoulders slumped and I rubbed my eyes. "It's not anything to worry about. Most people won't even care."

He took off his grungy straw cowboy hat and tossed it on the table. "Well I care."

I put a hand over his calloused palm. "Thanks for worrying. But, honestly? In a couple days everyone will have forgotten all about Phoebe Robinson, me, and the whole story."

He scanned me with jumpy eyes. "And what did she mean by 'expert witness' anyway? Loy isn't actually asking you to help him figure this out, is he?"

"He expressly ordered me not to get involved," I said.

"Which is why I keep voting for him."

"The only reason I got involved at all was because I found her body," I said reassuringly.

"Marley, that must have been awful and I'm sorry you had to be there. But don't take this as some kind of challenge, alright?" He squeezed my hand. "You promise not to go poking this rattlesnake?"

I balked and glanced down.

He shook my hand. "You've had too much trouble lately as it is."

"Dad, someone ran her down deliberately. It was more than just a stupid accident. What am I supposed to do? Pretend it didn't happen and just go on about my business like everything is fine?"

"That's exactly what you're supposed to do. You can't carry this. It's someone else's burden. You understand me? Let it go."

I stood up, jerking my hand away with more force than I'd intended.

My father's eyes flashed with fear for a moment. I felt horrible, but my anger was too powerful and I waved away his words with both hands. "How am I supposed to do that? I saw what someone did to her."

"And Loy will make short work of them. He's a good sheriff. I know in the past you have had a knack for poking into things and stumbling across the truth. But for once, for God's sake, leave it alone."

He wasn't angry, he was worried.

It twisted my guts but I managed to clamp down on my anger and I heaved a long, slow sigh. "Alright. Maybe it's better that way."

I eased into the chair and flipped the newspaper over so I couldn't see my pale photograph any longer.

My father smoothed the front of his plaid shirt and breathed out hard. We exchanged apologetic looks.

"Loy's got an applicant for deputy he says might work out," my father said quietly.

I felt my lip twitch. "That's good news. He's been going it alone for too long."

"Irene told me about it. She said to make sure and ask you if you had put in for that job, and if you had, to smack you on the back of the head."

"I didn't put in for it."

He let his shoulders drop down, the fight deflating out of him like a blown tire. "I told her it was crazy, even thinkin' that you would want to be a sheriff's deputy."

"Why is that crazy?" I asked.

He shrugged a shoulder. "You're a lousy shot."

That was no secret. I'd grown up on a ranch, and therefore

shooting was a common task I'd grown familiar with, but I'd never been proficient.

"Anyway, I came over to ask you if you'd be willing to take me and Irene to the airport in Billings tomorrow. You probably will want to just get a hotel and spend the night. Our flight don't leave till eight in the evening and that wouldn't put you home till after ten. I don't like the idea of you driving home that late. The deer'll be thick as grasshoppers and sure as hell, you'd smack one with that nice car of yours."

Driving at night in Montana brought an interesting assortment of road hazards. Deer, coyotes, the occasional bobcat. I'd been driving back to Killdeer from a late movie in Parkman once when I was a teenager and nearly plowed into a herd of Black Angus steers milling around on the highway.

"We could have dinner before your flight takes off," I said, wanting to make up for my harsh words. "Then I can drop you at your gate."

He squirmed in his seat. "I know dropping us at the airport is a hassle. It'll mean you have to come back over and pick us up when we get home. That's not a problem, is it?"

"No, no. Of course it isn't. Maybe I'll go shopping, buy some new clothes, get my nails done."

He studied me skeptically. "Uh-huh."

"Hey, I used to own a dress or two," I said defensively.

"I don't think it's right, Rose letting you go to work in blue jeans and boots," he grumbled. "Librarians are supposed to be professionals."

I gave a half chuckle. "She's not very picky when it comes to dress codes."

Since my boss at the library was in the habit of dyeing her hair two or three different shades of blonde, pink and red simultaneously, it was no shock she didn't give two hoots about my wearing casual clothing while working my shifts. I had no idea who she had roped into working my scheduled times during my leave of absence, but she had assured me my job would be waiting for me when I was ready to come back.

We sat in uncomfortable silence for several beats before my father slapped his hands on the tops of his thighs and stood up. "Got to go pack. Don't know exactly what's appropriate for storm watching. Waders, I guess. But Irene said I have to wear a suit for dinner at least once."

"I'll swing by the ranch house in the morning," I said.

I walked my father out and nodded obediently while he lectured me about locking my door while I was home alone, while I was gone, and generally instructing that I keep it locked at all times no matter what. I retorted that I'd nail it shut and simply climb out the window when I wanted to leave.

He gave me a firm hug as he left and I dutifully locked the door behind him.

As I watched him drive away I knew my promise to avoid looking into the events of Phoebe's death had been wasted breath. She deserved better. She didn't deserve to be forgotten so quickly.

Maybe it was a good thing my father and Irene were going to be gone for a week. They wouldn't be around to tell me to mind my own business. There was someone I planned to pay a visit to when I got back to Killdeer in two days: Phoebe's only living family member.

She was a drunk, and a slob, but I was willing to bet good money Louise Robinson would have a thing or two to say about her daughter that might be useful. With any luck, she might have some idea of who I should be looking for.

All I had to do was show up on her doorstep with a casserole and a fifth of Jim Beam and ask the right questions. If I was persistent and diligent, there was a strong possibility I'd be able to figure out who had killed Phoebe before my father and Irene even made it home from vacation.

Instead of falling into the couch and napping, like I'd done for the past three weeks, I pulled on my hikers and headed down the winding road for a brisk walk to blow the cobwebs out of my brain.

I had a lot of ground to cover, and not a lot of time. It crossed my mind that what I was planning could possibly be a very, very bad idea. But the unwanted side effect of all the anger I carried around inside me was that there wasn't room left for other emotions.

Like worry.

Or fear.

And the simple truth of it was that I really didn't care anymore what happened to me.

CHAPTER 6

I dropped my father and Irene at the airport without incident the next day. They had promised to call the moment they arrived at their resort hotel in British Columbia. Logan International Airport in Billings had been bustling with activity and I'd barely managed to hug them both before surrendering my spot to a honking silver Cadillac SUV nosing in behind me. I'd spent an uneventful night at a motel a couple of miles from the airport and the next morning I rolled out of bed at a shockingly tardy 9:30. No self-respecting rancher's daughter ever slept past 7, and I was slightly embarrassed to be creeping out of the motel on the verge of checkout time.

Since I knew Louise Robinson, Phoebe's mother, wouldn't be awake and moving until later in the afternoon, there was no need to rush back home right away. To fill the time I decided on a whim to actually do what I had told my father I planned, and I went shopping.

The mall would be too busy and nothing there appealed to me anyway, so I went downtown, fighting the odd arrangement of unexpected one-way streets, and struggled into a parking place at last. I caught myself staring up at the tall Sheraton Hotel like a hayseed who had never seen a building with an elevator before, and quickly cast my eyes about for a promising clothing store.

After wandering aimlessly for a few blocks I stumbled into a store with a helpful woman who cheered me up with her gentle demeanor and good taste. After quite a lot of resistance on my part, she managed to get me into a classy red dress she swore had been cut just for my shape, a new black wool coat and a pair of black leather boots that cost more than my first cutting horse. Two hours later I left the store with six neatly packed shopping bags filled with new clothes. It astonished me when she wrapped each piece of clothing in its own special little box, complete with pink tissue paper.

It struck me as silly to wrap something that was for me, but maybe Irene was right and I needed to do something nice for myself for a change.

My jeans were packed at the bottom of my shopping bag and I wore the red dress out of the shop, right off the rack. In an odd way, it made me feel a little more human again.

The last time I'd made a serious clothing purchase had been when I'd gone to the Goodwill in Parkman and picked up some secondhand jeans for work.

The girl standing in line behind me at the Parkman Goodwill had lamented to her friend the fact that her mother had discarded a particular favorite Carhartt coat she once owned.

"I had a real sentimental attachment to that coat," she'd said. "It still had the blood stains on it from my first deer hunt. Can't forgive Mom for tossing it."

As I loaded the bags of new clothes into the backseat of my SUV, I tried to imagine someone inside the shop I'd just left uttering a phrase like that. In Montana, it wasn't beyond the realm of possibility.

By the time I left Billings, after a quick stop to grab a chocolate shake from a fast food joint, it was pushing four in the afternoon and I would be getting back to Killdeer just in time to pay my respects to Louise Robinson. I occupied myself with formulating the right words to say. I was fairly sure Louise would have some insight into Phoebe's life that might help uncover who might want to cause her harm.

Not that Sheriff Loy Shucraft wasn't following up on that angle as well. By now he had probably talked to Louise and she'd told him everything she knew, or thought might be important. But time had a way of shaking things loose in our memory. Maybe she had thought of something more in the three days since her daughter had died.

By the time Parkman rolled into view over the top of the dashboard, I realized the only thing I'd had to eat all day was the chocolate shake. It slowed me down, but instead of trying to make it home on a growling stomach I decided to stop at a restaurant and treat myself to a nice dinner. I felt foolish wearing the shapely red dress. Being seen in expensive clothing was not my usual way and even though the woman at the shop had promised I looked like a million bucks, I felt self-conscious and out of place.

Dairy Queen was out of the question.

Instead, I sat alone at the bar of a new bistro that had only been open for a year or so. It was the same restaurant where Leif had proposed to me.

His way of proposing had been to ask me when my schedule would open up so we could get married. It was a bittersweet memory. I had been shocked by his forthright ways in the beginning, but I quickly grew to love his directness. With Leif, I had always known where I stood. He was simply incapable of bluffing or evasiveness. I'd always found his straightforward style refreshing.

The evening crowd moved around me like a blur, and it wasn't until my waitress asked me for the fifth time if I needed anything else that I realized it was past nine. I'd sat there for three hours, reminiscing.

So much for going to see Phoebe's mother.

Pink-faced, I left the restaurant and finally headed back towards Killdeer. On the outskirts of town I noticed my gas gauge was low again, and since the Gas N Dash was just up the road it seemed like a good idea to fill up.

As I pulled up beside the gas pumps the station looked more sinister to me than it had in daylight. Night made the yellow lights inside the store waxy and bleached the life out of everything. The parking lot was deserted.

A quick glance told me Phoebe's car had been towed away. The parking place where the small red Volkswagen had been was now empty.

Beside the building a beat-up up Chevy Malibu was parked in the employee space, and I assumed it belonged to whoever was working the night shift.

The handle on the hose was chilly on my hand as I slid the nozzle free, and while the pump ticked and burbled away I glanced up and saw Betty inside, busy stocking the overhead cigarette dispenser and talking to someone I couldn't quite see.

A picnic-style table with bench seats sat beside the coffee machine opposite from Betty's counter, and three figures milled in the area listlessly. A man sat at the table with his head down, his mass of brown dreadlocks spilling from a red bandana and coiling like escaped serpents on the beige Formica.

Another man paced around the table, his jerky movements and darting eyes betraying his agitation. He was tall and lean, and wore a Kansas City Chiefs baseball cap sideways. Wisps of dirty blond stuck out from either side of the hat.

The third figure was rounder and shorter than the other two. He wore his black hair cropped so short it was nearly shaved, and his right hand held a Styrofoam coffee cup. He extended two fingers and jabbed the air while he spoke. Whatever he was saying, he clearly thought he deserved his companions' full respect and attention.

All three of them wore various shades of grungy black. Not one of them was over the age of thirty.

"Vampires," I muttered.

The men were probably members of the night-shift crew of regular misfits Betty had told me about. As I watched the three I could see why she had referred to them as the living dead. Each one of them looked as if he had just woken up.

Another car pulled slowly into the parking lot and as I finished filling my gas tank I saw Rebecca Winthrop, the auburn-haired pediatrician, eased into an empty space and go inside the store. She disappeared inside the restroom behind the picnic table and I replaced the nozzle on the pump.

A drop or two of pungent gasoline dribbled onto my fingers.

"Dammit." I held my hands at my sides, determined not to touch my new red dress and soil it with the stink of petrol.

There wasn't a paper towel to be had. Every dispenser was empty, forcing me inside the store in search of a napkin.

I approached the counter and Betty blinked at me. "Wow. I didn't recognize you."

"Got a Kleenex or napkin back there?" I asked, waving my hands like a toddler. "I spilled."

She hastened to snatch me a paper towel and I gratefully accepted it.

I gave her a forlorn smile. "You working graveyards now?"

A commotion from the picnic table grabbed Betty's attention.

She peered around me and set her eyes on the three men. "Dustin, that's enough. You've already got him riled up. Stop it already with the conspiracy theories."

The lanky man in the Kansas City Chiefs hat ceased his pacing long enough to argue with her. "But—Animal thinks it's all his fault."

"He thinks what is all his fault?" Betty asked.

"Phoebe getting killed," Dustin said.

"Don't start up with that nonsense again," Betty said. "He doesn't know what he's talking about."

I turned slowly and stared at the three men with earnest curiosity. The distraught man with dreadlocks threw back his head, mumbling something unintelligible.

"They knew Phoebe?" I asked.

Betty nodded, her face betraying her distaste. "She worked graveyards before me and these three came in every night. Animal, his real name's Marty but we just call him Animal because you can't understand a thing he says, he's got it into his head that Phoebe dying was because of something he did, but he won't tell me what it was."

Another round of noisy squabbling erupted from the table.

"Do you think he would talk to me?" I asked.

Betty blinked at me like I'd asked her if Elvis had been in earlier to top off his Big Gulp.

"You want to talk to Animal? What for?"

"Maybe he saw something the night Phoebe died," I said.

She shook her head. "I don't think it's a very good idea. He's . . . odd."

"So am I." I turned towards the picnic table with purpose.

The three men stopped their rant when I approached and stared at me.

64

"Excuse me," I said.

They looked like three possums caught in a spotlight.

Dustin, the lanky pacer, swallowed a few times and coughed, looking me up and down with suspicion in his eyes. "You must not be from around here."

My sleek red dress was not doing me any favors. The three men stared at me like I had just walked off a spacecraft of some sort.

"Did you know Phoebe Robinson?" I asked.

Animal slid sideways from the bench and shook his head frantically, mumbling and slugging his fist against his temple.

"Whoa, whoa buddy. Take it easy," said Dustin.

He put a steadying hand on Animal's shoulder and eased the distraught man back down to the bench.

"Sorry," I said earnestly. "I didn't mean to upset him. But Phoebe was a friend of mine and I just want to figure out what happened to her."

"My fault, my fault," Animal said, rocking back and forth in place. A distinct odor wafted through the air whenever Animal made any sudden movements.

The man with the buzz-cut hair shoved thick glasses back up on the bridge of his wide nose and patted Animal's shoulder reassuringly. "It ain't yer fault. Geez, it was an accident s'all."

Dustin continued to pace around the table. "Man, maybe it was his fault. He said she went up on Jim Creek because of what he told her."

My interest was definitely piqued. "What did he tell her?"

Dustin and Buzz Cut stared at me with open hostility.

"Sorry. I'm Marley, Marley Dearcorn. I was raised there."

"I'm Larry," said Buzz Cut.

He didn't offer to shake my hand, but simply nodded towards me once, with unblinking eyes, like every action movie hero who had ever graced a big screen.

"It's good to meet you, Larry," I said.

"How come we've never seen you in here before?" asked Dustin suspiciously.

"I don't get out much," I said. "Were you friends with Phoebe?"

At the mention of her name, Animal jumped up again, flapping his arms. "I told her. I told her where they were."

The soda machine clicked behind me and I caught a glimpse of Rebecca, the pediatrician, filling up a large cup while she rested one hand on the counter. From the slump of her shoulders, it was plain to see things were not going well with Cecilia, and the drive back and forth between Killdeer and Parkman's hospital was obviously taking its toll. She looked exhausted.

Rebecca snapped a lid on her drink and haphazardly wandered the aisles, looking for something in the chocolate family. She glanced my way and I gave her a small wave. She returned it with a tired smile and resumed shopping.

Animal pointed a finger at Rebecca and mumbled something. Dustin and Larry were apparently fluent in his language and both of them pondered his words.

"You think so?" asked Dustin cautiously.

"What did he say?" I asked.

Larry pointed at Rebecca with two fingers, still holding his Styrofoam cup. "He said that woman comes in all the time now, since Phoebe got killed, and he thinks she did it."

"What?" I asked. "Why would he think that?"

"Animal says the front of her car has a dent," Dustin said, interpreting the mumbles.

"Who doesn't have a dent in their car, driving at night in Montana?" I asked.

The three men took time out of their busy schedules to glare at Rebecca, and a wave of concern filled me at seeing their open hostility.

"Animal," I said, leaning a hand on the table and peering at the strange man. "What was Phoebe doing up on Jim Creek Hill that night?"

He rocked back and forth, shaking his head wordlessly.

"It's important," I said.

"Hey man, we want to know too. So answer her." Larry used his two fingers and poked Animal on the shoulder. "What'd she go up there for?"

"Quarters."

I looked at Dustin. "Did he say quarters?"

Dustin rolled a shoulder and turned away. "Yeah. Beats me."

A waft of gasoline filled my nostrils and I realized I hadn't managed to clean my hands very well.

Animal resumed his silent rocking and Larry proceeded to ignore me in favor of casting an angry look towards Rebecca.

Dustin sat down at the table across from Animal and the two of them began a quiet, conspiratorial conversation.

They weren't going to talk to me any longer, that much was clear.

I went into the restroom, turned the hot water on full and started scrubbing. My hands were pink and raw by the time I reached for a paper towel, but they didn't smell like fuel any longer.

I dried my hands slowly, contemplating Animal's strange admission. He'd told Phoebe about quarters? What could he possibly have meant? He seemed fairly convinced that it was his fault she'd gone up on Jim Creek Hill that night, but how quarters fit into that equation, I could not even begin to understand.

Undaunted, I decided the three men probably bad witnesses, but there seemed to be something here worth pursuing, and maybe if I bought him a petrified hamburger off the day-old discount warmer, Animal would feel compelled to explain things a little bit better.

I tossed the paper towel into the trash and pushed through the bathroom door with determination. When I glanced towards the picnic table I was disappointed. It was completely deserted. Where had everybody gone?

I headed for the counter and stopped still when I saw that Betty wasn't there either. Where was everyone?

I spun a slow circle around and searched the small store for Rebecca, and sudden movement from the parking lot caught my eye.

"Oh no."

I could see the whole thing clearly through the glass.

Rebecca was backed against the store window in the parking lot, surrounded by the three misfits. Betty shouted at them from the sidewalk, but it didn't seem to have any effect. They hurled accusations at Rebecca, and kept moving closer.

I sprinted for the door.

Betty was shouting. "I'm calling the cops!" She hurtled past me and made for the phone.

Rebecca Winthrop had always been on the shy side, and I doubted very much she had the stomach to deal with confrontation at the moment.

I stepped between the three vampires and Rebecca with my hands held up. "Hey what's the problem?"

"She's been coming in here all the time since Phoebe died," Dustin said hotly.

"Yeah? So have you," I said.

He stammered. "I, I don't have a car. She's got a car."

"What if she fell asleep?" asked Larry. "Look at her. She can hardly keep her eyes open. What if she fell asleep driving and hit Phoebe?"

Rebecca inched behind me, her voice ragged. "I would never do such a thing!"

"Go inside," I said, motioning for her to make a run for it.

"Don't you move a muscle," Dustin warned. "Tell us what happened."

"Look." I gave each one of the misfits a fierce glare. "I understand that Phoebe was your friend. But this is not helping."

"We want the truth," Larry barked.

"Quarters!" shouted Animal.

"Jesus, man. Let it go," Dustin said.

"Just tell us what happened," Larry said. "Start talking."

"Nothing happened," Rebecca said with a whimper. "I wasn't even driving home then. I was at the hospital."

Larry lifted his chin. "She's lying." He slugged Dustin on the shoulder. "She knows what happened. She's just too ashamed to admit it."

"Why'd you drive off? How could you do that to her?" Dustin demanded.

Larry threw his coffee cup to the pavement. "By God, you are gonna tell us what you did."

The three men closed ranks and Rebecca was plastered to the window behind me.

"Get inside now," I told her.

In her panic, Rebecca totally misunderstood me and instead of making a run for the store she sprinted between the men and ran for my SUV.

Luckily it was still unlocked and she bolted for the passenger door, climbed inside and scrambled to slam it shut behind her. The doors clicked a dozen times as she frantically pressed down on the door locks again and again.

The three vampires surrounded the vehicle and taunted her, waving their arms and yammering.

Animal pressed his hands and face to the glass, smearing nose prints on the window like a sheepdog.

I felt my hands turn to fists and the blood boiled in my ears like a river of lava.

"I have had just about enough of you," I said. "You three have about five seconds to get away from her."

"Or what?" snapped Larry. "Whatcha gonna do, lady?"

Sitting on the sidewalk beside me was an old metal trash can. It was the type of trash can that had been phased out in most places. It was made from galvanized steel, and the heavy lid was shaped like a giant Frisbee.

Larry stood motionless, looking at me as I grasped the metal lid with both hands. Then his face twisted into an expression of disbelief as I hurled the lid at him with all my strength.

It hit his forehead with a teeth-rattling clang, and Larry fell over backwards with a thud.

Dustin shouted something and darted back and forth, completely at a loss for what to do.

Animal ran for the back of the SUV and dove behind it. He mewed like a frightened kitten and tried to climb under the bumper.

Before Larry could regroup I made for the buckets hanging on the side of the gas pump and grabbed one of the long squeegees used by the semi drivers to reach their tall windows.

Brandishing the squeegee like a sword, I stood between my SUV and Larry as he scrambled to his feet.

A siren wailed in the distance and I could see the faint outline and blue lights of a sheriff's truck racing towards us.

"Want to see what I'm gonna do *next*?" I asked through my teeth.

The sheriff's truck advanced, but they seemed oblivious. Larry and Dustin stood shoulder to shoulder, drawing courage from each other.

"Jesus, lady, you're crazy!" Dustin said.

Larry took a menacing step towards me, rubbing his head. "Man, it's just a window scrubber. We afraid of window scrubbers?"

The horn of my SUV went off like a Klaxon and startled me into spinning around. Rebecca was trying to climb into the driver's seat and her elbow leaned on the wheel.

When I turned back Larry had my left arm in an iron grip and was trying to strip me of my weapon. Dustin flailed about, attempting to snag my right arm, and I slammed my boot down on his instep as hard as I could.

He howled and pulled back a fist, aiming straight for my face. The blow never landed. Dustin's feet seemed to crumble beneath him and he fell sideways, defying the laws of gravity as his legs and shoulders seemed to float in midair. He was on the ground before I knew what had happened.

Larry turned sideways just as two hands that moved like lightning effortlessly blocked his vain punches.

Before I finished drawing a single breath, Larry was on the ground beside his friend, groaning and rolling in pain.

I'd never seen Loy move so fast in my entire life.

Then I really looked up and focused on the sheriff. I wasn't even sure Loy *could* move that fast. Come to think of it, when had he found the time to grow a beard in the last two days?

The man in front of me was not Sheriff Shucraft.

A pair of ice-blue eyes shone back at me from beneath a tousled mass of blond hair.

Angus Finn stood there, staring at me. He reached for me as if he would hug me to him, then stopped and held his arms at his sides helplessly. He looked down at the tangle of Larry and Dustin, and a momentary flash of anger shot from his eyes.

When Finn looked back up again, his face was an unreadable mask of restraint. "I came as fast as I could."

CHAPTER 7

I sat at the picnic table inside the store and looked up with embarrassment as Loy Shucraft eased into the seat across from me.

He rubbed tired eyes. "I see you met my deputy."

Finn was outside comforting a rattled Rebecca Winthrop with a very strained expression plastered on his face. She was sobbing. Still. He glowered at the three misfits where they stood by the lidless garbage can. Not one of them dared to look at him.

"Loy, I can explain."

"Nice dress."

I felt my cheeks blaze with heat. "Listen, I was only asking them about Phoebe, if they knew anything that could be helpful, and Animal started raving about quarters and how it was all his fault she—"

"Marley, ease off the accelerator a minute."

Loy rested his chin in his wide palm and yawned.

I shut my mouth and leaned back. The very least I could do at this point was stop talking.

"Was all this before, or after, the garbage can incident?" he asked mildly.

"Ah, before."

"Alrighty then. Whose bright idea was it that Rebecca was responsible for the accident that killed Phoebe Robinson?" he continued.

"That would be Animal."

"Otherwise known as Marty Flexner. Yeah. We know each other," the sheriff muttered.

I studied his expression. "Something tells me you have been out here before to talk to these three."

"Larry Hagel, he's the short round fella. Disabled vet. Let's say he's got anger issues."

I slumped a bit in my seat. "Don't we all."

"Mr. Kansas City Chiefs is Dustin Larson. Can you believe he's the great-nephew of old Sheriff Larson? He's also the most accomplished shoplifter in the distinguished and long line of criminals the family has produced over the years."

"All three of them are loonier than a three-toed squirrel," I said.

Loy's lip curled up. "For Killdeer, they are pretty mild in terms of their level of crazy. Listen to this. Last week I got a complaint from Randy Newman that someone had broken into his place."

"What'd they steal?" I was grateful to be talking about someone other than myself at the moment.

"Not a thing. Apparently, someone broke into his house a month ago and *left* this huge, ugly orange recliner just sitting there, in the middle of his living room."

"They broke in and left a recliner?" I asked.

"Yup. But whoever it was, they changed their mind and wanted it back for some reason. They broke in again last week and stole it back from him. He wondered if I could do an investigation and recover this orange recliner for him. He'd become fond of it, you see."

"What has this got to do with Phoebe?" I asked.

He looked down at his shirt and frowned at a newly discovered stain. "Nothing. I'm just telling you what I've got to deal with on a daily basis."

"So what you're saying is, folks around here are nuts."

He smiled. "Those three idiots in the parking lot? Last fall they decided they wanted to go out into the woods and play paintball. Only trouble was, none of them could afford the gear so they decided to improvise."

"How do you improvise paintball?" I asked.

"By putting on twelve T-shirts, a jean jacket and some welding leathers, and going out into the woods wearing motorcycle helmets while armed with .22 pistols."

I felt my mouth drop open. "They shot each other with .22 pistols?"

"Dustin very nearly bit the dust," he said with a wry smile. "The Parkman emergency room doctor said he'd never seen a bullet actually sticking out of a guy's sternum before."

"Loy, I sense you are trying to slow walk me to some sort of a point here, but if you could just jump to it, I'd be grateful."

He patted my hand. "Marley, whatever it was those three yahoos out there said about Phoebe Robinson was most likely nothing more than the ravings of creative and paranoid imaginations. There isn't a week goes by one of them isn't into trouble of some kind, or swearing the FBI is tapping their phones or they are being followed by the Russian Mafia."

Betty was chain-smoking at the counter directly underneath the sign that said *No Smoking*.

Animal and company were arguing again. I could see them through the glass window and they looked like they were on the verge of another breakdown.

My shoulders slumped. "It does sound a little bit odd, come

to think of it."

"What did they say, exactly?" Loy didn't particularly look like he wanted to really know, but duty demanded the question.

"Animal said something about it being his fault that Phoebe was up on Jim Creek Hill the night she died."

The sheriff shifted his big frame uncomfortably in the tight seat. "Did he say why?"

"All I could get out of him was something about quarters."

"Quarters. As in the money kind, or the unit of measurement?"

I shook my head. "Who knows? With him it could mean just about anything."

Loy shifted his gaze to the window and quirked a small smile when he saw Finn standing on the sidewalk outside. He turned back to me with a meaningful look. "I guess that's all the damage I can do here for one night. Go home, Hun. And maybe you should gas up at the station in Killdeer for a while and try to avoid this place till those three forget who you are. Since the three of them hardly have two brain cells to rub together, that shouldn't take long."

I didn't have the strength left in me to argue. "Sure. I can do that."

Loy stood up, snagging his gun belt on the corner of the table and causing the entire bench to buck. He closed his eyes for a moment, apparently willing himself to remain patient. "I'm going back to bed. If there is anything else you can think of that's important, tell it to my deputy."

He left, pausing in the parking lot long enough to spare a few words to Finn before climbing back inside his sheriff's truck and disappearing into the gloom.

Rebecca had long since gone home, not willing to do much more than give a statement and leave as quickly as she could. I couldn't blame her.

Betty stood defiantly behind the counter, watching the sheriff with an angry look as he drove off. "He isn't going to arrest them?"

I held out my hands. "What for?"

She harrumphed. "Assault. They scared the hell out of that pediatrician woman."

"Well, technically, I guess it was me who assaulted them," I said with a tinge of shame.

She glanced back and forth between me and the parking lot with a sour look. "Yeah, but I'm the one who has to put up with them for the rest of the night."

"What time does the morning girl come in?" I asked.

"Marianne? She gets here at 6 today."

I realized it was already 12:30, technically the next day, and felt tired all over again. "I would imagine Finn will tell them to go home and not come back tonight."

Which was exactly what he was doing when I pushed through the door.

Larry was rummaging inside his pants pocket for car keys, and I noticed a very tired-looking powder-blue Ford pickup truck parked around the side of the gas station in the shadows.

The three misfits trailed off together, deliberately not looking at me as they piled into the cab of the truck and rumbled away.

A stiff breeze blew a swirl of dust in circles at my feet.

Finn stared at me, his face carved in wood. He looked away at last and scanned the parking lot with unblinking eyes. "You cut your hair."

I reached up and self-consciously ran a hand through my short locks. "It was easier."

The air felt heavy between us. Seeing Finn again had shocked me into silence, and now? I had no idea what I was feeling.

"Thanks for breaking up the mess earlier," I said.

77

He watched me with what might have been like concern. "I'm not entirely sure if I was rescuing you, or them."

It occurred to me this was the first time I'd seen Finn wearing a color other than black. His khaki shirt was tucked into brown pants and he wore a county-issue gun belt with all the standard gear a deputy carried around. He even wore a badge. His name tag was nothing more than an adhesive address label stuck on the pocket flap of his uniform shirt. It simply said *Hiser* in neat black letters.

I'd known him for more than a year before learning his full name. Angus Finn Hiser, originally from South Africa, had never been in the habit of volunteering any information about himself.

Most people who heard Finn speak wrongly assumed he was British, because the accents were similar, and he didn't make a point of correcting the mistake. Finn never explained anything, even when the questions were so obvious they didn't need to be asked out loud.

After a painful few minutes of enduring his silence, I wrapped my coat tighter around my shoulders and examined him with what probably looked like a glare.

"Finn, what are you doing here?"

"Working," he said.

I felt my lips press together. "I don't mean what are you doing at the Gas N Dash. What are you doing in Killdeer?"

He opened his mouth a few times, obviously struggling to come up with the right words. Failing, he shrugged almost imperceptibly and studied his hands. "I'm working."

A thousand questions sprinted through my head. Why had he fled Killdeer so suddenly after I'd gotten married? Where had he gone? And, more importantly, why had he come back again?

Standing in the middle of a gas station parking lot in the wee hours wasn't the right time or place to sort it all out, and I was too exhausted to care, in any case. If he wanted to be evasive there wasn't much I could do about it.

Wordlessly, I walked to my SUV. It still sat at the pumps where I'd parked earlier. I hadn't heard him follow me, but when I stopped at the driver's side door, Finn's hand reached around me and pulled it open.

"I'll follow you home." He kept his palm on the handle.

"You don't need to do that."

"Yes," he said with deliberate care. "I do."

Whatever words he'd failed to say wouldn't be spoken tonight. I climbed inside and let him close my door. I could have been belligerent and pulled out quickly before he could get his truck started, but I waited for him, and let him follow me home down the deserted stretch of highway.

It probably came as a surprise to him when I turned up the winding road towards my new house. The last time Finn had been in Killdeer, I'd been living with Leif in the beautiful home at the very end of the road that snaked through the valley. It might be news to him that I'd moved into the old Nesbit place that wasn't quite so far down the lane.

I parked in the driveway and locked my SUV, more for my father's sake than anything else. Nobody came this far down the valley, usually. But this way I wouldn't have to lie to my father and tell him I was being responsible and locking everything like I had promised when I wasn't actually doing it.

It surprised me a little when Finn walked me up the steps to the front door. I could see his expression plainly in the glow of his truck's headlights.

He looked weary, and sad. Deeply sad.

I turned the key in the door lock. "Good night, Finn."

"Marley," he said, hesitating.

I paused, but didn't turn to look at him. I simply waited.

"I'm here," he said. "I'm back now. If you need anything . . ."

"I don't," I said abruptly. "I especially don't need anything from you."

I went inside and slammed the door, leaving him standing there, his face frozen with concern.

It wasn't a very kind thing to do. But I was fed up with being kind. I was fed up with not knowing where Finn stood, or what he thought or felt. Our relationship had been torrid and brief, and had ended with hard feelings on my side. We'd managed a tacit friendship afterwards, but there had always been something that he held back, that he simply couldn't come to terms with when it came to me.

I was surprised by the sudden crushing pain of loss that washed over me. I missed Leif more than ever at that moment. My marriage had been far too short. Leif Gable had always been forthcoming with me, unlike Finn. It was never a guessing game when it came to where I stood with my husband.

My heart was simply not able to accept that Leif was gone. And now, here was Finn, suddenly reappearing in Killdeer as if nothing had happened at all.

I was furious with him. Why had he even bothered to come back?

My feet carried me upstairs and I fell into bed after shedding my new dress and leaving it in a crumpled pile on the floor.

The last thing I thought before drifting off to sleep was that I hadn't heard Finn's truck pull out of the driveway. More than likely, he was still sitting there outside my house, waiting for whatever odd reason. I wasn't sure if that knowledge gave me comfort, or not.

CHAPTER 8

Morning sunlight warmed my face as I stood looking out the front window. I'd half expected to see a sheriff's truck still parked in the driveway, so when I saw a vehicle there I wasn't quite as surprised as I should have been.

What did surprise me was the man wandering around the front yard, stooping over, looking at the ground and generally making himself at home.

His car was parked exactly where Finn's truck had been the night before. But this was yellow. Bright yellow. A black stripe decorated the side and the hood. It was an older model, probably from the seventies, but it looked well kept. It wasn't a Camaro or a Trans Am, but it looked similar to the old muscle cars still rumbling around these days. The tire rims were so clean they sparkled. In fact, the entire vehicle shone with polish and gleamed like it was straight off the showroom floor. The license plate said it hailed from Kentucky.

I sipped my coffee and pondered the license plate, unaware of any person that I'd ever known of who lived in Kentucky. As far as I could remember, Leif had never mentioned anyone he was an associate of who came from there either. So this man roaming around my front yard was a stranger to me.

In spite of that fact, he acted as if he belonged there. He suddenly seemed to sense me looking at him and glanced up from the ground. His mouth fell open slightly when he saw me standing in the window watching him, and for a moment I thought he would wave or nod, or otherwise offer a gesture of welcome, but instead he slowly placed both hands inside the pockets of his tattered jean jacket and simply stood there, apparently waiting for me to make the first move.

He was wiry with a lean face and dark eyes set slightly too close together. His black hair stuck straight up on the top of his head like a stiff bristle brush made of hog's hair. He looked about fifty to me, or maybe in his late forties. Either that or he was younger and had experienced a hard life.

We stared at each other for a moment, like two wild animals who'd accidentally stumbled onto one another in the forest. Finally I lost patience with the situation and walked out on the front porch.

"Mornin'," I said, keeping my tone even and unwelcoming. "Help you?"

He walked carefully to the bottom step and stopped. "Mrs. Gable?"

My lip twitched. "I'm Marley Dearcorn. Did you lose something?"

He allowed one corner of his mouth to quirk up. "I'm assuming you are the wife of a Mr. Leif Gable."

"The widow of," I said.

His face registered neither shock nor surprise. "I am so terribly sorry to hear that."

His accent was unmistakably southern. Whoever he was, Kentucky had probably been home to him for most of his life.

"I don't believe I know you," I said.

He lifted one hand, placed it over his heart and gave me a crooked smile. "Forgive my manners, Mrs. Dearcorn."

"You can call me Marley."

His smile evened out. "I believe I'll call you ma'am until such time as you feel more comfortable being on a first-name basis."

This caught my attention. "Alright. Who are you and what are you doing on my property?"

"Why, my name is Thomas Dunne, ma'am."

"Which means absolutely nothing to me," I said.

In spite of my upbringing that had encouraged something resembling manners, I felt a pang of hostility towards him.

"Of course it won't mean a thing to you," he said. "Your husband hired me, after all."

"Hired you to do what?"

"To install the underground sprinkler system in your yard," he said mildly.

"I don't need an underground sprinkler system. Thanks. If that's what you are selling I'm not interested."

My hand was already on the doorknob.

"No, no, you misunderstand," he said smoothly. Every word out of his mouth was smooth. Like he was reassuring a frightened child. "I've already been paid for the job. My task here today is simply to determine the extent of the supplies I will need to purchase in order to start work by tomorrow morning."

I looked at him with irritation. "You are telling me my husband hired you to put in a sprinkler system for this house? What in the world for?"

He closed both his eyes for a moment and nodded his head once for emphasis. "Why, to provide your home with a barrier of live grass between it and the tree line."

"And he has already paid you for this?" I asked.

He pulled a crumpled invoice from his back pocket and held it up. "I have a receipt."

"You see where I live?" I indicated the surrounding forest and wild brush. "What do I need a yard for?"

Thomas Dunne slowly put both hands back inside his jean jacket. "He mentioned that your previous home had succumbed to an unfortunate fire. Mr. Gable indicated to me he wanted to prevent the possibility of another fire incinerating you property, perhaps one that originated in the woods surrounding your home instead of one that had been started from within."

My hands tightened on my coffee mug. Obviously this man had spoken to Leif after all. He was aware of the fact that our old house had been deliberately burned down.

My feet were starting to chill inside my fuzzy slippers, and more than anything I wanted the conversation to be over. "How long is this supposed to take, exactly?"

He kept his expression passive. "Perhaps a week, or ten days. It depends on the number of large rocks I might encounter while trenching for the line, and the availability of supplies here in your small hamlet."

Hamlet? Who talked like that anymore? "Why don't you have a truck with all of your gear inside it? If you are a professional, why don't you already have your supplies?"

"I am a recent import to your fine state," he said without missing a beat. "Your husband, and might I just say he was quite a magnanimous individual, took pity on my situation and hired me to do this job while I find my footing here, as it were."

"So why have you taken so long to get to it?" I asked.

"I was making arrangements with my previous employer, back home. Your husband allowed me a generous amount of time in which to settle my affairs before starting on your job. Mr. Gable was . . . most flexible."

That sounded exactly like something Leif would have done. He had been shockingly generous sometimes. He had been the sort of person who bought the beat-up brown-looking bananas in the grocery store so the manager wouldn't have to throw them away. And somehow he had managed to build an empire working as a president for an import/export company, and had made a small fortune managing trades for corporations exchanging international currencies. While simultaneously hiring a down-on-his-luck gardener to put in a sprinkler system.

Yes. That sounded like Leif.

I sighed. "Alright. You wanted to get started tomorrow morning?"

Thomas Dunne bowed his head slightly. He smiled faintly, looking relieved. "If that is an acceptable time for you."

"It's fine. But if I catch you peering in my windows like a gargoyle, this arrangement will come to a very sudden end."

His eyes widened. "I would never invade your privacy, ma'am."

"Right. Just keep on thinking like that and we will get along fine."

I slammed the door behind me and left him standing in the yard.

It was a sad side effect of my anger, but lately I had lost the ability to be nice to anyone. I hated the world so much it left a sour taste in the back of my throat.

I was angry at Leif for getting killed. I was angry at all the trouble I'd been forced to deal with over the last two years. And the old pain and rage from losing my mother to a drunk driver when I was a child was welling up to the surface again like a blast furnace had just reawakened inside my chest.

I hadn't meant to be abusive towards Thomas Dunne. It was simply a by-product of my internal turmoil. He was probably just a regular man, down on his luck, doing what he could to make it through the day.

I watched him as he unrolled a long tape measure in the yard and jotted notes on a small pad of paper. His hands moved with care, and in spite of the bright sunlight he seemed oblivious to the glare and worked on without sunglasses, concentrating fully on his task.

I showered and dressed in normal clothes, then felt guilty about leaving the red dress in a crumpled heap on the floor and hung it up in the closet carefully.

By the time I was ready to leave the house, Thomas Dunne was gone. The bright yellow car no longer sat in the driveway, and a small toolbox was nestled beside the stairs leading up to the porch. He'd obviously left it, intending to come back later in the day.

I drove towards town, instantly forgetting about my new gardener, thinking instead about Louise Robinson and what I might say to her that wouldn't sound insensitive, or prying. There was zero chance of coming up with questions that wouldn't make me out to be anything other than flat-out rude.

I talked to the windshield, trying out my test phrase. "Hey, Louise. I was hoping you have somehow managed to stay sober for more than one or two hours out of the day, and that you might know something helpful about your dead daughter who got murdered while you were passed out next to the sofa."

Oh, sure. She'd warm right up to me.

I shook my head, mocking myself and my pointless trip with a judicious eye roll.

Why was this so important?

Because life hadn't been fair to Phoebe and I hated that for her. She hadn't deserved what had happened, and seeing her body on the side of the road propelled me towards seeking justice. Even I knew it was misguided. But at least it gave me something to focus on other than my own troubles.

And there was the possibility I might actually be able to do some good here. Even if all I accomplished was helping Loy get one step closer to finding out the identity of the person responsible for the murder, that was something. Wasn't it?

I drove through town, convinced even misguided help was better than no help at all, and turned down the lane leading to the dilapidated trailer park the residents of Killdeer called The Burbs.

Louise Robinson owned a battered gold Buick, and I knew I didn't need to know the trailer number in order to find the right place, I just needed to spot the car.

"Son of a—" I said under my breath when I caught sight of the gold Buick.

A sheriff's truck sat outside the trailer, parked conspicuously on the street directly in front of the sidewalk leading to the front door.

I tried to gun my SUV to the end of the road and make a U-turn getaway, but before I could dart past the trailer, Loy was already leaving the place. He stopped mid-step and waved me towards him.

I let my chin fall on my chest for a moment. There was no sense doing anything other than pull over and deal with the consequences of my own stupidity.

I rolled down the window and eased to a stop behind Loy's truck. He leaned inside, resting his elbows and letting his arms dangle inside.

"How much sleep did you get last night?" I asked.

"'Bout four hours," he said. "I gather you wanted to pay your respects to Louise."

His tone was thick with sarcasm.

I threw my SUV in park. "Actually, I wanted to pump her for information about Phoebe."

Loy's eyebrows lifted with surprise. "Since when did you decide to start being honest with me?"

"Since telling the truth started being easier than making up a bunch of fibs to make you feel better about my snooping."

The sheriff laughed outright and scratched his forehead. "Alright. It might make you feel better to know that I looked into Animal's story about it being his fault Phoebe was up on Jim Creek Hill."

"And?" I asked, practically blinded by the shock of Loy openly sharing something with me.

"And, it turns out, he was telling the truth. Or something akin to the truth."

"You mean what he was saying about quarters?" I asked.

Loy picked at a scab on the back of his knuckle. "Early in March, Marshall Shelly was coming back to Killdeer from Parkman. You know that big blizzard we had at the beginning of the month? Well, the roads were pack ice and it was like a skating rink. Marshall owns that coin-op laundry over by the bowling ally in Parkman and he hadn't been able to go collect the money from the machines for three days. Finally he gets over there and fills up two plastic pickle buckets with quarters, sticks them in the backseat of his car and proceeds to roll the vehicle at the top of Jim Creek Hill at one in the morning."

"Two pickle buckets? That doesn't sound like a lot."

"Something like twenty-five hundred bucks," Loy said.

"Wow."

"Marshall collected the insurance on the money, since it was considered irretrievable due to snow. And those quarters supposedly sat up there all summer. Animal was in the Gas N Dash the night Marshall rolled his car, and he got the story secondhand from the tow truck driver."

"When Phoebe ran out of gas, Animal told her about the quarters so she could find some money to fill up her tank."

The sheriff nodded. "But Marshall is such a cheap bastard.

He went back up on Jim Creek a couple days after the snow finally all melted off and spent the whole damn day picking up all that change."

"So there wasn't any money up there anymore," I said.

The sheriff shook his head. "Animal didn't know that. Neither did Phoebe. You know she has a lock on the inside of her bedroom door?"

"On the inside?"

Loy cast a hard look over his shoulder. "I sometimes think there ought to be a law against being a worthless human being. Anyway, I got the impression from how Phoebe left her room that sometimes her mother likes to go in and help herself to her daughter's cash. Let's just say I think I know who was really paying the rent every month."

I looked towards the house and saw Louise standing in the window, smoking a cigarette and holding herself upright by leaning against the frame. She'd had enough presence of mind to apply lipstick, but not enough to keep it from spilling outside the lines of her mouth. She looked a little like a rodeo clown who'd taken a few bad hits.

Louise had been pretty once. Before alcohol and hard living had taken their toll. Her hair, once a smooth black mane that had turned more than one man's head, had now become a wicked mess of bleached strands. She was skinny, from lack of food and an abundance of vodka.

I wondered sadly if the death of her daughter had really managed to sink in yet.

"Loy," I said, peeling my eyes away from Louise. "How did she get up there?"

"Phoebe?" he asked.

"If she didn't get off work that night until 3 a.m. and started

89

walking, she wouldn't have made it to the top of Jim Creek Hill till well after sunrise. A person doesn't walk much faster than a couple mile an hour, and it would have taken her at least until 7 or 8 in the morning just to get there. But when I got there at 7:30 I could tell she had been dead for several hours. How did she get up there so fast?"

"Yeah, I thought of that too. She died sometime shortly after 3 so she had to have caught a ride with someone. My deputy is running down that angle for me."

I stared at my steering wheel so Loy couldn't see the bitter expression on my face. "You don't have to call him your deputy. You can just call him Finn."

"It's nice having backup again," he said casually, peering at me with a sparkle in his eyes.

"Your radio is talking inside your truck," I said.

I could hear the buzz and squawk from the cab.

Loy ambled to his vehicle and reached inside to key the mike. He chatted with Valerie, his dispatcher, and replaced the handset and came back to my window. "Got an angry tom turkey menacing patrons in the breezeway down at the library."

"Take your gun. My father had an old brown leghorn rooster on the ranch once. Meaner than a disgruntled government employee. He said that rooster was the best guard dog he ever had."

"Hey, I'm a government employee and I'm not disgruntled."

"Yes, but you have a sense of humor," I pointed out.

"That does come in handy sometimes," he said.

Loy lifted his eyes and lost his smile. He gave me a stern look. "Hun, I've had a sense of humor about you coming over to speak to Louise, because I know you sort of feel involved in this whole deal on account of finding Phoebe's body. But I'd like it very much if you called it quits now and left things alone. Louise couldn't think of a thing that might be useful. She knew almost nothing about her daughter's personal life. Honestly, it won't take us very long to figure out what happened. And before you say anything, no, I don't think it was just an accident."

I fiddled with the strap of my seat belt. "You have any ideas about who it could have been?"

"We've got a short list of names," he said reluctantly. "We found something at the scene that narrows it down a lot."

"I didn't see anything," I said with surprise. "What was it?"

"You know I can't talk about that. Let's just say we managed to get a good idea what sort of vehicle the killer was driving at the time based on how things were left."

I knew better than to rattle off more questions. Loy reached through the window and pinched my cheek with teasing affection. We were old friends, and sometimes he unabashedly showed his familiarity towards me even when it was not very professional. Our friendship afforded me a great deal of leeway with the sheriff, and it occurred to me at that moment, Loy was one of the reasons there was a glimmer of hope that I would climb out of my dark blue hole of grief. The support from my friends and my father had been unwavering, and sometimes I thought to myself their staunch loyalty was the only thing standing between me and a complete meltdown.

"If you and Wendy have too much leftover turkey, call me," I said.

"Why, I would never dream of taking a game bird without the proper license," he said with mock sincerity.

I'd once worked as an office manager at the Montana Fish and Wildlife branch office up in Helena. I still had the regulation book practically memorized.

He drove off to deal with the latest crisis and I spared one last glance at the trailer. Louise had disappeared, and I'd suddenly lost my desire to ask her a bunch of questions she probably wouldn't know the answers to anyway.

I'd already fixated on what Loy had let slip in our conversation. Something about identifying the type of vehicle based on what it had left at the scene.

Maybe I needed to go back up there and have another look myself, just to get a fresh perspective.

Before that, I decided to head back home for a quick lunch. The last thing I wanted was to end up looking like Phoebe's mother. In spite of what fashion magazines peddled, being a skeleton wasn't attractive.

CHAPTER 9

After rummaging inside the freezer for something I could pop in the microwave, I thought long and hard about what Loy had said. He'd told me something left at the scene had allowed him to identify the type of vehicle Phoebe's killer had been driving.

I thought back to that morning and tried to remember the place. I'd been fairly observant, but I couldn't quite recall seeing anything that revealing about the scene.

It was possible I wasn't qualified to understand all the particulars. Because of my upbringing, I knew a little bit more about cars than most women my age, but I was by no means an expert.

The rumble of a car engine alerted me. I set my half-eaten plate of White Castle hamburgers on the kitchen table and peeked outside to see who had just arrived.

Thomas Dunne, apparently freshly returned from checking on sprinkler supplies in town, was just shutting the door of his car when I stepped out on the porch.

"Did the Big R have everything that you need?" I asked.

He tilted his chin to the side. "Not everything. The pump they carry in stock will work just fine. And the pipe is more than I need. But the sprinkler heads were substandard, not the kind that filters debris, so I will need to backtrack to Parkman in order to purchase DWS heavy-duty versions."

My eyes drifted towards his bright yellow car while he spoke. My train of thought only had one track, and my questions popped out before I could stop myself.

"Do you know anything about cars? Like make and model. That sort of thing?"

He saw me looking at his pristine vehicle. "I know a fair amount."

"It's just that your car looks old, and you seem to take very good care of it. You sort of strike me as a gearhead," I explained.

"You might say that. I am self-taught but it's safe to say I know a great deal more about automobiles than I do people."

I sat down on the top stair and wrapped my arms around my knees. "What kind of a car is that, anyway?"

He rested his palm on the hood. "This is a 1974 Plymouth Barracuda."

"Is it fast?"

He seemed to be suppressing a grin. "It's been upgraded a little."

"So it's not what you would call a stock vehicle," I said.

"I replaced the shocks and leaf springs with geometry correcting sport leaf springs that reduce the roll steer, and dropped the overall profile by two inches. The engine's a 440, dual exhaust, with four-barrel intake upgrades. I like the fifteen-inch wheels, and a 3.73 gear ratio. The 4.11 gear ratio gives you a quicker initial launch, but you sacrifice higher rpm's at speed."

I blinked at him. "Thomas, I have no idea what you just said."

He spared a chuckle. "It's fast."

"I know you are probably trying to get organized so you can start work tomorrow, but could I ask you a favor?"

He heaved a sigh, and I knew I was on the verge of being an inconvenience, but my brain refused to let go of the fact that there was something up on Jim Creek Hill I'd overlooked.

"You aren't going to ask me to tune up your car for you, I hope?" he said. "I don't have much to do with the newer models. They lack soul."

"Oh, no, that's not it at all. Would you be willing to take a drive with me and look at something? I'm trying to figure out what happened to a friend of mine and I was hoping you could help me."

"Would this friend be a young woman who was killed in a hit-and-run?" he asked.

"You must have read about it. The story was all over the papers and everyone is talking about it."

He scuffed the ground with one boot and glanced toward the yard. "I've got a lot of prep to do before tomorrow."

"It won't take but a half hour. If you don't see anything we can come right back," I said hopefully.

Thomas rubbed his jaw with one hand, taking in my expression while he mulled it over. "I suppose a half hour out of my day won't make a difference one way or the other."

I stood up and headed for the door before he changed his mind. "I'll grab my keys."

We drove through Killdeer and up to Jim Creek Hill in near silence. Thomas looked acutely uncomfortable, not ever looking directly at me, even when responding to questions.

I assumed where he was from in Kentucky, strange women didn't often make it a habit to harass him while he was trying to work.

When we crested the hill I slowed down and pulled to the side of the highway to park. Straight across from the nose of my SUV, I could see the last downed reflector post, and knew we were in the right spot.

"I'm not exactly supposed to be doing this," I confessed.

Thomas let out a long breath. "Sometimes we find ourselves caught up in events that are bigger than we are."

He threw open his door and stepped out.

We crossed the highway and I stopped beside the bent post. "Here's where I found her. The girl who was killed. Phoebe Robinson. She was only twenty-three years old. That's too young to die."

Thomas let his eyes drift across the pavement, looking anywhere but the place I pointed. "Ma'am, I'm not entirely certain I understand exactly what it is you expect from me."

I waved a hand vaguely. "I don't know either, I guess. Maybe you could just look around and tell me if you can identify the type of vehicle that ran her down? There are three highway reflector poles that got flattened, and I thought it might be possible to tell what color the car was."

His jaw muscle twitched a few times. "To what end? What do you, personally, hope to gain by this?"

The question surprised me. Thomas's expression seemed pained somehow.

I hated to tell him the truth, because it was not something I was terribly proud of, but there was nothing to lose by admitting it so I decided it was better than making up some dumb excuse.

"My husband and I weren't married for very long before he got killed in a plane crash," I said quietly.

Thomas didn't interrupt, or ask any questions. He watched me in silence, holding his dark eyes steady, almost as if he was listening to someone giving confession.

It was utterly against my nature, but for some odd reason I felt compelled to confide in someone, even if that person was a total stranger. I'd kept it bottled up for so long, my feelings came rushing out.

I cleared my throat and continued. "I can't . . . it's not . . ."

I shook my head, the words not coming in any coherent fashion. "Why did Leif have to die so soon? We didn't have any *time*."

"Do you believe in God, ma'am?" he asked.

I blinked back a tear and gave a sharp laugh. "After everything that I've been through? What do you think?"

"Maybe if you prayed, asked for guidance, or help, you would receive the peace you are seeking."

"If I prayed?" I asked derisively. "Even if I thought God was listening, what is prayer supposed to do? It can't bring back my husband."

Or my mother, I thought to myself.

Thomas's eyes softened. "Ma'am, I don't believe I completely understand why you wish to come up here and revisit this place where a terrible event occurred."

My hands clenched and I bit down on my words. "Because it isn't right. Somebody needs to do something."

"I believe I noticed a sheriff's office on Main Street as I rolled into town."

My cheeks flushed. "Loy is a good law enforcement officer."

He studied me with concern. "Perhaps you should let him do his job. Why is this so important to you?"

"Because I *need* it to be."

I must have looked deranged, furious or half-crazy. Even to me, I sounded like a woman out of balance.

My voice was ragged. "I need it to be important because I need to do something besides sit at home and wish I'd be able to wake up the next morning and have everything back to normal again. I know things will never be back to normal. It just doesn't work that way. But maybe if I can help, do something that will tip the scales back, things won't seem so ugly."

"Tip the scales back to what?" he asked.

"Justice? Harmony? I don't know. The thought of some bastard running around on the loose, going about his life like nothing happened right after he killed some innocent girl, that's just way too much for me to stomach."

He closed his mouth and gave an almost imperceptible sigh of resignation. "Well then, I suppose I should take a look."

He turned his back on me and bent to the task. He didn't ask any questions, or prod me for information, he simply studied the ground carefully, moving with slow purpose over the disturbed grass and occasionally kneeling down to scrutinize a particular area.

The smashed reflector post occupied his attention for several moments, and he ran a thumb over the rough surface of the metal thoughtfully.

After he'd exhausted the post, he stood up, turned away and walked purposefully down the highway until he reached the next post. He studied it for only a moment, then crouched down and examined the ground around the post where the grass had been smashed flat.

I wondered what he could see that I couldn't. He seemed to be getting a great deal more information than I'd been able to decode. After he walked with his head down, toeing the dirt around the first downed reflector post, he marched back to where I stood and walked several yards past the place where I'd found Phoebe lying in the dry grass. He walked nearly fifty feet before stopping and squatting down on his heels.

I squinted against the bright fall sunlight, watching him while he pulled his tape measure from his belt. He unrolled the tape along the packed ground carefully, laying it flat against the grass and then holding the result closer to his face so he could note the distance.

He stood up, and it was obvious he had reached some sort of a conclusion. He didn't hesitate, but simply walked back to where I stood with a grim frown.

"I gather the local lawman has had a good look at this place," he said, easing to a halt beside me.

"Our sheriff went over it pretty thoroughly."

His tone was passive, but his eyes looked hard. "I need to know what it is that you intend to do with this information."

"Does it matter?" I asked.

"It matters. What are your intentions concerning this affair?"

Not that it was any of his concern, but if his help was conditional that was fine by me. "I suppose if it's something Sheriff Shucraft might have missed, I would tell him about it and let him add it to his stack of evidence."

I must have given the right answer. Thomas slid his hands inside his battered jean jacket and nodded at the smashed reflector post at our feet.

"He straddled all three posts," he said slowly. "I'd say he hit them directly with the leading edge of his grille guard. Chrome paint flecks are all over the metal, and since they don't have any other color of paint in the surface, it's safe to say we are talking about a pickup truck."

My face must have looked disappointed. "I sort of came to the same conclusion myself."

"That's not all," he said. "The track is too wide for standard trucks to have made. We are looking at a dually."

"You mean, trucks with two wheels on the back end for pulling trailers?" I asked.

"And not just any dually. It's an extended crew cab. If I was going to guess I'd say it was a newer model Ford Super Duty."

My expression shifted from disappointment to disbelief. "How could you possibly know that? There's no way you can tell what model it was."

"Well, of course there is," he said.

"And how in the world did you figure that out?" I asked.

Thomas looked pale. He swallowed a few times, but managed to continue. "After he ran down your unfortunate young lady, he pulled over and got out of the cab and stood next to it for a moment. There is a tread mark where he jerked the wheel too hard as he stopped. And when he jerked the wheel he left tread where his rear tires weren't in line with his front tires. That allowed me to figure the wheel base of the truck."

"Is the wheel base the distance between the front tires and the rear tires?" I asked.

He shook his shoulders once and closed his eyes, casting off the pallor that had suddenly gripped him. "That's right. And his wheel base is at least 172 inches. Way too long for a regular cab truck. It's got to be an extended crew cab. Most ranchers want a Chevy or a Ford, and since the wheel base was longer than 167 inches, which is a typical Chevy crew cab, I'd say it's probably a Ford."

I was impressed in spite of myself.

Thomas reached up quickly and wiped a layer of sweat off his upper lip. "Was that helpful?"

"You could say that," I said.

"If your sheriff has anything closely resembling intelligence, he'll have already determined these facts. But you might want to clue him in, just in case."

"That was . . . impressive. Thank you."

"Might we return to your home so I can resume my work?" he asked slowly.

Thomas still looked pale, and I felt a wave of pity for him. I'd become numb to things that usually upset normal people. Discussing the circumstances of a death appeared to be something that genuinely bothered my new gardener. Maybe I'd asked too much of him.

"We can go. I know you probably won't be crazy about this idea, but there is one more stop I need to make before we head back," I said.

He grimaced. "As you say, ma'am."

"It won't take long," I promised. "I need to go talk to the second to the last person who saw Phoebe alive the night she died."

He frowned. "The second to the last?"

"Her name is Marianne. She was the girl who came on shift right after Phoebe clocked out. And I am hoping she saw whoever it was who stopped and gave Phoebe a ride up here that night."

"Ma'am, do you know how many disasters end up with someone explaining to a judge that nobody was supposed to get hurt?"

"What?" I asked, fumbling for my car keys.

Thomas trudged to the passenger side of my SUV and shook his head. "Never mind."

He climbed inside and closed the door softly.

CHAPTER 10

I drove a little faster than the speed limit allowed, hoping to catch Marianne before her shift ended.

I kept glancing between Thomas and the speedometer, trying to determine if my driving was making him nervous. If anything, he seemed calmer than I was.

We pulled up in front of the Gas N Dash and left a small cloud of dust in our wake. I felt a small bit of satisfaction when Marianne was still holding court behind the checkout counter. There was no other way to describe it. Her pert turned-up nose and tight red curls made her stand out against the squadron of coal miners like a dove in a flock of magpies. The men were all gathered around her with bright smiles and the banter was obnoxious. Marianne was pale-skinned and cute, and her bright green eyes seemed to take in every single move around her. She was slender and rosy-cheeked, but she chirped out cuss words so vile even the coal miners honked with laughter.

She spared me a glance as I pushed through the front door and pretended to search for a pair of sunglasses on the spinner by the window.

I studied the coal miner who was goading Marianne. He wore the standard workingman's uniform. Heavy boots, safety glasses looped over his neck on a cord, filthy canvas pants and Levi shirt tucked in beneath a belt that was one size too tight.

He was a duplicate of the other three men. Aside from their various ages, they all looked pretty much the same.

I noticed Thomas had wandered to the back of the store and was trying to avoid the mob. He disappeared behind a magazine rack.

The cheerful miner nodded at Marianne. "You'd make a lot better money if you danced over at the Northern Lights club."

"You'd take home a lot more money if you didn't blow it on strippers who love you for your personality," she shot back.

The other miners laughed raucously.

"Well you won't ever come home with me so I got to hope you might show me your goods someplace," replied the miner.

Marianne jerked her chin at him. "I think your girlfriend has a better chance of seeing my goods."

The others jeered him relentlessly.

This went on for what seemed to me like forever. When the show finally came to an end, the miners straggled to the parking lot one by one and a chorus of pickup trucks roared to life and sped away. It was obviously the midday shift change and they were on their way to work. Finally, the store was deserted and quiet once again.

Marianne was scrutinizing me when I set a small bag of pumpkin seeds on the counter. She didn't bother to look at the bag, and simply rang it up with her eyes still trained on me like lasers.

"One twenty-nine," she said. "I saw your picture in the paper the other day."

I glanced up from rummaging in my jeans pocket and gave her an embarrassed smile. "I didn't think the reporter would actually print that."

"Are you kidding? That was golden," she said quickly. "Wish I'd said it."

"Were you and Phoebe friends?" I asked. This was going to be much easier than I'd originally thought.

"Course we were friends," Marianne said. "I loved that girl."

"Were you the one who relieved her shift the night she died?" I asked cautiously.

Marianne took my money, dropped it in the register and slammed the drawer shut. "Yes."

She blinked at me and folded her arms. Her face wasn't open and friendly anymore. Now she looked angry and hostile. Maybe this wasn't going to be easy after all.

"Look, I don't mean to upset you," I began.

"Then maybe you should shut your mouth and quit talking about it," she said.

I took my pumpkin seeds and fiddled with the corner of the bag, stalling. "I was hoping you might be willing to answer a question."

She turned away and snatched a worn dishrag from a small sink behind the counter. Her hands moved deftly and she wiped down surfaces that were already clean.

"Marianne, I know this can't be easy for you," I said, doing what I could to try and sound diplomatic.

She threw the rag in the sink and whirled on me with eyes flashing. "What do you know about it? You aren't the one who just lost your best friend to some stupid accident. How could you possibly know what I'm going through?"

I took a long breath in and let it out slowly, willing myself to stay calm. "I thought you might know who gave her a ride up to Jim Creek Hill that night."

"Who says I know anything about that?"

"I'm not saying the person who gave her a ride killed her," I said evenly. "But he probably was the last one to see her alive. He might be able to shed some light on what happened."

She leaned against the counter and folded her arms once again. "I already told Loy, I don't know who it was."

My temper was starting to fray around the edges. Phoebe was this woman's best friend? If I knew anything about best friends, it was that they told each other everything. "Yeah, you do."

Her pale skin blotched with a red rash on her neck and it was obvious she was lying. She stared at me like an angry rattlesnake. "Why don't you kiss off?"

Being nice obviously wasn't working any longer, and I took a moment to really think about everything I knew about Marianne.

Her last name was Morgan, I knew that much. She was about the same age as Phoebe. She'd lived in Killdeer for a few years with her mother before moving to be with her father, who lived in Parkman after her folks got a divorce. The only reason I knew all of this was because of my best friend, Irene.

Irene had painted a picture of the Morgan family one afternoon over ham sandwiches at the café. The gossip was that the Morgans had split up because Marianne's father had crossed the picket line at the Big Bear coal mine after the regular workers went on strike. The union miners called the men who crossed picket lines scabs, and Marianne's mother had decided she couldn't stomach being married to one. As far as I knew, Mr. Morgan still worked at Big Bear, but the strike had left bitter feuds that existed to this day.

There was one thing about living in a small town like Killdeer. You knew everything about everyone, whether you wanted to or not.

"Your dad still work the night shift out at Big Bear?" I asked.

Her lips tightened but she didn't reply. She simply glared at me with such spite I could almost feel the heat.

"Okay," I went on, not giving her an inch. "I can understand you not wanting to tell Loy it was your own dad who gave Phoebe a ride that night."

"It *wasn't* my dad," she said.

"The sheriff is going to go talk to somebody about it," I told her. "It's either going to be the person who picked her up, or I'll tell Loy you got really upset when I mentioned your father."

Her lips worked with anger, but she shook her head and finally scanned the store carefully and didn't see anyone close enough to hear us. Thomas was still lost behind the magazine rack.

She chewed her thumbnail. "I could lose my job."

That admission surprised me. She wasn't angry any longer, she was afraid. Now her reluctance was starting to make more sense.

"It was your boss? Adam?"

Marianne didn't respond, but she closed her eyes and nodded a couple of times to indicate I'd guessed correctly.

"Please, please don't say that I told you. I lied to the sheriff because Adam was fricking standing *right there* when he came in."

I had a hunch her lie had been pretty transparent, if her behavior now was any indication of how she had acted then. So it was a safe assumption that Loy had already put it together who had given Phoebe a ride up to Jim Creek.

"Thanks, Marianne. I wouldn't worry about Adam if I were you. Loy is always careful."

"Yeah, but Adam has a way of making a girl's life awfully damn miserable," she said.

"He won't hear it from me," I assured her.

I turned towards the door, but stopped before leaving. "What kind of a car does your boss drive?"

She laughed. "He's got a Saab. Can you believe it? What are we, in Aspen or something?"

A Saab was not the kind of car that had killed Phoebe, if Thomas was right. So he probably wasn't the one who had killed her. That didn't mean he wouldn't have something useful to say.

"Why do you and Betty hate Adam so much?" I asked.

"We call him Adam Creeper, even though his last name's actually Beecher. He's always pawing Phoebe. It's gross. He is old enough to be her dad."

"That's what Betty sort of told me too," I said.

Add another item onto the list of things that made me angry. Pervert bosses who took advantage of poor women was quickly making it to the top.

Marianne leaned across the counter, her face imploring. "Look, I know I told you all about him giving her a ride, but I've still got one more semester of dental hygiene school before I can get a real job. And until I graduate, I can't get fired. I mean I really can't. Do you know how much just the textbooks for that program cost?"

"More than Adam's Saab," I said.

She waved a hand in the air with frustration. "We all hate him, but this is the only job I could find where the boss was willing to work with me on my schedule. He's a real douchebag, but if you need a day off to cram for finals, he gives it to you."

"When Adam isn't in here making your life miserable, where does he go to hang out?" I asked.

She lifted her eyebrows at me. "Seriously? You want to go talk to him?"

"It crossed my mind."

"As long as you don't tell him I ratted him out," she said.

"Not a peep," I promised.

She made a face like she'd just bitten into an apple and spotted half a worm. "He likes to hang at the Broken Spoke."

"What? In his wingtip shoes and three-piece?" I asked.

"He might drive a Saab, but he dresses like a surfer bum. Adam thinks it's like he's slumming when he goes to the Broken Spoke, you know, hanging out with people he thinks are beneath him. It makes him feel rich."

"So he goes to the biker bar in Killdeer so the alcoholics in there thinks he's what, a trust fund baby or something?" I asked.

"God, who knows? Maybe he wants to keep in touch with his drug dealer? I shouldn't be talking about him like this."

"It's okay," I said. "I think you've helped a lot. I'll let the sheriff know what happened, but I'll keep your name out of it, alright?"

She shrugged. "Whatever. Adam's said some things to me sometimes. You know? Creeper. Maybe getting fired would be the best thing that could happen to me."

I gave her a faint smile as I left, mulling over her confession and trying to weigh the cost of confronting Adam about the night he dropped Phoebe off on the side of the road and just drove off without her. If I asked him directly, would he even bother to tell me the truth?

Probably not.

At least I knew how she had gotten up there.

The parking lot was empty and I had to force myself back to the present. Where was Thomas?

The door opened behind me and he sauntered out. "I was washing my hands."

"For ten minutes?" I asked.

His mouth twitched. "I thought it best to allow you some privacy."

"Thanks for being patient," I said.

He slid his hands inside his jean jacket pockets. "Have you satisfied your curiosity as to the events?"

"Almost."

He studied me with a tight jaw. "I see. Maybe it would be better if I allowed you to continue with whatever it is you are doing, and I went back to work on the yard."

"I'll drop you off," I said.

Like most folks living in Montana, I'd really racked up the windshield time the last few weeks. I'd traveled back and forth so many times to see Mr. Toomey in Billings it was almost time to get my oil changed again.

When I pulled up in front of my house, Thomas stepped out and put both feet on the ground, but lingered with his hand on the door.

"Ma'am. It is not typically my policy to involve myself in the affairs of my employer. But might I make an observation?"

"Observe away," I said snidely. Obviously he was about to tell me I was making a bad error in judgment.

He took in my cavalier expression and his resolve seemed to shift. "Well now, never you mind. I'll just get back to the sprinkler system if that's alright."

He shut the car door gently and took up where he had left off, bending to the task of mapping the yard.

I left him alone to work and went back inside to kill the remainder of the day. It was only a couple hours after lunchtime, and there had to be something I could do at home until the witching hour arrived. I'd decided to have a chat with Adam Creeper over at the Broken Spoke saloon before filling in Loy about everything I had learned from Marianne. I wasn't about to clue Adam in to the fact that I knew about him giving Phoebe a ride that night, but if I asked the right questions maybe he would make a mistake and let something useful slip out.

I had to think carefully about what to say.

And, on top of that, I had to figure out something that truly was beyond my usual comfort zone. What, exactly, was considered appropriate attire for a biker bar?

CHAPTER 11

The Broken Spoke sat, fittingly enough, at the very end of Cemetery Road just off of Main Street in Killdeer. During rodeo weekend the bar became the state's worst offender of fire code regulations concerning occupation limits. Since the fire marshal from Parkman was typically entrenched in the rear of the bar diligently defending his mini-shuffleboard championship title against the encroaching bull riders, citations for overloaded capacity were not usually issued.

Throughout the course of the remaining months after August, the Broken Spoke regulars did everything within their power to re-create the mystical, magical feel of rodeo weekend. On any typical Tuesday evening, it was not unheard of to see an ambulance parked in the load-'em-up position in front of the front door, or to see the Parkman city police surrounding the building, taking their tiny SWAT team out for some exercise. Loy had said once the Parkman police were quite fond of the Broken Spoke. They had confessed to him the bar was considered a tactical training site. And where else did you get to see two half-naked women catfight on amateur stripper night? The loser of that particular altercation had lost half her nose when the winner had bitten it off.

I walked into the Broken Spoke at a quarter to ten and felt

like I'd stepped into another world. Since it was Saturday night, a blue cloud of smoke hung in the air above the mash of bodies. Smoking inside was against the law in Montana, but in Killdeer, nobody cared enough to complain. Or, more likely, nobody reported them for smoking, because at least for a few hours on weekends the riffraff of the valley were safely locked up inside the bar and the local law-abiding citizens could breathe a sigh of relief, knowing where most of the troublemakers were currently passed out.

A single bar stool remained open, and the reason nobody had taken it was apparent. Two heavyset men dressed in black leathers flanked the stool, and no one else in the saloon was stupid enough to squeeze in between them.

Almost no one.

The moment I sat down I could practically feel the gaze from half a dozen inebriated men, and at least a couple women. The two men on either side of me barely spared me a sideways glance.

The place was loaded to the rafters with bodies. A pool table in the back seemed to have a waiting list.

"What'll it be?" asked the bartender.

I focused on the man in front of me. The first thing that stood out was his shirt. It was pink. Not just pink, it was tight, threadbare, and PINK.

His hair was bleached blond, practically white, making his tan stand out all the more. If he had been an Olympic athlete, the drug-testing committee would have taken one look at him and disqualified him simply for showing up. Even his muscles had muscles. When he moved it looked like two boa constrictors were fighting underneath his shirt.

"Ah, Shirley Temple?" I asked.

He looked at me. "How about a raspberry Stoli and lemonade?"

"I don't drink," I said automatically.

He ran his tongue around the inside of his cheek. "You are in a bar, you know that, right?"

"I'm waiting for someone," I said.

He took in my outfit. "Girl, if you aren't careful tonight, when you leave someone will be waiting for *you*."

I'd fished around in my new bags of clothing before coming, and dug out a sheer burgundy blouse that looked absolutely fabulous in broad daylight, but in half-darkness the thing turned practically invisible. Wearing a black bra underneath it hadn't helped matters much. I'd shimmied into a tight pair of Wranglers and pulled on a pair of old cowboy boots to top off the look. Even with my hair cut short, I had to admit, I looked like a girl who wanted someone to get her drunk and take her home.

I beamed an innocent smile.

"I'll get you that Shirley Temple," the bartender said.

He went to work, ignoring the shouts from staggeringly drunk customers and mixing me my drink with one hand while casually refilling a glass of beer for a biker sitting to my left with the other.

He slid the glass down the bar, and I marveled that it came to a stop inches from the end. I didn't recognize him, but the bartender had obviously been doing this for a while.

I studied his calm demeanor. "I don't mean to sound rude, but what kind of a guy wears a pink shirt in a place like this?"

He showed me a row of perfect white teeth. "One tough son of a bitch, that's who."

I sipped my drink through the tiny straw. "I don't suppose you know Adam Beecher?"

His eyes widened slightly, but he regained his composure almost instantly and shrugged. "Sure."

"Is he here yet?"

I'd searched the parking lot for a Saab before coming in, but hadn't found it. I was hoping he hadn't already left for the night.

"Adam usually doesn't get here until eleven or so," the bartender said. His eyes had hooded slightly and he searched my face. "What do you want to talk to him for?"

"I'm Marley Dearcorn," I said, trying to deflect the question.

"I know who you are," he replied tartly.

I leaned back a bit and ran my finger over the ancient wooden bar. Obviously my reputation in Killdeer had been made. The past two years I'd been in the middle of some serious trouble, but through a combination of determination and sheer stupid luck I'd managed to navigate my way through it and come out the other side with something resembling a knack for solving mysteries.

"I'm Jaycee," the bartender said. He polished a glass. "Adam is a friend. Sorry if I came off sounding like an ass."

If Adam Beecher was a friend of his I had to be careful about what I said. But then again . . .

This man already knew who I was, and with that information he had most likely already made up his mind about me. No matter what I said, I doubted very much I could come up with a story convincing enough to snow an experienced bartender. He had probably heard every lie under the sun at least a dozen times.

"The night Phoebe Robinson was killed up on Jim Creek Hill, Adam was there," I said.

Jaycee's eyes popped. "He was?"

I held up one hand to placate him. "Now, I don't believe he was the one driving the vehicle that ran her down, but I do think he was the last one to see her alive."

I let that sink in.

Jaycee's left leg bounced up and down a few times, causing his entire body to vibrate. "Uh-huh."

"Adam's got a reputation," I went on. "Some of his employees—"

"I know what they say about him," Jaycee said bitterly. "It's all a bunch of hogwash."

Apparently, even manipulating perverts had their side of the story.

"I just want to know one thing," I said.

He held up one finger. "Hold on."

A broad-shouldered roustabout was hollering for a Moose Drool brown ale from the other end of the bar. He hammered a fist on top of the sticky surface until Jaycee relented and pulled a long neck from the cooler.

"Another round for the home team," a frazzled waitress shouted. She stood between the steel divider rails that prevented bodies from lining up at the bar and blocking her access to the bartender.

In the dark recess of the far corner, a tableful of cowboys sounded a chorus of whoops in unison. They had been carrying on since I'd walked in, and their raucous banter was so loud it even carried over Merle Haggard's jukebox favorite, "Workin' Man Blues." The three Stetson-wearing cowboys were not ashamed of their command of the crasser words in the English language, and they apparently thought that "yee-haw" could be used as an adverbial clause or a compound verb, interchangeably.

Something about the tone of one particular yee-haw managed to penetrate the fog of noise permeating the bar, and I turned slowly to get a look at the table of drunk cowboys.

"Oh fudge."

Three rowdy hands from the Lazy Ox Yoke ranch sat together, celebrating the recent release of their short but angry leader from jail. Willie Pittman, a small man with a big opinion of himself, sat with two of his best friends at a rickety round table a few yards from the mini-shuffleboard table, pounding down beer enthusiastically.

I turned away fast and ducked my head. Willie Pittman had

done his last stint in jail due in no small part to the efforts of my father. Willie was a convicted felon, and had not bothered to stop carrying his rifle in spite of that fact. After Willie and I had shared a nasty encounter up on a secluded mountain trail in the wilderness area a year and half ago, my father had let Loy know about the rifle Willie kept. His arrest shortly thereafter came as no surprise to my father, or me. To say Willie had a grudge against me was like saying wolves were not fond of coyotes.

Sometimes the coyote got the better of the wolf if he was damn lucky, but usually, it was the other way around.

At that moment I was still flanked on either side by the larger than average men with black leather jackets, who displayed their political party affiliation with pride. The two of them were currently active members of the Hell's Angels caucus. They shielded me from the cowboys through their sheer bulk, but the moment they got up to leave I'd be visible.

My common sense managed to override my feelings of anger, and though I hated to admit it, I wasn't in any shape to handle harassment from Willie Pittman. The evening was officially over. I needed to get out of there before the Lazy Ox Yoke hands saw me.

Jaycee breezed back to his post in front of me, scrutinized my expression and frowned. "What's wrong with you all of a sudden?"

"I'm just realizing what an incredibly bad idea this was," I said. "Do me a favor, would you? If Adam really is a friend, tell him he needs to go to the sheriff and admit he was the one who gave Phoebe a ride that night."

Jaycee mulled it over, his jaw working hard while he appeared to think about it. "That's not going to look so good."

"As opposed to Loy coming to question him about it after a few days have gone by? Sure, it won't give the impression at all he was trying to hide something."

He rubbed his neck with one hand. It looked like a band of steel cables was strung underneath his skin. "Okay, okay. I see your point."

A commotion behind me almost caused me to turn and look, but I forced myself to keep my back turned. Willie Pittman and his buddies sounded like they were on the move.

"Hey, that tableful of cowboys?" I asked.

Jaycee kept his head straight while his eyes pivoted over my shoulder. "What about them?"

"What are they doing? It's getting awfully noisy back there."

"They are getting up," he said. "Now they are walking towards the door. Nope, they stopped. They are feeding some dollar bills into the English Mark darts game."

My head dropped forward. "How long does it take to play a round of darts?"

"About twenty minutes. But, they are pretty sloshed. It could be awhile."

"That's fantastic," I said, shaking my head.

"Not friends of yours then?" he asked.

"What are you drinking?" asked a woman's voice.

I blinked with surprise and turned to look past the Hell's Angel on my left.

The frazzled waitress stood at his shoulder, but she was talking to me. She held a battered brown serving tray with one hand and her makeup was starting to run from the heat.

"Sorry?"

She rolled her eyes. "What are you drinking? The guy waiting to play pool is buying."

I cautiously peered around the biker and saw my gardener, Thomas Dunne, lift a Corona beer to me in salute. He gave me a slight nod and I grimaced, lifted my hand and tried to wave back without looking like I was waving.

The waitress leaned on the bar. "I don't have all night, lady."

"Tell him thanks, but I'm just leaving," I said.

"He's buying, so make her a Long Island Iced Tea, Jaycee," she said.

"But I don't want it," I said.

"It's for me, ditz," she replied before disappearing again.

Jaycee pulled a tall glass from the bar and started to build the drink. Before he was half finished, I sensed someone standing behind me and turned cautiously.

"Ma'am," Thomas said. "I did not exactly take you for the type to set foot in such a place as this."

I craned my neck awkwardly over my left shoulder, hoping my profile wasn't visible to the cowboys.

"I don't usually," I said.

"Is something wrong with your neck?"

"She's trying to keep those three rednecks from seeing her," said the Hell's Angel on my left. His voice rumbled like an avalanche.

Thomas leaned sideways and studied Willie and his two misdemeanor buddies. "I see. They appear to be standing beside the only exit. You could be here awhile."

"Yes," I said with irritation. "I know."

"What do those gentlemen have against you?" he asked.

"One of them spent a few months in jail because he made my father angry."

"In my experience," Thomas said evenly, "oftentimes it all starts with someone offending the wrong person."

"If they see me, it could start looking like rodeo weekend in here in a hurry," I said, my face grim. "All three of them are beyond smashed. I have no idea how I'm going to make it back to my car."

Thomas took a slow swig from his beer, his eyes sliding around the room like he was taking inventory. "Does the bathroom in this establishment have a substantial door with a sturdy lock?"

"I've never been in the bathroom in here," I said.

"Maybe you should proceed to the ladies' restroom and freshen up," he said, pointing the way with his eyes.

"Thomas, you aren't planning on pulling the fire alarm or something stupid, are you?" I asked cautiously. "Or starting something with those three just so I can slip out?"

Thomas placed a palm over his chest. "Why, I am a nonviolent, Christian man. I do not believe in sullying my hands with the blood of others."

The biker next to me laughed out loud.

"Ma'am. If you would," Thomas said, holding out his hand towards the back of the bar.

"I can't hide in there until the bar closes," I said, scrambling off my stool and hurrying through the crowd.

"If things get competitive out here," he said as he pushed me inside the bathroom, "I suggest you keep the door closed."

I turned back. "Competitive?"

But he was already gone.

I paced the floor for a few minutes, listening intently but not hearing any change in the sounds coming from the bar. After nearly ten minutes had passed I stopped and looked at myself in the grimy mirror. "This is ridiculous."

I put my hand on the door and turned the handle, but stopped when I noticed something strange.

The handle was vibrating.

I felt it in my feet, then it traveled across the floor and the grimy mirror started to jiggle against the wall.

Someone shouted outside the door. Glass shattered off in the distance. A woman screamed.

I stepped into the hallway and saw every man, woman and biker inside the bar running madly away from the entrance.

The front door had been peeled off it's hinges and hung from a single bolt.

But I wasn't paying any attention to the door. I was paying attention to what was running through it.

A gooseneck trailer had been backed up to the front steps of the Broken Spoke, and a dozen seven-hundred-pound steers gleefully sprinted down the ramp and onto the dance floor at full speed. They tossed their heads, flinging snot wildly into the crowd and scattering everyone on two legs like bowling pins.

Jaycee stood on top of the bar and was shouting incoherently.

From the bathroom door I could see two waitresses and a few customers heading towards me at a dead run.

A steer darted past the bathroom, shied frantically when he saw me, spun away and crashed against the pool table. Pool balls spilled onto the floor and people were scattering everywhere.

The waitresses seemed to know better than to try making it out where the steers were spilling inside. They put their heads down and ran past the bathroom where I crouched, ran down the hallway and disappeared around the corner.

Instinct kicked in and I chased after them.

When I rounded the corner the waitresses were shoving open a door. They practically fell through it and I followed them. The three of us screeched to a halt inside a tiny break room with a small desk and a single office chair.

Behind the desk a tall door was partially blocked by a coatrack.

"Go!" yelled one of them.

The waitress with smeared makeup paused. "But it's an emergency exit door."

"There are *cows* in the bar," said the other waitress.

"Good enough for me," she replied and pushed on the handle.

In spite of the sign telling us that an alarm would sound if the door was opened, nothing happened as we piled out the back door and into the lot behind the bar.

The three of us stood there for a moment, listening to the sounds of splintering wood and thumping hooves.

The waitress wearing makeup now had a series of dark streaks dripping down her face, and the first waitress heaved her shoulders and shuddered. "I'm moving back to Wichita."

I made my way back to the parking lot as fast as I could and thanked my good fortune that my SUV was parked furthest from the bar. Last one in, first one out.

The stampede was slowing down. The gooseneck trailer appeared to be empty. Steers trotted inside the bar but had lost their momentum, and the hardier patrons were busy rounding them up.

I tore out of the parking lot and turned off Cemetery Road just as a sheriff's truck rolled by behind me in a blur of lights. For his first week on the job, Finn was sure earning his paycheck.

My foot eased off the accelerator and I actually laughed out loud when I pulled into my driveway.

"Crazy son of a bitch."

Thomas was nowhere to be seen. My driveway was empty. But as I went inside and locked the door behind me, it occurred to me I had just laughed for the first time in nearly a month. He'd just broken six or seven state statutes and violated at least two federal laws, but Thomas had helped me avoid Willie Pittman and a near-certain rough altercation.

His help had been appreciated, but it seemed to me Thomas had gone to a great deal of trouble to assist someone he hardly even knew. If he was capable of pulling off a stunt like that without a bit of hesitation, I suddenly found myself feeling very grateful that he seemed to be on my side.

CHAPTER 12

"You know I never could figure out why you didn't bother to get married at some point," I said.

Tatiana Phelps, who looked nothing at all like a Tatiana, snorted and tossed her battered straw cowboy hat on the kitchen table.

"Marley, why would I want to go and do a stupid thing like that?" she asked.

"The Deep Creek is prime ranchland, and I know you had offers from more than one man who wanted to come live there with you and work it," I said, baiting her shamelessly.

She fiddled with her long, sun-bleached braid with weathered hands. "Men are too damn emotional. They have such fragile feelings. You can't trust 'em not to go all cockeyed on you after you've said just the teeniest little thing."

"That's not how my father is," I said, suppressing a smile.

She stared at me. "It was only 'cause of your mother that he turned out alright."

Tatiana had pounded on my door at the crack of sunrise, and we'd made coffee and traded barbs for a while. As usual, she looked like she had just climbed out of a hay wagon. Knowing her as well as I did, I figured that was exactly what she had done.

"Leif was stable as a rock," I said, feeling a lump in my throat.

"Your Leif Gable was not at all like most fellas," she said. "He was what I like to call a man. The rest of them are boys, as far as I'm concerned."

I sat at my kitchen table and looked at my hands. They were wrapped around a coffee mug, and it was a good thing they rested on the table or Tatiana would have seen that they were shaking a little.

"Besides," Tatiana said with a wave of a hand. "I'm past being interested in sex. If I wanted to get back in the game it would take some weapons-grade hormone replacement therapy."

"Some women say their libido increases after they go through the change of life," I said.

She pulled a cocklebur off of her shirtsleeve and flicked it on the table. "I don't have time for that anymore. My foreman and I are going round and round about the plans we got for the ranch."

"You aren't thinking of selling, are you?" I asked with concern.

Tatiana Phelps had been my mother's best friend when she had been alive. After my mother's death, Tatiana and I had kept our relationship. She had been a steady, strong female presence in my life since as far back as I could remember. I couldn't imagine life without her, especially now.

"I'm not ever selling the Deep Creek. But my foreman wants me to get out of the sheep business and into the wheat business."

"Do you have enough irrigation to pull that off?" I asked.

"We don't have water rights that would let us raise catfish commercially, but we got enough to raise grains," she said.

"I hear in China they grow fish on fish farms, just like we grow wheat here in the U.S."

"Yeah?" she said, rubbing her chin. "That must be a mess going through the combine. I guess the scales go in the hopper?"

124

I laughed at her and took a long sip of coffee.

Her expression turned serious and she laid a hand on top of the table like she was trying to comfort a flighty horse. "Your father told me to come by and check on you while he was gone. So, here I am, checking on you."

The familiar weight of sadness settled back on my chest. "I'm alright."

"You don't look it," she said.

I couldn't quite meet her gaze. "I'm getting by."

"Figured out who killed that Robinson girl yet?" she asked.

I glanced up. "You know about me looking into that?"

Tatiana leaned back in her chair and the muffin-top of her belly rolled around on top of her tight jeans. "Sweetheart, there isn't a man, woman or child in Killdeer who doesn't know about that."

"So you came over here to tell me to back off and let the sheriff handle it," I said.

She shook her head once, with feeling. "I know better than to tell you what to do. You got your mother's sense of righteousness."

My tone wasn't as combative this time. "I haven't figured it out yet."

"I was in Lil's yesterday and got all the facts from Harvey Wilson," she said.

"Harvey Wilson's facts may or may not be correct," I said.

"Just not the same without Irene in there running the café," she said. "That girl she left in charge? Judy Isley? She's come a long way, but she can't hold a candle to Irene's management style. Anyway, Harvey Wilson said the scuttlebutt was that whoever killed the Robinson girl was driving a pickup truck."

"Probably an extended-cab Ford," I said.

She clucked her tongue. "How in blazes did you figure that out?"

"My gardener is some sort of mechanical genius. He seems to know an awful lot about cars, and I asked him to go up on Jim Creek with me and look at the tire tracks."

"I wondered why there was a trencher sitting in your yard," she said.

"He's just putting in a sprinkler system for me."

"You know how many extended-cab Fords there are in Killdeer?" she asked.

"A couple hundred?" I said. "But it wasn't a light-duty truck. It was heavy-duty, and a dually."

"So something that can pull a gooseneck," she said.

"That still leaves a lot of people on the list," I said.

"Dozens," Tatiana mused.

I was finally able to meet her eyes. "Tatiana, why are you here, if it's not to talk me out of digging around in this Phoebe business?"

She sighed and rubbed her wind-worn face with a dry hand. "Look at yourself. Marley, you are skin and bones. You don't go to work at the library anymore and you hardly leave the house. I was hoping you'd have come to me before this, but I can tell you are in a bad way."

"It hasn't even been a whole month yet," I said.

"I'm not saying what you've had to go through ain't terrible. More than any one person should have to carry. But cutting yourself off from the rest of the world? That's no way to live."

"Better I do that than subject the rest of the world to me," I said.

"What are you goin' on about?" she asked, leaning forward.

Even now I could feel my temper tilt dangerously towards anger. I breathed a few times to settle myself down again.

"Marley, what's inside your head? I can't see in there. How am I supposed to know what you are thinking unless you tell me?"

I slid my coffee cup away and stared at the palms of my hands.

"I appreciate what you're trying to do. But I really, really don't want to talk about it."

"Why not?" she pressed. "What's keeping you away from folks?"

My hands balled to fists in an instant and I slammed them on the table. "Because if I don't, I'm liable to start strangling people. I can't stand all the looks. The *pity*. It makes me crazy."

She watched me with a rigid expression for a moment.

After I'd taken a few more breaths, Tatiana pointed her chin up. "You done now?"

I shrugged. "Sorry."

She grunted a bit and stood up. "I was expecting this. So, I brought you a therapy dog."

"A what?" I asked, feeling a surge of panic.

"Let's go. Outside," she said, nodding towards the door.

We stopped side by side on the front porch and I could see that Tatiana had driven out to my place in her own dually pickup truck, pulling a horse trailer.

"That," I said, staring at my front yard, "is *not* a therapy dog."

She had hammered a stake deep in the ground and tethered a long lead rope to it securely. Harnessed at the other end of the rope, a spry little paint mustang stood beside my black SUV, cheerfully chewing off the windshield wiper. It hung out of his mouth as he nibbled it up like a rubbery blade of grass.

"Dammit, Peanut," she said. "Forgot he likes to eat cars."

Peanut had belonged to Tatiana's niece, but now that the girl spent more time at the university than she did in Montana visiting her aunt, the little mustang had become a bit neglected. He was a special case, after all. Peanut was deaf. And he hated dogs. Hated them with all his soul. He couldn't be around dogs because if he spotted one he would stomp it into the ground, and for a horse living on a sheep ranch, that was a problem.

"He ate my windshield wiper," I said.

Peanut and I were already very well acquainted. It was no exaggeration at all to say that the feisty mustang had saved my life.

I grumbled and folded my arms over my chest. "Tatiana, I can't."

"Well, I went out and got me a couple Great Pyrenees pups, so I guess the expression I'd use here is, tough beanie weenies. He's yours."

"What?"

"I'm giving him to you. Drew up a bill of sale. You owe me a dollar, by the way."

"You aren't joking, are you?" I asked with my mouth hanging open.

"Nope."

She limped down the stairs, compensating for her trick knee, and pulled open the door of her truck. With one hand she heaved a saddle onto the ground and threw a dusty saddle blanket on top of it. She came back up the stairs and handed me a well-used bridle. "Here's the keys."

I looked at the bridle and looked back up at her. "A dollar. For a horse."

"It's a bargain," she said brightly.

"What am I supposed to do with a mustang?"

"Take him down to your dad's pasture, turn him out with some oats, and go down and ride him once in a while," she said.

"But I don't—"

"And make sure he's got fresh water. Until your dad gets back and can help you set up the stock tank, you will have to go down every day to fill his barrel."

"Tatiana," I began.

She stifled my protest with a massive hug. "Marley, child. Your mother meant the world to me. But she's gone. Losing your husband like that, well, all's I can say is that's a tragic thing. I know you must feel like the whole world is sitting on you."

She held me at arm's length and forced me to look her in the eye. "I know you're angry. Hell, I'd be too. But holding it all inside like this ain't gonna do nothing but turn you into a spiteful human being."

She let me go and tapped the side of my temple. "You gotta get out of your own head and stop living in such a dark place."

I hadn't even noticed I was crying until the tears fell on my hands. "Are you sure about this?"

"Peanut's all alone in the world," she said. "He's got nobody. He needs someone to look after him. Can you do that for me?"

I wiped my face off and nodded. Even to me, my voice sounded small. "I can take care of him."

She took my elbow and led me down the stairs. Peanut was still jawing the windshield wiper when we reached him, and I grabbed what was still hanging out of his mouth before he could swallow it. "Give me that."

"Now remember, he's deaf so don't ever walk up behind him or he'll lay you out. He doesn't like to be snuck up on."

"I know how he feels," I said.

Tatiana took my hand and put it on the little mustang's neck. "Just give him a good pat when you are ready to put the saddle on. He doesn't deal with change all that well, so once you get him settled in a new routine, don't mix it up much. He likes to know what to expect next."

"Don't we all," I mumbled.

"I got to get back to the ranch now."

I wiped my nose on my shirtsleeve. "Tatiana," I began.

"Don't thank me. I'm not doing this out of charity. I needed to unload this animal and you are the one who's doing me a favor."

"Okay," I said quietly.

"Oh, and he's used to being around other critters, so you might want to think about getting a goat or something to keep him company."

"A goat?"

"Or another horse if you want. Peanut likes having someone to talk to."

"Dad's head's going to explode when he gets home and sees that I've opened up a petting zoo."

She wiggled her lips back and forth like she was trying to dislodge a wad of chewing tobacco. "I doubt it."

Tatiana worked her truck keys out of her front pocket. "I'll come by and check on you two in a few days."

"I'm going to have to go back to work now," I said. "It looks like I'm going to have a couple mouths to feed."

She grabbed the top of her head. "Forgot my damn hat. I'll be right back, then I got to skedaddle."

She bounded up the stairs with a bit more vigor than one would expect.

After she went inside I found my eyes drifting to the grille guard on her truck. It was chrome, and covered nearly the entire front end of the vehicle.

It was also completely splattered with bugs. I went to examine the grille guard more closely. It had to be very similar to the type on the mystery truck and maybe I could get some idea of what to look for.

As I picked at the layer of bugs I noticed a spray of blood and a wad of hair glued to the sharp corner on the right-hand side of the grille.

"Damn deer," Tatiana said. She stood beside me and crammed her hat on.

"When did you hit one?" I asked.

"Week ago Thursday. The Fish and Wildlife need to sell more whitetail licenses. They are thick as field mice this year."

"How fast were you going?" I asked.

She folded her eyebrows together. "Oh, fifty, maybe?"

"That's a lot of blood for only going fifty," I said.

She nodded. "Hit it broadside. Ran right out in front of me a block away from the grocery store."

"You were going fifty miles an hour on Main Street?" I asked.

"I had to pee," she said. "And Loy was up on Parachute Avenue giving a ticket to Old Lady Harrison so I hustled."

"He's got a deputy again," I said.

Tatiana gaped. "No kiddin'? I'll remember that next time I'm breaking the speed limit at strategic places. Who'd he hire?"

"Finn," I said.

She closed her mouth and watched me for a moment. "The South African fella?"

"Hired him Friday, I guess."

Her eyes drifted towards the trees and it was clear she was pondering that recent development. "Son of a gun."

Peanut tossed his head and snorted at us. He nudged Tatiana with his shoulder and she pushed him away. "Get off, you big mooch."

I took his halter and pulled him back a few steps. "I'll hold him while you drive out."

Tatiana gave Peanut a hearty scratch behind one ear and the little mustang leaned into it with delight. "He needs a good curry. After you ride him down to the pasture, brush him down so he knows you are looking after him."

"I will," I told her.

She turned to leave, but stopped and slid one hand inside her back pocket. "Marley, your father is coming back in six days. He's gonna raise high hell with you if he finds out you're searching for the man who killed that Robinson girl."

"I know. I'm not exactly sure what to do about that just yet," I said.

"I can tell you what you need to do about it," Tatiana told me.

"What's that?"

She pulled her hat down over her eyes. "Catch him before then."

CHAPTER 13

Peanut settled into our lower pasture willingly. As promised, I gave him a good going over with a currycomb, picked a couple rocks out of his hooves, and generally did what I could to make him feel at home.

I'd ridden him down from the house, and in spite of the cool air drifting over the landscape from the north, Peanut was damp with sweat beneath the saddle when I pulled it from his back. He danced to and fro, nodding his head with excitement, and darted back and forth sniffing the air and generally getting his bearings.

Tatiana said Peanut didn't cope with change very well, but I suspected she'd only said that so I would feel more protective of the little mustang and heap attention on him like a banty hen worrying over a clutch of chicks.

The sun was easing into evening, leaving a splash of orange behind in the low white clouds that hung over the mountaintops like displaced snowcaps.

My father's little red barn was empty. He had sold all the hay in late summer and so that was one more thing to put on the list of things I needed to do. I decided to make a couple of phone calls after I got back to my place and get a flatbed to deliver a load of bales as soon as possible. This late into October, it could snow at any minute and I wanted there to be plenty of hay in case we got hit with an early blizzard. Then there was the issue with water. We would need to set up a stock tank with a heater to keep the surface from icing over.

That, and try to find someone to keep Peanut company.

It was a problem. I didn't need two horses to ride. And what was I going to do with a goat? Goats had a habit of slipping outside the fence line and making themselves a nuisance. They ate things they shouldn't eat. I'd once seen a billy goat walk right up the side of a giant cottonwood tree, leap straight over a six-foot-high board fence and climb inside the backseat of a woman's Subaru like he was a golden retriever.

No goats.

Maybe I could find someone with a retired cutting horse that needed a soft place to land after years of hard labor?

It would work itself out. Living in Montana certainly meant I'd have my pick of unwanted horses if I looked hard enough.

After giving Peanut a final scratch behind the ears I headed back home on foot. Sunlight glinted off the remaining golden leaves in the aspen grove. The bugs were taking advantage of the few remaining warm days before winter arrived and swarmed around me gleefully. It never ceased to amaze me how durable insects could be. We'd already had hard freezes, but give them a single warm day and it was suddenly like they had risen from the dead. A persistent horsefly was making himself a genuine pain in the butt, and it took me three attempts before I managed to swat him with my floppy hat.

The sound of tires on gravel made me turn. A brown sheriff's truck rolled to a stop behind me.

Finn sat behind the wheel, watching me with not even a hint of an expression on his face.

After I studied him silently and folded my arms, he leaned out his window.

"Want a ride?"

Every instinct told me to refuse, but if Finn was living in Killdeer and working as a deputy from now on, I'd be running into him from time to time. Might as well get the awkward encounter over with sooner rather than later.

I climbed inside the cab and closed the door.

He drove slowly, not uttering a word. The front of my T-shirt was covered with horse slobber. Peanut had snagged my shirt, looking for more sugar cubes, and a grimy stain oozed across the formerly white fabric.

I was long past caring about my appearance and didn't even attempt to cover up the grunge.

"Nice day," Finn said.

"Hm."

"Was that a horse in your pasture?" he asked.

"Yes."

We drove a few more moments, the only sound a persistent hum of tires on packed dirt and gravel.

"Irene gone on vacation?" he asked.

"Yes."

He shifted in his seat, adjusting his rearview mirror, and I could see his jaw muscle flexing.

"Marley," he said.

"What was in the envelope, Finn?"

I turned in my seat to stare straight at him.

"What envelope?"

"You know what I'm talking about. The one Leif gave to you on the day we got married. What was inside it? You never did tell me."

My words sounded like sharpened steel. Even I was surprised by how angry I felt.

He took his foot off the accelerator and slowed down to round the corner leading up the hill to my house. He kept his eyes on the road.

"Directions," he said.

"Finn, I swear if you say one more goddamned cryptic thing I will jump out of this truck."

"I'm not being cryptic. It really was directions," he said quickly.

We pulled into the driveway and I saw Thomas Dunne's yellow car sitting in front of my house.

Thomas was squatting beside the rented trencher, fiddling with the starter mechanism. He barely glanced up as we rolled to a stop.

Finn cut the engine of his truck and kept both hands on the steering wheel, unwilling to look at me.

"Directions to what?" I asked.

"Why is this important?"

I jerked open the door and started to step out.

"Wait," he said, snagging my elbow with one hand. "Wait a second."

"So you can sit over there and think up another *Jeopardy* riddle?" I snapped.

"Why does it feel like a rail bang every time I talk to you?" he asked.

His South African accent always got worse when he was upset. At the moment he was barely intelligible.

"The envelope," I said. "Or this conversation is over."

He closed his eyes and rubbed them with one hand. It was the first chance I'd had to really get a close look at him. He was so tanned it was apparent he'd been repeatedly sunburned over the last few weeks. His hair was bleached from wind and exposure. Like me, he'd lost a few pounds.

"Leif gave me directions to a house in Namibia," he said at last.

"For the woman I talked to on the phone?" I asked.

He frowned. "Woman on the phone?"

"The number programmed into the cell phone you gave me. She didn't sound very happy to hear from me."

"That's just Terry."

"She said her last name was Hiser, like you. I sort of assumed you had gotten married."

He laughed and stared at me. "Terry's me mum."

It took a second for that information to sink in. "I called your mother?"

"She got in touch with me that night. That's why I came back. I knew you were . . . I knew you needed . . ."

He trailed off miserably and let his hands fall into his lap.

"You knew I was what?" I asked.

"Alone. I knew you were alone," he said flatly.

No doubt Finn was still in contact with his two acquaintances that had worked with him at his old job up at the station. Leif getting killed in a plane crash was such devastating news it had probably spread like wildfire via e-mail.

My voice had lost most of its venom. "I've been alone before."

"Not like this. Not so sudden," he said.

It didn't seem like a good time to remind him about my mother dying when I was seven.

"Wait, did you say Namibia?" I asked. "Why was Leif giving you directions for a house in Africa?"

He gave a half-shrug. "Well, more directions for a person than a house."

"Who?"

"The man who shot me when I was working there as a bodyguard."

I managed to clamp my mouth shut before peppering him with questions. The first time I'd met Finn, he had only lived in Killdeer for six months or so, and before that he had worked as a security advisor and bodyguard in South Africa. He'd been working in the Namib Desert before coming to Montana, doing freelance security for a group inspecting a fraudulent sale of faulty bomb detection equipment. Things had turned ugly. He had tried to get his team out, but hadn't managed to escape quickly enough. A woman had been killed, and he'd been shot in the leg. Finn's right femur had practically been shattered, and on cold days he sometimes walked with a pronounced limp. I suspected that Finn had nearly died that day, but the guilt and remorse he obviously felt over the death of the woman had damaged him. It was one of the primary reasons we hadn't been able to make it work as a couple. He had never managed to see beyond his failure to protect the woman who had trusted him, and with me he had overcompensated to such a degree it had become maddening.

It never had occurred to me that the man who'd shot him was still running around loose in the world.

"Did you find him?" I asked.

"I did."

My intuition told me not to ask any thing more. That and the look of savage satisfaction on Finn's face.

Questions buzzed inside my head. It made absolutely no sense to me at all that Leif would go to all the trouble of locating a man from Finn's past, and then deliberately set his feet on a path that would lead to confrontation.

Finn's admission raised more questions than it answered, but

I didn't have the stomach to ask them. My guess was that Leif understood all too well that I had taken my breakup with Finn rather badly. The only explanation that made any sense at all was that Leif had sent Finn off to deal with his past in order to get him out of Killdeer for my sake.

Leif was protective, but he knew I was strong enough to take care of myself. The answer didn't quite make sense, but it was the only thing I could come up with.

My husband lived a quiet life with me, but I had always known there was far more to him than I got to see on a daily basis. There were things about him I would never know and I would have to be content with that.

Whatever reason my husband had for his actions, they had to have been unselfish. That was his character. I had never questioned Leif's behavior while he was alive, and I wasn't about to start doing it now that he was gone.

"So that must mean you don't have any more unfinished business in Africa," I said quietly.

"All of my Africa business is finished," he said evenly.

Thomas had left the trencher and stood behind his car with the trunk open, rummaging inside for something. He'd been at it for a while, and I wondered what he could possibly be digging for in the back of his car that was so small it was taking ten minutes to find.

I saw Finn's questioning look as he scanned Thomas carefully.

"My gardener," I said. "He's putting in an underground sprinkler system for me."

"Nice wheels," he said.

Thomas apparently heard us discussing him, and sauntered over to Finn's side of the truck.

"Afternoon, officer," he said with his smooth Kentucky drawl. "Ma'am."

"If I was going to rob a bank, that's the car I'd use," Finn said, nodding to the pristine Plymouth.

"Not if you want to get away, you wouldn't," Thomas replied.

"It looks like it could outrun just about anything on the road," Finn told him.

Thomas gave a soft chuckle. "It can. But if I were tasked with driving an escape vehicle after a bank robbery, why, I'd drive a minivan. Older, beat-up. With a child's safety seat in the backseat and a couple bags of groceries in the hatch."

Finn gave him an impressed look.

Thomas lowered his eyes. "Not that I would ever consider doing such a thing."

"I smell like horse," I said, climbing out of Finn's truck. "I'm going to clean up. Thanks for the lift."

"Anytime," he said.

Finn fired up his truck engine and I gave him a wave as I headed up my front stairs. It was an abrupt departure, but I knew Finn well enough to imagine he wouldn't take a hasty end to the conversation personally. In fact, he probably felt relieved.

A great deal of the animosity I'd felt for Finn was evaporating quickly, leaving behind a fog of questions about my husband and his motives.

Since those questions were impossible to answer now that Leif was gone, the best thing I could do was forget about the stupid envelope, forget about his true motives for sending Finn on his mission, and get on with my day.

I hardly glanced back before going inside to take a long shower.

After I'd blow-dried my hair and thrown on a pair of sweatpants and a fresh T-shirt I wandered downstairs intent on heading for the kitchen. Voices caught my attention and I peered through the tiny window on the front door to see who was outside.

It had to have been at least a half-hour since I'd come inside, but when I looked out I saw Thomas still standing there, hands slipped inside his jean jacket pockets, talking to Finn.

Finn was nodding at something Thomas said, and with a final shake of his head, Thomas turned and went back to rummaging inside his car trunk.

Finn studied Thomas for a moment before pulling away. He drove down the road slowly, watching his rearview mirror carefully.

When the sheriff's truck had disappeared from view, Thomas slammed his trunk and leaned against it for a moment, his expression shifting rapidly between irritation and what looked like anger.

I ducked down before he spotted me. What had all that been about?

Most likely, Finn had given my gardener a verbal background check while he tried to work.

Something like that would make me a little irritated too. I forgot the entire incident and went into the kitchen for something to eat, so the next time Tatiana came to visit she wouldn't be able to complain about my skin hanging off my bones.

I had more important things to worry about at the moment than whether or not the new sheriff's deputy disliked my gardener.

Tatiana had mentioned there had to be at least a dozen dually extended-cab trucks running around Killdeer Valley. My task of figuring out who had run down Phoebe Robinson would be a lot simpler if I had that list.

Luckily, I knew someone who could probably get it for me. After dialing the phone and securing a load of hay to be delivered for Peanut, I hung up and went into Leif's office and located a certain business card.

I dialed the phone, realizing it was after normal office hours, but felt a bit of surprised relief when he answered.

"Mr. Toomey? It's Marley Dearcorn. I'm sorry to bother you so late in the day, but I need a favor."

CHAPTER 14

My eyes popped open and I rolled over and squinted at the clock beside the bed.

"Dammit dammit!"

I jumped up and darted into the bathroom, tripping on a pile of decorative throw pillows mounded on the floor, then recovered and stumbled into the shower like a zombie.

"Late, soooo late," I said, enduring the cold spray of water.

There was one good thing about having short hair. It washed much faster.

Mr. Toomey had set up an appointment to meet me in Parkman at ten that morning. It was already twenty after nine and there was no way I would make it.

I brushed my teeth with one hand and tried to put on some eye makeup with the other. I'd always tried to dress somewhat professionally when I went to see Mr. Toomey, but today he was getting the real deal. Jeans, worn-out sneakers and a flannel shirt with a hole in the armpit.

After this meeting I seriously had to consider getting some new everyday clothes.

I flew downstairs and snagged my car keys from the bowl by

the front door.

The moment I stepped onto the porch my heart sank.

"Thomas, of all the rotten places you could have picked."

Sitting on the ground squarely behind my SUV, a mound of sprinkler pipe blocked my path. I'd parked with the nose of my vehicle snug against the porch, and with the pipe directly behind my rear bumper there wasn't nearly enough room to back out.

The drive to Parkman would take at least a half hour.

There was no way humanly possible I would make it on time.

It was Monday. "Yeah, that's about right."

Cramming my car keys into my pocket, I hurried to the pipe and started shifting it to the side as fast as I could carry it.

After the third armload someone cleared his throat behind me.

"Ma'am, you appear to be in somewhat of a hurry."

"Thomas, I need to be in Parkman in twenty minutes and that is physically impossible. I hate to point out the obvious, but this was a really poor choice of places to put this pipe."

He turned slowly and nodded towards his bright yellow car. "I'll be more than happy to offer you transportation."

"Can you get me to the Java Junkie on Parkman Main Street in fifteen minutes?"

"How important is this meeting?" he asked, pulling open his passenger-side door.

I scrambled in. "Very. Mr. Toomey doesn't like to be kept waiting."

He eased himself into the driver's seat and carefully buckled his seat belt. He gave me a sideways smirk. "Please keep your hands inside the vehicle at all times."

"Okay."

Thomas lost his tilted grin and looked at me with sudden seriousness. "And ma'am, I'd like to ask you to refrain from grabbing the steering wheel. Is that something you can promise not to do?"

"Of course I can."

He started the engine and the entire car vibrated like an F-16 as he revved it up. "It will be better if you don't brace your knees against the dashboard at any time, ma'am."

"Why would I—?"

He hit the gas.

It was like being fired from a cannon.

The Plymouth growled as the rear tires bit into the ground and we spun 180 degrees before I could blink once.

Thomas shifted gears twice, and that was while we were still in the driveway.

The blood drained from my face as the trees flew by so fast they became a blur.

I caught a glimpse in the rearview mirror. A plume of dust higher than a three-story building billowed up behind us as we tore down the road like a bullet.

I wanted to scream but my mouth was too dry and my throat had squeezed shut. Every muscle in my entire body locked.

Storefronts flashed by my window and I realized we were already rolling directly down the center of Killdeer.

My brain couldn't process information that quickly. Bodies, cars, soda cans, all of it blinked by so rapidly all I managed to do was register what object we had just missed as they disappeared behind us.

In an instant downtown was gone and the interstate popped into view.

"Ahhh . . ."

"Ma'am, please don't put your hands on the dashboard like that," Thomas said. "It's much safer if you keep them at your sides."

I was grateful my stomach was empty.

Sheer terror prompted me to glance at the speedometer. The needle was buried.

"Thomas, are we actually going 110 miles an hour?" I managed to ask.

"Oh, no, that's not accurate," he told me quietly.

Instead of distracting him I decided it would be far more intelligent to let the man drive.

I clamped my mouth shut and tried to keep my hands in my lap.

The tires sounded like a coal train in eight-throttle. I'd never seen reflector posts go by so quickly. Then the hill came into sight and I could feel my legs shake with adrenaline.

It was impossible, but we were already close to Jim Creek. We started climbing. My brain did a frantic flip-flop when it pondered the consequences of hitting a deer at this speed. Luckily it was broad daylight and I didn't see so much as a ground squirrel.

At the top of Jim Creek Hill my gut felt like it had climbed into my rib cage. How we managed to stay in contact with the asphalt was beyond me. Every law of physics dictated that the Plymouth should have gone airborne. If we had launched into orbit I wouldn't have been at all surprised, but the wheels never left the road.

The Gas N Dash flew by on the left and Thomas tapped the brakes for the first time since he'd started the engine.

Downtown Parkman snapped into focus and I gasped when he pulled his foot off the accelerator.

"Can you tell me exactly where the Java Junkie is located?" he asked.

"It's . . . Um . . ." I sputtered. "You just passed it."

He hit the brakes and the rear tires slid sideways slightly.

"I see it," he said.

The tires chirped and we shot backwards, moving in the

opposite direction. The coffee shop was behind us on the opposite side of the road, and Thomas steered with his right hand, his left casually hanging outside his window. He shifted and worked the clutch in a way I had never seen done before.

A single parking place flanked by two parked cars was open directly in front of the coffee shop and before I could register what was happening, Thomas hit the gas, spun the wheel and braked hard. The rear of the Plymouth skated sideways, the nose rotated like an ice dancer and we slid into the empty slot like a hockey puck.

Thomas cut the engine and stepped out.

He opened my door and peered in. "You can take your seat belt off now."

"What was that?" I was panting with adrenaline.

"Technically, it is sometimes referred to a bootleg J-turn, or a high-speed reverse 270. But I like to call it a North Dakota grille-watchers stop."

A woman carrying a plastic shopping bag was staring at us from the sidewalk.

Thomas gave her a polite nod. "Ma'am."

She hurried off, looking back over her shoulder twice. Probably checking to see if we were busy pulling on ski masks.

I very nearly fell to the pavement and kissed it. As I wobbled inside the coffee shop, I caught sight of Mr. Toomey rising from a small table by the window. He was staring at the yellow Plymouth with razor-sharp eyes.

"Marley," he said, pulling a chair away from the table for me.

I sank into it gratefully.

"I hope you didn't have to wait very long." My knees vibrated underneath the table.

"I have just arrived," he said.

Mr. Toomey studied the license plate on Thomas's Plymouth

for a moment, nodded slightly and turned to me with a business-as-usual expression. "Here is the information you requested."

He slid an envelope across the table and I let it sit there while trying to get my hands to stop shaking.

"Thank you. I really appreciate it. How did you get this so fast?"

He ignored the question. "Friend of yours?"

I followed his gaze. Thomas stood on the sidewalk in front of the store next door. He amused himself by window-shopping.

"My gardener," I said.

Mr. Toomey leaned back as a young woman set two coffees on the table in front of us.

"I took the liberty of ordering. As I recall, you occasionally enjoy hazelnut?"

I took a polite sip and smiled. "Thank you. It's perfect."

Since my heart was on the verge of exploding the last thing I needed was a dose of caffeine, but I wasn't about to turn it down.

"You might be surprised to see that the list consists of over fifty-seven registered vehicles matching the criteria," Mr. Toomey said.

"Did you put the names of the owners on the list?" I asked.

He looked slightly irritated. "That was the point, was it not?"

I attempted a smile, but it probably looked more like I'd just stepped on a tack. "Thank you."

"This errand aside," Mr. Toomey went on, "Scott has contacted me and indicated he will be arriving in Killdeer a week from Friday to arrange for the dispersal of Mr. Gable's remains."

"Did he say he has decided where to scatter Leif's ashes?" I asked.

"Not as of yet. He indicated his idea was a bit unconventional in nature, and he wanted to discuss it with you in person before making his final decision."

"I will do whatever Scott wants."

Mr. Toomey's mouth twitched. "It seems your opinion is somewhat the deciding factor. Leif's stepson has grown fond of you. He values your input."

That information made me feel surprisingly good. "I guess I've grown pretty fond of him too."

"I need to be in Washington by nine this evening, so unfortunately, I must cut this meeting short," Mr. Toomey said, rising and grasping his tattered leather briefcase.

I managed to stand up and shake his hand without falling over. My heartbeat had returned to normal but I was fairly certain I now had a serious case of post-traumatic stress disorder.

"Ms. Dearcorn," Mr. Toomey said with a rigid expression. "About your gardener."

"He's not really my gardener," I said quickly. "His name is Thomas Dunne. I think he's had a string of bad luck. He's just putting in an underground sprinkler system for me and then he's probably going to look for a full-time job. Leif hired him as a favor while he gets settled here in Montana."

"That sounds like something Mr. Gable would do," he said.

"But I interrupted you," I said.

"I was simply going to point out to you how much effort and care Mr. Gable took in order to provide you a safe and comfortable life."

"And I am more grateful than he would have ever thought possible," I said.

"Then you should act like it."

I shook my head. "I'm sorry?"

"Your husband valued your life and well-being above everything else," Mr. Toomey said. "Perhaps you should behave as if you do as well. If not for your own sake, then for the sake of his legacy."

With that, Mr. Toomey lifted his briefcase and strode from the

Java Junkie with smooth, loping steps.

I stood there speechless for a moment.

Thomas watched Mr. Toomey leave, and the young lawyer didn't even spare him a single glance. Clearly my gardener was beneath recognition. But he did spare a long look at the license plate on Thomas's car. Unless I was mistaken, it looked exactly like he was committing it to memory.

From Mr. Toomey's perspective my arrival had probably seemed uncharacteristic to say the least. No wonder he was curious. To someone sitting at street level, the spectacle of our gravity-defying parking job probably looked incredibly reckless. Well it had felt that way too.

When I went back outside Thomas was standing by the passenger-side door, holding it open for me.

"We need to stop for gas," he said.

"Let's not break the speed limit from now on."

We rolled to a gentle stop at the Gas N Dash, and Thomas lifted the handle on the 87 octane.

"You don't use 91 octane?" I asked.

"It hardly ever gets purchased, so it ends up sitting around in the tank. The 87 turns over faster."

It had never occurred to me gas could get stale.

"I'm going to get a bear claw," I said. "You want anything?"

"If it isn't too much trouble for you, a small bag of Corn Nuts sounds good."

When I went to the counter to pay, I was surprised to see a man at the cash register.

His smooth black hair and good looks reminded me of a used car salesman. He gave me a once-over with his eyes, but not in a lascivious way. More like he was looking at my outfit with abject disapproval.

"Adam Beecher," I said suddenly. "You are the manager."

He looked at my face with a streak of worry. "Yes?"

"Phoebe's boss," I said.

His eyes darkened. "Oh, yes. The Dearcorn woman. I saw your picture in the newspaper."

"Did you tell Sheriff Shucraft that it was you who gave her a ride up to Jim Creek Hill the night she died?"

His lower lip shifted back and forth. "I did not."

"Don't you think that's some information he would like to have?" I asked.

"Why? So he can beat me over the head with it?" he asked.

We stared at each other.

"Let me start over," I said.

"If you think that will do you a bit of good at this point, go ahead."

I took a slow breath. "Adam, I know it wasn't you who ran her over." Truthfully I didn't know it for a fact, but I was fairly sure.

His face relaxed nominally.

Before he could get bent out of shape again I pressed on. "But you were the last person to see her alive. It would really help a lot if you told me what happened."

"I'm not saying anything." He folded his arms.

"She told you to leave her there, didn't she?" I prompted.

Adam's frown deepened.

I purposefully dropped my tone to let him know I was not angry. "She said she wanted to look for something. Didn't she? What excuse did she use to get rid of you?"

He shifted his feet. "Everyone here thinks I came on to her and she jumped out of the car."

"You can understand why," I said matter-of-factly. "You are sort of a dog, by reputation."

He blushed fiercely. "Phoebe isn't my type."

Outside, Thomas waited patiently beside his car and watched me with unblinking eyes. In a flash I marveled at his ability to indulge my erratic schedule without so much as a peep of complaint.

A red Mazda Miata pulled up to the pumps and a young woman got out to fill up her tank. She slid a credit card into the slot on the pump and pulled it out quickly.

"Adam, Phoebe went up there because Animal told her about the quarters that got spilled on the side of the road by Marshall Shelly the night he rolled his car."

"So that's what she was after," he said. "I thought it might have been a cell phone or something. But I couldn't figure out why she told me to take off."

"Why did you just leave her up there?" I asked.

He waved one hand defensively. "She said someone else was coming to pick her up. I thought it was weird but I'm not in the business of telling people how to live."

I latched onto that. "Did she say who? It might be really important, Adam."

"I have no idea. She never told me. Christ, if she was looking for gas money I would have spotted her twenty bucks from her next paycheck."

"And taken it out in trade?" I asked hotly.

He glared at me. "I'm in a committed relationship."

His anger was so genuine I almost believed him. "With who?"

"None of your damn business."

"Right. Committed relationship," I said. "Tell that to Loy. Or, better yet, I will tell him for you and we will see if he buys it."

Adam pressed both hands on the counter and leaned in. "You have no idea what you are talking about."

"I know your girls feel like they have to avoid going into the storage room with you alone," I said.

His cheeks flushed even more. "That's by design."

I must have looked utterly bewildered. "You want your employees to think you are a stalker-pervert?"

"Maybe it's better than having them think something else."

"Like what?" I asked with frustration.

"It's better than having them think I'm gay."

In an instant everything snapped into focus. I felt like an idiot. "Jaycee. You are in a committed relationship. But it's not with a woman. It's with Jaycee at the Broken Spoke."

His face twisted and he ran a hand over his sweating forehead. "I am trying to get transferred to Henderson, Nevada. But until that comes through?"

"You have to deal with the never ending line of coal miners and truck drivers that come in here," I finished for him. "Not the easiest place in the world to be less than a manly-man."

"You have no idea."

I took a moment to let the new information sink in. "Adam, I don't care about that. It's nobody's business. But you could try not being such a jerk to your employees."

He rang up my bear claw and my Corn Nuts. "I don't think that's a risk I'm willing to take."

"Rather look like a sleazeball than be honest, would you?"

"If those are my two choices? What do you think?" he asked. "That's two-seventy-nine."

I set three bucks on the counter. "Look, I'm sorry I pushed you so much. But it's still important. Did you see anything? After you dropped Phoebe off at the top of the hill. Which way did you drive?"

He lowered his eyes, remembering. For a moment I was convinced he wasn't going to say anything else, but he surprised me.

"I stopped in here that night because I had just left Jaycee's place and saw that both Phoebe's car and Marianne's were still here at the shop. Only one of them was supposed to be clocked in at that time, and I don't like them hanging around chatting when they should be working, so I came in to find out why both of them were still parked outside. That's when Phoebe asked me if I could take her back to Killdeer because she had run out of gas. When we got to the top of Jim Creek Hill she went ballistic and told me to let her out. She insisted she needed to stop and look for something, and then she told me she had a ride coming and I could just go. I left her on the right-hand side of the road driving towards Killdeer. Then I did a U-turn and drove back here and went home."

I wasn't sure if Phoebe had lied about someone else coming to pick her up or not. Most likely she had simply wanted to get rid of her boss so she could search for the quarters alone and not have to share them. I doubted very much that someone was coming for her. Considering the amount of traffic that streamed out of the Big Bear coal mine during the course of an average night full of shift changes I imagined she must have thought someone would come along eventually and she could hitchhike.

I searched his face. "Did you see anyone? Adam, please think about it carefully. Did you meet any other cars on the way back to Parkman?"

He shook his head a few times. "No one. It was three o'clock in the morning. There wasn't anyone out there except for me."

"What about here at the Gas N Dash. Was anyone parked here filling up or buying a soda? Anything?"

He stood up straight. "Loy already pulled the security camera tapes from the pumps. It was completely deserted for more than two hours after three that morning. Whoever it was, he sure as hell didn't come in here."

I felt my shoulders slump. "That's too bad."

"Are you finished giving me the third degree?" he asked.

I took my change and scooped up my things. "Sure, Adam. But I still think you need to go tell Loy everything you just told me."

He glanced outside as the red Miata sped away. The woman had used her credit card to pay at the pump and didn't need to come inside. A real time-saving convenience.

Adam stared out the window, watching as the Miata became a bright red dot off in the distance. "Alright. I'll make a phone call and ask him to come by this afternoon."

"Loy is smart. He'll figure it out anyway, and it will be better coming from you rather than him having to dig around for the truth."

He looked resigned and let his head drop forward. "Alright."

I headed for the door and stopped. "Where's Betty? I thought she was working extra now?"

"She quit yesterday," Adam said. "Why do you think I'm standing behind this cash register when I should be in the back doing inventory?"

I was genuinely surprised to hear that. "No notice or anything?"

"I'm lucky she even worked till the end of her shift. Betty said that she would never set foot in here again as long as she lived," he told me.

I heard Thomas start his car, but I paused and gave Adam a hard look. "She said that?"

"She said it would be better to go be a stripper down at the Northern Lights club than work here."

"Did she mean it?" I asked, bemused.

He slammed his cash register shut. "She meant every word. She was really upset."

"Why did she quit so sudden like that?" I asked.

Adam rolled his eyes. It was obvious he thought the entire thing was ridiculous. "I don't know. She said something though. Something stupid. She told me she was quitting here because it was too dangerous. Can you believe that?"

A tiny kernel of worry settled in my chest. "Yes, I can believe that," I said, and walked out without looking back.

CHAPTER 15

I spent the afternoon with Peanut, taking him for a good long trot around the pasture and ambling down the road to my father's ranch house to peek in and check that everything was fine. We rode back at a slow walk, the late fall sunlight slanting low and bathing everything with an easy gold glow. I brushed the little mustang down, cleaned a rat's nest of burrs from his tail and gave him a carrot I'd found in my father's refrigerator. He looked forlorn when I filled his water and left him alone, and it was sinking in that I needed to find him some company.

Tatiana was right, though. Taking care of Peanut was gradually pulling me out of my bitterness to some degree. My temper wasn't as frayed as it had been.

I'd taken a few minutes to glance at the list of names Mr. Toomey had given to me, and although the majority of them were familiar, none of them stood out in any way. I couldn't very well go to each one of them in turn and ask them where they were the night Phoebe had been killed. That really was a good way to get myself in trouble with Sheriff Shucraft.

For the time being, I would simply keep my eyes open and when I saw someone who I recognized from the list I'd try to find a way to check out the bumper on their dually truck. It was a poor strategy, but it was the best I could come up with at the moment.

To my dismay, Tatiana Phelps was on the list, but it was impossible for her to have done such a thing, and I discounted her almost immediately.

The news that Betty had quit her job at the Gas N Dash so suddenly sat under my skin like a splinter. I picked at the thought all afternoon, trying to see the deeper meaning behind her rapid departure, but try as I might, I couldn't make any sense out of it. It didn't get me any closer to figuring out who had run Phoebe down in the middle of the night.

In spite of being handed a list of names that most likely included a killer, it hadn't helped me all that much after all. It narrowed down the number of suspects, but subtracting Tatiana, that still left fifty-six people who drove dually pickup trucks.

Maybe I could narrow down my choices further if I had Thomas look at the list and tell me which of the trucks didn't match the make and model of the one he suspected. It was a place to start, at least.

I drove towards Killdeer and Peanut hung his head over the barbwire and nickered as I left. He dashed up and down the fence line, not happy about being left all alone. I felt suddenly guilty and decided it was time to search for a companion for the little mustang. Resolved, I drove straight to the Big R and went inside to check the bulletin board.

The posters tacked to the cork surface were all homemade. Some of the flyers advertised hay for sale, some showed a piece of farm equipment that needed work but could be had for a bargain price. One poster was simple a piece of paper with a hand-scrawled note indicating the man who had made it needed to either find a home for the three rattlesnakes currently in his freezer or get the telephone number for a divorce lawyer.

At the bottom of the bulletin board a row of horses were offered for sale.

I chuckled to myself over a postcard with a photo of a white goat that was being let go in trade to anyone with a good fly-fishing pole.

"No way," I said quietly.

The horses for sale were the usual. An eighteen-hands-high quarter horse with a new saddle had to find a home. From the wording on the poster it was pretty plain that the owner had purchased the big horse for an eager teenage daughter, and after a month realized the child was more interested in *getting* a horse than in *having* one.

Two mules were being sold. Their owner, a retired welder from Parkman, was moving into an assisted living facility and couldn't take the mules with him.

I shook my head. None of these animals would do. I didn't need working stock, I needed a companion animal for Peanut.

The last poster caught my eye. Harvey Wilson, ever-present regular at Lil's and self-appointed radio scanner monitor, was selling a six-year-old lame Icelandic pony, and if he didn't get the five hundred bucks he was looking for, the pony was going for dog food.

"Typical Harvey," I said.

But I'd already made up my mind and pulled the poster off the board. It was 5:30 and I knew Harvey would be bellied up to the counter at Lil's, Irene or no Irene, because after so many years of routine it would be practically impossible for him to do otherwise.

I drove to Lil's and parked outside. The lot was full of the usual suspects, and I saw the wide frame of Harvey Wilson squatting at the counter when I pushed through the front door.

Judy Isley, Irene's substitute, gave me a perky smile when I walked in. She wasn't the brightest girl in the valley, but she was honest and did her best to work hard. Irene and Judy had an on-again, off-again working relationship. When Judy wasn't trying to get through a term of cosmology school, she worked for the café. Irene had confessed to me that Judy would probably screw up a pile of invoices during her tenure as temporary manager of Lil's, but it was a small price to pay for a long vacation in British Columbia.

"Harvey, I want to buy that Icelandic pony of yours," I said.

He swiveled on his stool and looked at me from underneath his worn John Deere baseball cap. "Who says I still got it?"

"You want my five hundred bucks or not?" I asked, pulling out a checkbook.

His eyes lit up. "You got to pick it up yourself, then."

"Fine. I'll drop by first thing in the morning," I told him.

Harvey was not the easiest person to get along with. On a good day I usually felt like socking him in the nose.

I handed him the check. "Can he walk? The poster said he was lame."

"He can walk," Harvey said, snatching the check. "Just not very fast."

"You get a vet to take a look at it?" I asked.

He snorted. "Waste good money on a pony? Why would I want to go and do a thing like that for?"

I bit the inside of my cheek. "I'll be by at nine."

He wadded the check inside his pocket and as I turned to leave I saw Thomas sitting at a table alone at the back of the café. He smiled and gave me a nod as I headed for the door. It was a given that everyone in Killdeer eventually made it to Lil's. The food was simply the best you could get, and the atmosphere was pleasant.

As I reached for the door, Sheriff Shucraft pushed through and stopped when he saw me.

"Marley," he said tightly. "A word?"

He must have gotten that phone call from Adam Beecher, and I was about to get my head bitten off.

I went outside obediently and stood beside his truck.

Loy leaned his back against it and gave me a silent glare.

"I know it wasn't any of my business. But there was no way Adam was going to come forward about giving Phoebe a ride unless someone lit a fire underneath him."

The sheriff's expression twisted. "Hun, I have no idea what you are going on about."

"Adam Beecher. He's the one who gave her a ride that night," I explained.

"I'm not here to talk about Adam and his taxi service," Loy said.

Thomas walked out of the café, slowly ambled to his car and drove out of the parking lot. Loy gave him a piercing look, not taking his eyes off of Thomas once until he'd disappeared down the road.

"So, what am I in trouble for this time?" I asked.

"I need you to tell me who it was hot-wired a truck in the parking lot of the grocery store Saturday night and backed a trailer full of steers into the Broken Spoke saloon."

"What makes you think I know who it was?" I asked.

"Because my deputy saw you fleeing the scene," he answered. "And because everyone else I've talked to about it seems to have gone temporarily blind during the event."

I gave a noncommittal shrug.

"I see," Loy said. He shifted his gun belt, his face pink from the glow of sunset.

I shuffled my boot, toed a loose stone and tried to sound casual. "How did you know it was Adam who took Phoebe up on Jim Creek?"

His eyes pivoted towards me with warning. "We ain't the Keystone Cops, you know."

"Is it easier now that you have a deputy again?" I asked.

He grinned. "Finn's a bit on the rough side, but I've never seen anyone who can break up a domestic quicker."

"So he's working out," I said.

"I'm going to make him my undersheriff when he gets out of the academy."

"How long is the training for deputies?" I asked.

"Six weeks. He could teach the class on hand-to-hand. His biggest weakness is the defensive driving. I'm not worried about his shooting. Hell, I'm thinking about enrolling the Killdeer law enforcement staff in anti-terrorist training so Finn can qualify us for a bunch of government funding. He can hit a dime in midair with a .45."

"What are you going to do with government funding?" I asked with a smirk.

"Get a new truck."

We shared a grin and Loy turned to face me. His grin faded slowly and he ran his tongue around the inside of his cheek, thinking. "Marley, we are close to making an arrest in the Robinson case."

My mouth dropped open. "I don't believe it."

"I imagine it will only be a few more days. I've got two leads to check and when I get the information back, I'll have enough."

"That's good news," I said.

"You don't sound like you believe that."

"How did you narrow it down so fast? There are a lot of folks in Killdeer who drive a dually."

His eyes flashed. "How do you know about that? Has Finn been talking to you?"

"Are you kidding? I didn't know his first name for a year. Loy, if there is anyone in this valley who can keep a secret it's Angus Finn. I figured it out on my own."

Which wasn't precisely true, but hey . . .

"I need you to not say anything about this," Loy said flatly.

"I won't. But could you tell me one thing?"

He pulled open the door of his truck. "No, I can't."

"Why did they do it?" I asked quickly.

He stopped and looked at me, blinking in the last rays of sunlight. "What do you mean, why?"

"Why kill Phoebe? It doesn't make any sense. I've thought about it over and over, and I can't for the life of me figure out what motive anyone could have to hurt her."

"Maybe they were drunk. Maybe they were changing the CD in their stereo. Sometimes people do stupid things for no apparent reason. In this case, I am fairly well convinced there wasn't a solid *why*. It's more a question of who as far as I am concerned."

He climbed in his truck and drove away, leaving me alone with my thoughts.

Something about the entire scenario didn't sit right with me. It couldn't have been an accident. I didn't believe for one second that the driver had been changing out a CD, or that they had simply fallen asleep at the wheel or swerved to miss a deer. The reflector posts had been flattened too methodically for it to be anything other than a deliberate act.

Something told me the sheriff was about to arrest the wrong person, but until he actually named his suspect, there wasn't a thing I could do about it.

As far as I knew, Phoebe had lived a very isolated and limited existence. She worked, took care of her alcoholic mother, and what else? She was too broke to have much of a social life. Like mine, her reputation around Killdeer was that of a woman who shunned bars.

After seeing up close and personal what drinking did to a person, I could imagine Phoebe hated anything to do with liquor.

So what had she done for enjoyment? Had she been in a relationship? Those were definitely questions that needed to be answered.

That meant I'd be going back to the Gas N Dash to talk to the vampires again. As much as I hated that idea, I doubted anyone else in Killdeer would have a better idea of Phoebe's personal life than the crazies who saw her every day. If she was dating anyone, it was a safe guess Animal and company would know about it.

I drove home thinking about what Loy had said, and I couldn't have disagreed with him more. To my way of thinking, it was a mistake to discard the motive behind killing Phoebe Robinson. For all I knew, finding out why she had been killed would point a finger straight at the person responsible.

When I parked in my driveway I saw Thomas stowing his tools in the trunk of his car. The sun was down and only a shimmer of fading light remained, casting everything in a gray pallor.

The list of names and vehicles weighed heavy in my jacket pocket, and as Thomas closed the trunk of his car I went to stand beside him.

"I don't suppose you would do me a favor," I asked.

He turned to look at me with a flat expression. "Yes, ma'am. I would be happy to."

"Come on inside and I'll make you a cup of coffee."

He hesitated, but when I turned and walked away he trudged up the front steps after me.

We sat down at the kitchen table and I set the paper with names and vehicle registrations in front of him.

"Could you scratch off all the trucks that don't match the one you think was used in that homicide?"

Thomas looked pale as he turned the page around with one

hand. He hesitated before responding. "Do you think it will help?"

"I hope it does," I said.

"It's possible the person responsible isn't on your list at all," he said.

I sat down and rested my chin in my palm. "It's only a place to start."

I offered him coffee, but he refused and took a glass of water instead. He studied the list for several minutes and took a pencil I offered and started eliminating names.

When he was finished the list was whittled down to fifteen vehicles. Not too shabby.

"Ma'am," he said, handing me the paper. "It's probable the person you want isn't even here."

"You said that already," I told him.

"Yes, but you didn't seem to hear it."

I leaned back in my chair. "Well, I've got to do something. I can't sit around and pretend like it didn't happen."

"Have you ever considered how the man responsible must feel?" he asked.

I frowned. "I don't think he feels anything. If he did, he would have turned himself in."

"I'm simply suggesting that he may be filled with remorse. Perhaps the best way to handle this situation is simply to let things run their course naturally."

"Let things run their course?" I asked hotly. "Thomas, you sound like you actually feel sorry for this bastard."

His eyes looked sad. "No, of course not. I simply believe that pursuing someone who has killed another person is foolhardy. Maybe you should allow balance to return without trying to force it."

"I thought you were a good Christian. That sounds very much like a Buddhist philosophy to me."

He carefully folded his hands on top of the table. "I am a good Christian. I'm also a pragmatic man. In my experience, a man who has killed another person either accidentally or deliberately is in a very dark place. Do you really want to seek that person out intentionally?"

I fixed him with a hard look. "More than anything in the world."

He tilted his head to the side. "That tells me you are also in a dark place."

"What do you know about me?" I demanded.

He watched me with concern. "A great deal more than you could possibly imagine."

My eyes grew damp and I looked away. "I don't like feeling helpless. I need to do something besides sit around and wait for this murderer to grow a conscience and seek redemption. Not that I believe he could be redeemed in the first place."

"We are none of us beyond redemption," he said evenly.

I ignored his comment. "I just wish there was something I could do to make this whole thing more clear in my mind."

Thomas looked confused. "What would help?"

"You seem to know so much about vehicles, driving, that sort of thing. I wish I did. If I understood the mechanics of it better, maybe it would tell me something about the person driving that I can't see right now."

He looked surprised. "Well, now. I could teach you that."

"You could? How?"

"You take me to a big empty parking lot and I will teach you everything you ever wanted to know about driving."

Before he could change his mind, I stood up and held out my hand. His southern manners kicked in and he shook my hand purely by instinct.

"You know what, Thomas? You've got a deal."

CHAPTER 16

"**N**o, not like that," Thomas said patiently. "Sit with your back flat against the seat. Keep your legs in as much contact with the seat as possible, too. It helps because it provides you more tactile feedback from the car."

"I think cars probably talk to you more than they do to most other folks," I said.

"The only skill I possess that allows me a greater advantage concerning how to operate a vehicle is that I listen to them more."

I sighed and wrapped both hands around the steering wheel. "Okay, my butt is back against the seat. Now what?"

We sat at the very end of runway number 1 at the Killdeer airport, in total darkness, and it was closing in on midnight.

It wasn't exactly as if we had broken in. The fuel gate had been left open next to the hangar and we had simply pushed it wide and driven through onto the tarmac. Although I wasn't usually in the habit of trespassing, the airport runway was the only place I'd been able to think of that was big enough to accommodate the driving that I wanted to experiment with. Unless I wanted to go up to Jim Creek Hill in the middle of the night and tear around at ninety miles an hour, which seemed like an incredibly bad idea to me, this was the only place in the valley with enough pavement to show me what I needed to know.

Thomas sat beside me in the passenger's seat, not bothering with his seat belt, which concerned me a bit.

"Try to keep your shoulders in contact with the backrest at all times," he said.

"Tactile information?" I asked.

"It's sort of a safety thing. If you roll it, that is."

I swallowed. "I don't plan on doing that."

"Nobody ever does," he commented.

"Alright, I've got my hands at 10 and 2, just like they teach you in driver's ed.

"That's all a bunch of hooey," Thomas told me. "Your hands go at 9 and 3. Keep them there at all times. It gives you greater range of motion."

I shifted my grip obediently. "Like this?"

He reached over and shook my wrist. "Don't squeeze the wheel. Hold it firm, but you don't want your knuckles white. Contrary to what your instincts might be telling you, it is not possible to increase the traction of the tires by holding onto the wheel harder."

"Right."

Thomas took a deep breath and let it out dramatically. "It's not like shooting a high-powered rifle three hundred yards. You can't drive if you are holding your breath. So breathe deep and slow, and keep doing that so you don't deprive your brain of oxygen. Trust me, you will need all the oxygen you can get."

"Tell me about it," I said.

"Don't count on your thumbs to stabilize the wheel," he continued. "Use the heels of your hand. And I cannot communicate this enough. Do not, ever, under any circumstances, oversteer the car."

168

"Isn't that the cause of more traffic accidents than any other mistake?" I asked.

He shrugged. "I have no way of knowing that. But in my experience, it's been responsible for more rollovers than any other mistake."

The motor was silent. We hadn't graduated to actually starting the engine yet, and considering the lesson I was getting, it was probably a good idea.

"When you turn the wheel, don't pull it with your leading hand, push it with your trailing hand. Push towards the 12 o'clock position. You do it that way because your trailing wrist is locked and it gives you greater control."

I pushed the wheel to the left. "Like this?"

"That's exactly right. You want your wrist locked while turning, because it makes you focus on what you are doing and it gives you better stability. Jerking the wheel too quickly makes you lose traction with the road, and you don't want to do that. Every move you make needs to be smooth."

"Can we start the engine now?" I asked.

"I see you have your hand sitting on the shifter," Thomas said.

I glanced at him. "Is that wrong?"

"They do it in movies all the time, but that's not the way you want to drive a car. Never put your hand on the shifter unless you are actually gearing up or down. Leaving your hand resting on the knob prevents you from steering. And steering is the most important task you have."

"Okay. Can we start the engine now?" I asked.

He grumbled. "Don't wrap your fingers around the shifter knob. Use the heel of your hand because it gets your hand back up to the wheel quicker."

I reached for the key.

"Not yet," he said, waving my hand away from the ignition. "Look at the floor. How many pedals do you see?"

"Three," I said, without looking.

"Wrong. There are four. Look down there, don't just rely on your memory."

"I don't see a fourth pedal, Thomas," I said impatiently.

"Gas, brake, clutch and rest," he told me. "The fourth pedal is not a true pedal because it doesn't move. But it's crucial. You see that pad to the left of the clutch? It's the rest. You always keep the ball of your left foot resting on that while not shifting, because it helps to stabilize your body."

I set my left foot on the pad and pushed down. "You're right. It doesn't move."

"Don't lean on it like that," he said. "Set your foot there. It's a rest, not an excuse to get lazy."

"I got it, I got it. Can we start the car now?" I asked.

"As you wish. Press the clutch down with the ball of your foot. Don't use your toes to shift, or to operate the gas pedal. Use the ball of your foot, and your legs should never be fully extended. There needs to be a little bit of bend left in your knee even when you are pressing the clutch. Got it?"

I turned the key and the engine purred to life. "Wow. This car isn't exactly stock off the line, is it?"

"I've modified this car so that you can do a heel-toe downshift, but that requires you to perform five things at once, so let's skip that."

"No, I mean the engine," I said. "It doesn't sound like a normal car motor."

He ignored the comment. "Let's talk about traction."

"That's all you've been talking about," I said, tapping the gas pedal.

The engine growled.

"Even the best driver in the world cannot recover a skid if he loses traction. Because once your tires have lost their grip, there isn't anything to recover *with*. The trick to stopping, then, is to brake as hard as possible without losing grip. If you can do that, you can control a vehicle."

"Can I put it in gear?" I asked.

"Sure."

I slid the shifter into first, let out the clutch and killed the engine instantly. "Oops."

"Don't be wishy-washy with this car, Marley. When you brake, brake. When you release, release. I've got more than four hundred horses under the hood, close to six hundred if you need to know. And it's got a much stiffer suspension than a stock vehicle, but it only weighs three thousand pounds."

"So it's fast?" I asked.

"That's not the point I was attempting to make," he said.

I started the engine again.

"Easy," he said. "Nobody is chasing us. Let out the clutch nice and smooth, and give it a little bit more gas."

The Plymouth nosed forward a few inches. The big engine rumbled. It felt to me like it wanted to go faster.

I hit the gas.

The back tires squealed and we fishtailed quicker than a sockeye salmon spawning in a typhoon.

I pulled my foot off the gas pedal at once. "Oh my."

"The rear wheels give you power, the front wheels give you direction," he said. "They need to be in agreement."

"Right. Agreement," I said.

He grabbed the wheel and pulled it into the correct position. "Now, hit the gas again."

I did as he instructed and the Plymouth shot forward like a

spooked horse. Thomas held the wheel and forced it into the right position so we didn't lose traction. In a matter of seconds we were reaching the threshold of first gear.

"Back it off," he said.

I eased off the accelerator and could feel a grin spreading across my face. "That was great! Let's do it again."

"Wait a second, wait a second," he said. "What are you going to do once we get to the end of the runway?"

"Ah, turn?" I asked.

I could almost feel him rolling his eyes.

"Yes, but how are you going to do it? Cornering is an art, and a science. The idea is to have the fastest speed you can achieve coming out of the turn, and you do that by hitting the gas as your wheels start to straighten out, but not before."

"So when my hands are getting close to 9 and 3, hit the gas?" I asked.

Thomas was quiet for a moment. "I suppose that's as good a way to put it as any."

"Is there anything else I need to know?" I asked.

He slumped back in his seat. "One or two things."

"You are being sarcastic," I told him.

"A little. But I can't think of anything else I could actually tell you. The rest you need to learn by feel."

"I can't see what's in the rearview mirror." I craned my neck up but I was still too short.

"Good. You don't need to see what's in the mirror," he said sharply.

"I don't understand. Isn't that important? What's behind you, I mean?"

"The faster you go, the further ahead you need to look. Don't stare at the signs, the lines, or the mirrors. Look ahead at what is coming. It wastes time to look at the speedometer so don't bother with it. Look far ahead once, then look straight ahead twice, and keep that pattern up until you get where you are going."

"What if I want to pass someone? Won't I need to know where they are so I can flip on my blinker and get back in my lane?"

He snorted out a laugh. "If you are driving like I've just taught you, the last thing on your mind is going to be your blinker. Listen. This car is fast enough to pass just about anything on the road, as long as it's street legal. If you really want to get by someone, all you have to do is follow the look-once, watch-twice pattern and wait for the other driver to hesitate. Then you slip on past."

"Alright," I said as I braced my left foot exactly like he had instructed. "Let's light this candle."

The Killdeer airport runway was deserted. It was typical to see more deer and rabbits inhabit the area than airplanes. For two hours we had runway number 1 completely to ourselves, and Thomas instructed me on the finer points of high-speed turns. I asked him to teach me how to perform his signature North Dakota grille-watchers stop, but he flatly refused.

I learned how to control a car going into a sharp corner, and how to keep the wheels from slipping. I learned how to deliberately lose traction and flip the car around 180 degrees without rolling it over, and most importantly, Thomas taught me the difference between too little and too much when it came to acceleration.

I was sweating like a summer hog by the time we were finished.

After we had burned through almost an entire tank of gasoline, I pulled to the side of the runway and put the car in neutral.

For a few moments I simply stared ahead, thinking about the real reason I'd dragged Thomas out to the impromptu driving lesson in the first place.

"Are you alright, ma'am?"

I shook myself back to the moment and gave him a tired smile. "Why didn't he jerk the wheel?"

"I beg your pardon?" he asked.

"The man who hit Phoebe. Why didn't he jerk the wheel? If it was an accident, you would think he would have panicked after running over a person, and jerked the wheel back towards the pavement. Why didn't he do that?"

Thomas fell into a dark silence.

I turned and really looked at him. He seemed upset, but I needed an answer even if the topic was making him squeamish.

"Thomas, wouldn't someone who had drifted off the road, accidentally, jerk the wheel after hitting something? It would be purely a reflex, right? But he didn't do that. He drove straight ahead, stopped, got out and stood by his truck looking back. That's what you said. You said his tire tracks indicated that he pulled over and parked, then got back in his truck and drove away."

"Turn the engine off," he told me.

I rotated the key and the car died.

He sat beside me in utter silence, and even though I couldn't see his face any longer in the near total darkness, I could feel the heaviness of his words.

"You surmise that the man deliberately aimed for his victim," he said.

"That's exactly what I surmise," I said.

"What if you are mistaken?" he asked.

It was my turn to be quiet. I thought hard about what he had just asked me, but I shook it off, disgusted. "I can't believe it was an accident."

"Because you have already made up your mind about the person who was responsible."

"Because he needs to be held accountable for what he did,"

I replied.

"Please don't get yourself upset," he said quietly. "I am only asking a question."

"If it was an accident, the man driving the car would have swerved. He didn't. That tells me everything I need to know."

To my astonishment Thomas threw open his door and clambered out of the car. He walked a few paces away, shaking his arms like he was trying to shake off a swarm of bees.

I stepped out and watched him, silhouetted in the dim glow from the hangar lights. He came to a halt with his back to me, and reached up quickly with both hands, looking to all appearances like he was wiping away a shower of tears.

I didn't follow him, but simply stood where I was until he was composed enough to return.

Wordlessly he came to the driver's side of the car and I stepped aside to let him climb back into his seat.

He waited until I was buckled in the passenger's side, started the engine with practiced confidence, and drove us back to the hangar gates in total silence. I hopped out and swung the gates closed behind us, making sure to lock it this time so no other hooligans could come joyriding on the tarmac tonight.

Thomas drove us back to my house without so much as uttering a single word. When we came to a stop in the driveway, I reluctantly climbed out, but before closing my door I peered at him.

"Are you alright?" I asked.

"I know that you disdain the ways of the faithful," he began. "I won't judge you for your lack of belief in the Lord. But for some of us, hope for redemption is all that we have to hold onto."

"I don't understand," I said.

His jaw muscles worked hard as he seemed to be suppressing unspoken words. After a moment he finally looked up, managing to give me a slight nod. "I'm just fine, ma'am. I understand why you hold such contempt for religion. It has, after all, let you down in the past. But for me? I do not hold to my beliefs so that I may use them as a club. I do not need to prove to others that I am righteous in order for it to be so, and because of that I do not blame you for your anger at God. But in my case, the hope of redemption is sometimes all that stands between me and oblivion."

His confession was a surprise. Not that I thought of Thomas as a Boy Scout, exactly, but I hadn't ever gotten the impression he was as bad as all that. "Redemption for what?"

He looked away and shifted the car into gear. "I have not always been a good person during the course of my travels. That's all changed now, and there might be hope for me yet."

Before I could reply he started to back out of the driveway and I had to scramble to get the door closed.

I watched him drive away, a feeling of utter sadness hanging over me that I simply could not explain.

CHAPTER 17

"How long has his hoof been like this?" I asked.

Harvey Wilson shifted the toothpick in his mouth from one corner to the other. "About a month."

"Jesus, Harvey."

I dropped the Icelandic pony's left rear hoof and straightened up. It took all my strength to keep from saying something that I might regret later.

"You bought him, he's your problem now," Harvey said.

"He's got thrush. You ever think it might be a good idea to muck out your stalls once in a while?"

The chubby rancher grunted. "I think I got a halter around here someplace."

Harvey ambled off, searching the barren stable for a halter, and all I could do was shake my head after him.

The pony had a bacterial infection surrounding the frog in his left rear hoof that was caused by standing in wet, dirty conditions for too long. Thrush, probably not the technical term but the word we had always used on the ranch, was curable. Clean, dry stable conditions and a twice-daily dose of iodine would clear it up. But it chafed my nerves to see it on an otherwise healthy animal.

"Don't worry." I stroked the pony's neck. "I'm getting you out of here."

By way of thanks, the pony flattened both ears and bit my elbow.

"Ow! Thanks a lot."

"He's called Lil Nipper," Harvey said, handing me a halter and lead rope.

"Yeah, that's just great."

I slipped the halter over his head and snapped the lead rope to the O-ring. Lil Nipper blew out a long snort, shook his head and stamped. Horse-speak for *let's get this show on the road.*

He was gorgeous, if a pony could be described as such. All long blond mane and shiny tail, chestnut-colored and bright-eyed. Aside from his limp, he was a truly beautiful animal. He was so small, compared to the working horses I'd grown up around, only standing as high as my waist. Pocket-sized. Or portable. He was mean, but cute as all get-out.

I led him out of the disgusting stall and into the courtyard. I'd borrowed my father's gooseneck trailer and battered old pickup truck, and they were parked just outside. Lil Nipper limped eagerly to the back of the trailer and loaded himself right up. I got the distinct impression he knew he was making a break for it, and he walked directly to the front of the trailer and waited for me to fasten his rope, swishing his tail impatiently.

"Thanks, Harvey," I said. "You don't have any other horses here, do you?"

He eyed me suspiciously. "Why you want to know?"

"In case I need to inform animal welfare," I told him.

His round face spread into a grin. "That's funny. You should be a comedian."

It was lost on him that I wasn't kidding.

"Pleasure doing business with you," I said.

As I dug in my jeans for the truck keys, the problem of what to do about the thrush in Lil Nipper's hoof reminded me that I had very little in the way of horse gear back at the ranch house.

"Harvey, you got a hoof pick around her anywhere? I would just as soon not have to go into the Big R today if I can help it."

He fiddled with the toothpick, not moving. "I guess I got one you can take."

The things cost three dollars. But that was three dollars out of Harvey's pocket that he was not happy about donating to the cause. I suppressed a tart comment as he waddled back towards the barn.

As I closed up the trailer it occurred to me that I'd not gotten a bill of sale, and in the case of doing business with Harvey Wilson, proper paperwork was a really good idea.

I trailed after him into the stable, glanced around, but didn't see him in any of the stalls or in the little junk room at the back. A wide door opened into the corral behind the stable and I glanced outside, but didn't see him there, either. How could a man who weighs close to three hundred pounds disappear so quick?

"Dammit, Harvey, I'm not searching your entire four thousand acres looking for you."

I stomped back outside and noticed the door to his steel building was slightly ajar. The implement garage, as my father liked to call it, was the staging area for broken tractors and beat-up hay swathers, and doubled as an oil-change station and general all-around repair area for the myriad machines it took to operate a ranch. As I approached I heard him rummaging around just inside the door and I pushed inside.

Harvey leaned over an ancient wooden box that sat on top of a workbench at least sixty feet long. His back was to the door, and I cleared my throat loudly.

He jerked his round head towards me. "What in the hell are you doing in here, girl?"

"Sorry," I said, a little taken aback by his sharp words.

"Get out. I'll bring you the damn thing. Just give me a minute."

It was dark inside the steel building, and for October, pretty hot and stuffy. The ghosts of tractors past occupied the concrete floor, dripping various fluids and generally looking like they had seen better days.

"I need a bill of sale," I said.

He practically lunged for me, reaching for the open door. "Get. I'll bring it. Just wait by your damn truck."

I started to back out. As my foot hit the packed dirt outside I glimpsed a flash of something shiny leaning against the wall at the far end of the steel building. In the half-light of morning it was not easy to see clearly. I stopped, trying to focus on the shiny object, but Harvey glared at me and I took three steps back until I was behind the door. He slammed the door closed, but it was slightly off-hinge and didn't quite fit. In between the door and the frame I could see a sliver of space.

I heard Harvey trudge back to his workbench and before he could return I pressed my face to the crack.

There was something inside that he didn't want me to see, which made me want to see it.

I peered through the crack, scanning the area as best I could. The shiny object at the very back came into focus and I finally managed to make out what it was.

Grinning like a shark, a heavy-duty chrome grille guard was propped up against the back wall of the building like it had just been put there a few minutes ago.

The newness of the silvery metal had caught my eye. Everything else inside the building was worn and rusty. It was half hidden behind the fleet of mothballed machinery, but it was there.

Harvey had apparently found the hoof pick, and I heard him hitch up his bib overalls and toss the wooden box aside. He lumbered for the door.

Before he heaved his bulk around the corner I spun quietly and planted by butt against the wall, my thumbs hitched in my belt loops like I'd been standing there waiting for him for hours.

He stopped when he saw me, looked me up and down once and held out the pick.

"Here. I've done my civic duty for the day."

"What about that bill of sale?" I asked.

His tone was harsh, but his eyes flickered with worry. "It's in on the kitchen table. You want me to make you a sandwich and a milkshake too, while I'm in there?"

"When was the last time you washed your hands?" I asked, flipping his sarcasm right back at him.

He relaxed a bit when it was apparent I was as irritated and impatient with him as usual, and he lumbered towards the big white house that sat across the courtyard. He heaved himself up the front steps and I heard the screen door bang.

I stayed exactly where I was, never moving a muscle, and once I saw him peer through the kitchen window at me like a ghoul. He was obviously checking up on me, but I kept my stance, and deliberately avoided looking inside the steel building again.

I didn't need to, after all. I'd seen the chrome bumper and knew it for what it was. Looking twice wouldn't change anything.

Harvey came out through the front door and walked across the packed ground holding a piece of ratty paper in one hand.

He stopped beside me and thrust a pen at my nose. "Sign."

I took the bill of sale, resting the sheet against the wall of the building, inked my name and handed it back. He did the same.

"I'll send you a copy," he told me.

"I want the original. I'll send you the copy," I said.

He looked like he was about to argue, then his piggy eyes shifted to the door of the steel building and he made a face.

"Fine. Here, and you might want to think about getting a companion animal for that pony. He likes company."

"You don't say," I said. "So, why didn't you?"

Harvey shoved the bill of sale into my palm and turned to walk away without bothering to reply.

I climbed back inside my father's truck and the engine roared to life. An embarrassing amount of blue smoke shot out the tailpipe and all I could do was shake my head as I ground the thing into gear and lurched from the courtyard, the truck groaning with each turn of the tires.

It was a long haul back to the ranch, but when I pulled to the side of the road in front of the barn the drive seemed to have gone by in a flash.

My mind had been occupied, after all.

Harvey Wilson had a brand-new heavy-duty chrome grille guard sitting useless in his junkyard. Now, in all the years that I had known the man, never once had Harvey struck me as humble. If he had access to a new piece of equipment, he would use it. In fact, he would use the ever-loving hell out of it. Especially if it looked sharp. Harvey wasn't the type of man to keep a low profile if he could help it. The fact that he had a new accessory like that and wasn't using it meant something to me.

It meant that he didn't want people to see that he had it.

I dropped the gate on the trailer, and when I went inside, Lil Nipper turned one eye towards me gamely. He waited while I untied the lead rope and followed me out of the trailer, tossing his head. He stopped at my shoulder and nudged me impatiently with his head a couple of times while I strained to open the tight gate.

Peanut was already trotting towards us as we made our way inside the pasture. I let the two of them sniff each other like cats for a moment before taking Lil Nipper into the barn and segregating him inside a makeshift corral. The two horses touched noses, snorted and pawed, and generally said hello to each other.

Peanut looked happy to have company. Lil Nipper looked like he was pleased to have a servant on staff he could order around. From the glint in the pony's eyes, it was obvious who would be in charge in this outfit.

I gave him plenty of water and some hay before making sure he was secure. Horses took time to sort out the pecking order, and I wasn't about to let the two of them abuse each other. After a few days I'd let them have some time without a fence between them. But for now, particularly while Lil Nipper was gimping around on a thrush-infected hoof, it would be better to keep them apart.

They were already settling in nicely. Peanut stood beside the corral attentively, but wasn't making any rude charges for the bars, and Lil Nipper was nosing his hay happily and didn't seem at all concerned about the mustang.

"So far, so good," I said.

My boot heel thumped as I rested my foot on the wooden beam of the corral. I stood watching the two horses, but my mind was elsewhere.

My list of suspects had just gotten whittled down to one name.

I had no idea why he had done it, but I knew that he was guilty as sin.

Harvey Wilson had killed Phoebe. There wasn't a doubt in my mind. Everyone in the valley knew that Harvey drove a big burgundy Ford Super Duty dually pickup truck. And he had become so agitated when he'd seen me looking around he'd about blown a fuse.

Only a guilty man acted that way.

I felt a wave of sickness weaken my stomach. I'd known the man all my life, and though Harvey wasn't exactly a friend, he was familiar. That he had done such a thing and not come forward about it twisted my guts.

The sound of tires on gravel made me leave the barn and drew me into the subdued October sunlight.

A sheriff's truck pulled up and parked behind the trailer and Finn stepped out.

He watched me for a moment, unmoving, before dropping his chin to his chest unhappily and walking my way.

Finn stopped at the barbed-wire gate and studied it carefully.

Like all country folk I always got a great deal of amusement watching a city-dweller try to operate a gate, and I leaned against the side of the barn for the show.

Finn completed his assessment of the wire and wood, and wrapped his arm around it like an experienced cowhand. In a matter of seconds he was through the contraption and had it closed behind him like he'd done the task a thousand times.

It rankled me that no matter what Finn turned his hand to, he always did it like he was born to the job. He walked to the front of the barn, looking official in his brown uniform, and it occurred to me I still hadn't gotten used to him wearing a color other than black.

"We have made an arrest," Finn said as he stopped in front of me.

I stood up straight. "What? When did this happen?"

"Yesterday morning. It has not been made public, as of yet."

He stood looking at me with his mirrored sunglasses.

"Well who was it?" I demanded.

"The woman. Betty Newman."

"The day shift worker at the Gas N Dash? Finn, I may not be a cop but I can sure as hell tell you she didn't do it."

He seemed mildly surprised by my vehemence. "Yes, you are right. You are not a cop."

"Look, it's impossible that it was her. And anyway, she didn't have any reason to kill Phoebe."

"We have found otherwise," he said evenly. "It was not impossible. And she had a very good reason to kill her coworker. She lied to us from the very beginning."

"She lied about what?" I asked.

"Her story was inconsistent. And then there was the fact that she was using a skimmer to steal from the Gas N Dash. She attached the device to the gas pumps during her shift using Super Glue and Popsicle sticks. When the customers chose the pay-at-the-pump option, she stole their credit card information and skimmed from their accounts."

I felt a lump form in my stomach. "Is that why she quit her job so abruptly?"

"Yes. And it is also why she killed Phoebe Robinson. The young woman discovered what Betty was doing and threatened her with exposure if she didn't share the proceeds."

"But it doesn't make any sense," I said. "Betty wasn't even there the night Phoebe died."

"We have a witness that will testify otherwise," Finn said.

"Who?"

"That is none of your concern," he told me. "I only came by to tell you this as a courtesy."

Finn's lips twitched into an unconscious smirk and I wanted to smack him.

"Why are you so damn smug?"

He broke into a broad grin. "For the first time since I have known you, I have been able to prevent you from getting yourself shot, or stabbed, or rolled on by a horse, all in pursuit of the truth. In this case, I managed to discover the truth first. It feels good."

"She didn't do it, Finn. You arrested the wrong person. Betty may have been skimming, but she did not kill Phoebe. I can tell you that with the utmost certainty."

His grin faded and he removed his sunglasses slowly, piercing me with his ice-blue eyes. "Marley, you have been wrong before. You are wrong now."

I couldn't respond. All the anger that I'd managed to tamp down came rushing back to the surface again and my hands clenched.

My face felt hot with rage and I hissed a reply. "We will just see about that."

Finn put his palm on my shoulder and squeezed. "Stop. Just stop. I know you are angry about the death of your husband. But this is not going to bring him back and all it will do is make you into a crazy person."

I slapped his hand away. "You have no room to talk about being crazy, Finn."

"I know better than to say you are acting in a way that is stupid," he replied.

"At least you learned *something* from our relationship," I said.

"I only wish you had a greater capacity to learn."

"You aren't the one who just had your new husband taken away." My voice was sharp as a switchblade.

"He was not taken from you," Finn said. "It was his choice. Marley, listen to me for a moment, would you?"

I stared at him. "What do you mean, it was his choice?"

Finn's face instantly closed down and he slammed his sunglasses back on so quickly his hands were a blur. "Nothing. To fly, I meant to say. It was his choice to fly. He knew the risks."

Before I could stop him, Finn spun around and strode away, leaving me standing there like a tree that had just been struck by lightning, with shock and rage and disbelief turning my world upside down.

He drove away and as I watched him go, a feeling of utter panic swept over me with a tidal wave.

It was his choice.

Finn never said anything that was not calculated or carefully thought out. But for once in all the time I'd known him, he had just made a verbal mistake. He'd said something that he wasn't supposed to say. I could see it plainly. He'd backtracked so fast the statement couldn't have been anything other than a slipup.

That meant he had accidentally just told me the truth.

I didn't bother closing the gate on the trailer before jumping into my father's truck, and I drove straight back to the ranch house with it crashing back and forth on the hinges. I parked and killed the engine, ran for my SUV and drove back home in record time using every high-speed maneuver Thomas had taught me.

The key refused to turn in the lock of the front door, and I swore again and again as I jimmied it until it finally opened.

I turned towards Leif's office and ran to the oak desk, fulfilling Finn's prophecy and acting like a crazy person.

The safe deposit box key was precisely where I'd left it, resting inside the desk drawer in its little envelope. Without a moment's hesitation I snatched it up and shoved it inside my jeans pocket, slammed the drawer closed and drove into Killdeer leaving a rooster tail of dust so high in my wake it looked like the prairie was on fire.

The wheels screeched as I pulled up in front of the local bank and braked so hard something in the backseat hit the floor with a thud. I ignored it.

It was Tuesday, and practically deserted at the teller stations. One of the women sat at her computer, filing her fingernails and looking bored.

I slammed the key on the desk in front of her.

"I need to get inside this safe deposit box," I said.

She jumped and practically threw her nail file. "Oh!"

She looked at the key, looked back up at me and smiled with her customer service expression.

I smiled back. "Now."

CHAPTER 18

I sat at a private table inside the safe, the box at my elbow. It was practically empty, except for one very telling item.

A baseball card had been set on top of a file folder carefully. It hadn't been tossed in haphazardly; it was placed there with care.

I could see that it was old. The back of the card was printed with the baseball player's vital statistics and said that he led the American League in runs scored in 1933.

The player was Lou Gehrig.

I knew enough about baseball to realize the card was probably worth a fair amount of money, but Leif had never really been a fan, so the careful placement of the card didn't make any sense to me.

I set the card aside on the leather blotter and pulled out the file. The folder was filled with a stack of papers, and when I opened it the first thing I saw was the cover page and letterhead of an insurance company from Boston.

One of Leif's companies had been based in Boston. But he had sold that business several weeks ago, not long before his death. The stack of papers turned out to be an accidental-death life insurance policy in Leif's name, and the beneficiary of the policy was someone named Jaroslaw "Jarek" Legerski.

There was only one Legerski I was familiar with, and his name was Roger. He owned Legerski Processing, and they sold a variety of local sausages and meats, and generally had been in existence as long as I could remember.

That couldn't be a coincidence. What were the chances that Leif would know someone named Legerski who wasn't in some way connected with a local man with the same last name?

Pretty damn slim.

I scooped up the baseball card from the table, stuffed it inside the file folder and checked the safe deposit box for anything I may have overlooked. It had been tipped up on its edge inside the box and I almost missed it, but as I tilted the heavy box to the side a photograph flipped down and I saw a picture of Leif and me on our wedding day, looking at each other as we recited our vows.

My throat tightened up and if I hadn't been sitting down at the table I would have sunk to my knees. My hand shook as I lifted the photograph and held it up. He looked so happy. I looked flushed and overwhelmed and slightly shocked. But I was smiling nonetheless.

When I turned the photograph over I could see that Leif had used a fine-point Sharpie marker and had jotted a note on the top.

"We had no time"

The blood in my veins turned cold and for the second time in a matter of weeks my world felt like it had just tilted on its axis.

An accidental-death life insurance policy for some Polish man I had never even heard of? A Lou Gehrig baseball card, and now this note written by Leif on the back of a photo of our wedding day?

Leif Gable had known me well enough to guess that if he laid out a trail of bread crumbs this blatant that I would be stubborn enough to follow them to the end.

He was trying to tell me something from the grave.

I left the empty safe deposit box on the table and told the safe manager I was ready to leave. She signed me out and I tried to think about what to do next.

The day Leif and I had been married, Finn had spoken to him. My intuition was telling me that Finn knew something that he had not told me yet, and I would need to confront him about it at some point.

I wasn't ready to face Angus Finn just yet, because there was a small chance I would fall apart and do or say something stupid. Instead, I set the file on the front seat of my SUV and drove straight to Legerski Processing.

There wasn't a chance in hell this was simply a coincidence. There had to be more to it than that.

When I parked outside I didn't see old man Roger leaning on the counter smoking his trademark cigar, but I went inside anyway, pushing through the front door and stopping at the counter with what had to have been a pretty desperate expression painted on my face.

When Roger ambled out from the back room he stopped at the sight of me. "Marley. You look like you need a shot of Vajunka."

"Who is Jarek?"

He blinked and wiped a hand on his greasy white apron. "Who?"

"Jarek Legerski. Who is he, Roger?"

The old man produced a cigar from thin air and lit it unapologetically. He puffed, inhaled deeply and blew out a blue trail of smoke. "You really want to get into this?"

I responded by folding my arms over my chest in the universal signal of all womankind that I wasn't leaving without some answers.

He studied my stance, gave a single nod and strolled to the front door. With the cigar held between his teeth, he shut off the lights and locked the front door. "Why don't you come on back, then."

I followed him through the door leading to the back room, probably one of only a very select few of Killdeer's residents to ever do so, and forced myself to sit down at a small plastic table that occupied a cluttered office area. The table shared the space with a couple of old metal file cabinets, a rickety desk and a mustard yellow rotary telephone set on a stack of ancient phone books a yard high.

Roger eased a bottle of the infamous Wyoming-made Koltiska KO out of a desk drawer and poured himself a generous shot into a coffee mug. He gestured towards me with the neck of the bottle, and I held up a hand.

"No thanks."

"Suit yourself." He replaced the bottle and sat with me at the small table. "Didn't Leif ever talk to you about his time in Iraq?"

I leaned back in the chair, my heart fluttering like a bird's wings. "Let's pretend he didn't tell me a thing."

Roger scratched his scalp where the thinning white hair looked like cake frosting beside his blacker than black eyebrows. "Alrighty then."

He took a long drink from the coffee cup and set it aside carefully. His gray eyes lost their focus and he stared off into some distant time and place that I couldn't see.

"Roger, why don't you start at the top and work your way down to the here and now?" I suggested.

He glanced at his hands, folded them and set them in his lap like he was getting ready to make a confession. "I am not really sure where the top starts."

"There is a life insurance policy sitting in the front seat of my SUV with Jarek's name on it. Leif took it out on himself. And if I am reading the thing correctly, he has held this policy for over six months. Maybe you should start with that?"

Roger let out a snort and shook his head. "Gable always did pay his debts."

"The policy is for half a million bucks, Roger. What kind of a debt are we talking about here?"

He drained the coffee mug of its contents and set the cup at his elbow. "You don't think it was chance that Leif Gable ended up in little Killdeer, Montana, all the way from Washington, D.C., do you?"

"He said it was pretty here," I told him.

"Jarek is my sister's oldest," Roger began. "She and I keep in touch. I go back there once in a while. Jarek, *Jaroslaw* Legerski, is my nephew."

"You go back where?" I asked.

"Poland."

"Okay, tell me about him."

"Jarek is a sniper with Polish Special Forces. Or he was until he gave it up and started working for the intelligence service instead. GROM was busy back in 1991 and Jarek was only twenty-three at the time. GROM is a Polish military unit dedicated to snipers. He and Leif worked together during Gulf I. Back then, before Shock and Awe, back when Saddam Hussein was still running the show, the Americans had restrictions on when they could and could not shoot on the streets of Fallujah. That's where Jarek and his team came in."

"Wait, Leif told me he was in Iraq during the first Gulf War, but he said that all he did was move money around and fund projects for the State Department."

Roger drew deeply from his cigar. "Sure, in a manner of speaking."

"But he was more than that?" I asked.

"You know about the roadside bombs that are set off with radio signals? GROM could shoot anyone on the streets of Fallujah after eight p.m. who was holding a cell phone. The Americans couldn't fire on someone unless they saw the person holding a weapon. The Polish government had looser restrictions about who could shoot whom and when. So, since GROM could pretty much clean house when the American military had its hands tied by regulations, the State Department aided the Polish snipers with cash. Lots and lots of cash."

"So Leif didn't sit in an office building in liberated Kuwait and make wire transfers?" I asked.

"He rode camels, donkeys, motorcycles, and got shot at, chased, almost kidnapped and pretty much did everything the GROM soldiers did. Except he did it carrying around a couple hundred pounds of Benjamin Franklins."

"But why did he have to haul around money? That doesn't make any sense."

"It does if the United States government doesn't want anyone to know we were helping the Poles," Roger said.

"No paper trail, or electronic records of transfers," I said. "So he was working with a team of snipers?"

"And he would have died but for my Jarek. The kid was fond of Leif. Well, everyone was. But for Jarek it was personal. He liked Leif Gable, looked up to him in fact. And during a midnight operation your husband found himself stuck in a difficult position."

"What do you mean stuck?" I asked. This information was starting to help me make sense out of my husband's strange past and I wanted to know everything.

"Alright. He was trapped in a complete fiasco. Leif was traveling back with the GROM team to a new assignment and they got hit with friendly fire from a squad of Americans who didn't know who they were. I guess they couldn't tell the difference between Polish and Arabic on the radio. Goddamn miracle nobody got killed. But while they were getting shot at, Jarek took it upon himself to make sure Leif made it out of there alive. The kid sort of designated himself as a personal bomb shelter for Gable and took a bullet. He lost the feeling in his left arm from nerve damage for six months after that. But he survived. Leif probably felt like he owed Jarek his life."

"That's what the life insurance policy was for? He was repaying a debt?"

"Seems that way," Roger said.

Something tickled my memory and I sat up straight. "I found a rifle in Leif's office once when I was cleaning. It was like nothing I had ever seen before. Could it have been a sniper rifle from his time in Iraq?"

"Do you still have it?" Roger asked.

"We lost it in the fire," I said.

Our first house had burned to the ground, along with everything inside. I'd forgotten about the rifle that I'd seen inside a cabinet in Leif's office, or I might have tried to save it. He had kept it in a discreet place, almost hidden. It seemed important, somehow.

"Probably a Tantal," Roger told me. "That's the rifle they were using at the time."

"It couldn't have been an easy thing, getting something like that rifle back into this country."

"Your husband was pretty high up on the food chain after the war," Roger said. "For someone like him, there might have been exceptions to normal rules."

I ran a hand over the surface of the worn plastic table as all the information sank in. "How do you know all of this?"

He flicked cigar ashes on the floor casually. "Jarek talked about Killdeer to Leif constantly when they were working together. Told him all the stories I'd passed along over the years about what a good place it was to live. If he ever wanted to drop off the face of the earth and start over, the middle of nowhere Montana was the place to do it."

"So when Leif was finally ready to get out of D.C. for good, he came here," I finished for him.

"Leif looked me up the first day he came to town. Relived the old times. We haven't talked since. He thought it was better that way."

"Was Jarek one of the Polish men who came to our wedding?" I asked.

Roger chuckled. "So, you do you remember him?"

I shook my head, not entirely certain I remembered a great many things about our wedding day. Not only had the ceremony been a complete surprise, but Angus Finn had shown up at the wedding and he and Leif had shared a private conversation that had prompted Finn to flee Killdeer almost immediately after.

The entire incident had puzzled me at the time, but now I felt like I was on the verge of getting some answers.

"I remember a group of Polish men showing up and doing their best to drink Leif under the table, but they also treated him like he was practically family."

"If Leif hadn't taken the risks he did, ferried that money all over the damn desert, that GROM unit might not have been able to operate so successfully. So, you could say they were tight-knit."

"Roger, could you get me a contact number for Jarek? Not that Eric Toomey wouldn't be able to find him, but this might speed things along. He's got some money coming to him."

Roger nodded and clamped his cigar back between his teeth. "I'll see to it."

I stood up and thanked him for his time, wandered back to my SUV in a daze and sat inside for several minutes before I was able to finally start the engine and drive back to town.

Legerski Processing sat on the outskirts of Killdeer and it took me a few minutes to make it to the sheriff's station on Main Street.

When I went inside it was plain to see that Finn wasn't there, and I left a message with the dispatcher, Valerie, for him to get in touch with me as soon as he got back to the station.

I drove home, feeling a bit numb, and went back to Leif's office once more. I lifted the telephone and dialed Mr. Toomey in Billings. He'd given me his extension number and it rang straight through to him, bypassing the secretary.

"Ms. Dearcorn," he said after picking up on the third ring.

"Mr. Toomey. I'm afraid there is one more thing I need you to take care of concerning Leif's estate," I told him.

"And that would be?"

"I found a life insurance policy in a safe deposit box," I said.

He let out a soft sigh. "I see. When can you bring it to my office?"

"How about tomorrow?"

"That will not be possible. I am currently in Washington."

"I just called your office," I said with confusion.

"My work phone is forwarded to my cell number. Will you be able to come to the Billings office on Friday? I will be at my desk then."

It was my turn to sigh. "What time would you like me there?"

"Noon. There is something we need to discuss."

That sounded ominous.

"You aren't having any more problems with Virginia, are you?" I asked.

"Hardly. She is not a concern of yours any longer. This has

more to do with your gardener."

My day was getting stranger and stranger. "What about my gardener?"

"Well, to begin with, Thomas Dunne is not his real name."

"How do you know that?" I asked.

"I took the liberty of investigating his license plate number, and it belongs to a man named Eugene Reisner from Clay County in Kentucky."

"Maybe Thomas is borrowing a friend's car?" I asked quietly.

"Hardly. I will brief you on my findings when you can be in my office. I need to go. If you could bring the insurance policy we will deal with it at that time. And, might I suggest that you not associate with Thomas Dunne any longer? It would be prudent to fire him immediately. I will see you Friday."

He hung up the phone and I sat there staring at the receiver like an idiot, listening to the dial tone as if it would bother to give me any answers at all.

Finally, I placed the receiver back in the cradle and rested my face in my hands.

The revelations about Leif were not a total shock. I'd always known he had been involved in some sort of operation in Iraq back in 1991. But the nature of his work was a surprise, to say the least.

I'd been married to the man, but I couldn't help but feel that in spite of that fact, I'd hardly known him at all.

CHAPTER 19

Thomas had been conspicuously absent from work all day Tuesday, and after I stumbled downstairs Wednesday morning, making a beeline for the coffeepot, I looked outside to see if he was back on the job.

The screaming yellow Barracuda of his was parked outside and he was busy hauling pipe. Hard at work once more.

I sipped steaming coffee and studied him for a while. He worked methodically, setting the sprinkler pipe into the trenches smoothly, and his lean frame was probably a lot stronger than appearances would suggest.

I'd slept hard that night, in spite of the thoughts and troubles working my brain like a buzz saw. For the most part I'd managed to finally piece together the clues that Leif had left for me inside the safe deposit box, and I'd come up with an explanation that made sense. There was one more person I had to go see before I could be certain of my guess, but I was fairly confident that I had the answers now. Finn's cryptic comment wasn't as much of a mystery to me now.

After breakfast, I showered and took my time getting ready for the day. I threw on a pair of gray slacks and a red sweater. Fall was descending and mornings were chilly. It would not be much longer before the first snows began.

Thomas was hunched over a sprinkler head when I came down the front steps. He stood up when he saw me and if he'd been wearing a hat, I was sure he would have tipped it.

"Ma'am."

"Good morning. How's the project going?" I asked.

He slid his hands into his tattered jean jacket pockets and shrugged a reply.

"How many more days will you be at this?" I asked.

"That all depends," he said.

"On what?"

It was his turn to scrutinize me. "How is your investigation into the death of that unfortunate young woman proceeding?"

I kept my expression carefully neutral. "Well, I was sort of hoping you might be able to help me with that again."

He looked me up and down and a flicker of exasperation clouded his features. "If I can, I'd be happy to assist you in any way."

"How hard is it to remove a chrome grille guard from a dually pickup truck yourself?"

"It's a one-man job," he said.

I thought back to Harvey Wilson's steel building. The heavy-duty chrome guard had been propped against the far wall like it had been carried there by someone. I remembered from the sheen glinting off the metal that the thing looked practically brand-new.

"Would a big grille show signs of impact from hitting a person?" I asked.

He didn't hesitate at all. "Absolutely. Even someone who only weighed a little over one hundred pounds would cause damage. It might be slight, but it would be visible."

"That helps me a great deal," I said.

"Is there anything else I can be of assistance with?" he asked. "I have a lot of work yet to do this afternoon."

"What was your line of work before this?" I asked. "I mean, before you came to Killdeer what did you do for a living?"

His mouth twitched ever so slightly. "Demolition."

I shook my head. "What sort of demolition? Like, heavy equipment?"

"Tunnel coal mining explosive demolition," he said.

"I would have thought you were a limo driver or something," I said smoothly, "with all of your skills behind the wheel."

"Oh, that's just for personal improvement, a hobby, like crochet or brewing beer. Those skills are not something the average person uses to make a living."

The gleam in his eye suggested to me that it was much more than a hobby.

"How do you even know what crochet is?" I asked, teasing.

His eyes drooped sadly. "My ex-wife was an enthusiast."

"I didn't know you were married," I said.

For someone who was living in a quasi-on-the-run state of being, Thomas certainly did volunteer a lot of information to me.

"Kids?" I asked.

He beamed then, lifted his wallet from his pocket and held out a photograph of a smiling, gap-toothed little girl wearing a pink shirt and pigtails. "My Ellie. She's gone and turned eight years old already. I can't hardly keep up."

"She's beautiful." I handed the photograph back to him. "Does she live back home?"

"Yes. I still get to see her regularly. Or I did before I relocated here to Montana."

I watched his features stiffen when he spoke. He wasn't being completely honest, but he concealed it so well it was only because

I was looking for evasiveness that I actually saw it. I couldn't tell if he was lying about the ex-wife, or the daughter, or if he was lying about getting to see them regularly. But something wasn't quite right. Probably he was lying about relocating here to Montana. Something told me that Thomas had no real intentions of becoming a registered voter in Big Sky country. This was a temporary gig for him, at best.

"The sheriff has arrested a person he thinks may be responsible for killing Phoebe," I said.

Thomas blinked with surprise. "Well, that is good news."

He looked immensely relieved, which made me suspicious at once. Why did he care so much about who got the blame for her death?

"So that means you will be abandoning your inquiry into the circumstances of her killing?" he asked.

"Not yet. I think the sheriff has the wrong guy. So to speak."

His face twisted as though he was filled with irritation, but he managed to hide it with a grimace and bent back to the sprinkler head at his feet. "I had best get on with my work. You will let me know, won't you, if there is any new information about your young woman?"

"Sure I will," I said.

Mr. Toomey had suggested I fire Thomas at once and get as far away from him as possible, but I had absolutely no intention of doing that just yet. There was a lot more to my gardener than he was letting on, and until I figured him out I wasn't about to let him out of my sight.

"I've got some errands to run, but I should be back this afternoon. Do you need anything from town?" I asked.

He glanced up. "Not a thing that I can think of."

"I'd give you my cell phone number, but here in the valley

it's practically impossible to get a signal. But if you need to get in touch, you could always go to Lil's café. They are usually in the loop about where folks around town have got to."

"I'll keep that in mind," he said without looking up.

I turned to go but he stood up quickly. "Ma'am? Were you asking me about a single grille guard in particular? Or were you simply curious in general?"

My answer popped out before I could restrain myself. "One in particular."

"So one of the names on the list of vehicle registrations," he said with narrowed eyes, "belongs to the person you suspect."

My cheeks colored. "I believe so, yes."

"And would you be willing to share that information with me?"

I laughed. It was involuntary and I almost slapped a hand over my mouth purely by reflex. "Not a chance. I could be totally wrong."

His eyes hadn't wavered from my face a centimeter. "But you are fairly certain you are not mistaken."

"Let's just say that out of those fifteen people on that vehicle registration list, I would bet a million bucks that one of them is our man."

"So that leaves eleven," he said.

"I don't understand."

"There are fifteen names on the list and four of them are women," he explained. "You seem confident the person you are looking for is a man. So you have eleven men to sort through."

A warning bell went off inside my head. "You know, for a gardener you sure do have a devious way of thinking about things, Thomas."

"Must be from all that time I spent in jail."

"What did you go to jail for?" I asked.

His expression darkened. "Homicide."

The warning bell turned into a siren. "Probably a little bit more information than I really needed."

He looked at me unapologetically. "I have never tried to conceal my past. It was a long time ago, and I have taken responsibility for the wrong that I committed. I was very young, and very misguided."

"I suppose you are a changed man," I said, a tad bit sarcastically.

"By God's grace, I have been given an opportunity to atone for my transgressions."

We studied each other for a moment, both of us thinking our own thoughts.

There was a lot more to Thomas Dunne than he was letting on, but I wasn't in any position to quiz him on his past.

I wouldn't need to ask him any more awkward questions, in any case, because I had Mr. Toomey on speed dial. In two days I'd be getting a complete rundown from the Billings attorney. Maybe Thomas had fallen on hard times and gotten mixed up with a bad crowd, or he had been involved in some fast getaway and had accidentally hit a pedestrian. Still, I didn't think I'd need to fire him right away. He didn't seem dangerous. Until I heard the whole story from Mr. Toomey I would keep him on. It wouldn't hurt anything to hold off letting him go for another forty-eight hours.

I left him to his work and drove to the barn to see to Peanut and Lil Nipper. I'd stopped the previous day at the Big R, purchased iodine and supplies, and after feeding and seeing to the water I set to work doctoring Lil Nipper's thrush.

The pony's thrush was caused by a bacterial infection, and the iodine and clean, dry stable conditions would clear it up.

Lil Nipper and Peanut stood nose to nose on either side of the corral. They looked relatively acclimated to each other but I wasn't about to turn the pony out into the general population until I was convinced he wouldn't take a beating.

Peanut was a genial enough mustang, but in the past I'd seen him act like a gangster and to be on the safe side, I'd let the two of them get to know each other better before letting them cohabit.

I gave them both a good curry before leaving, and for once Peanut didn't run the fence line nickering with alarm as I drove away. He seemed happy to have company.

It was nearly noon by the time I drove into Killdeer and pulled up in front of the insurance office.

Like many of the businesses in town, Harrison Auto-life Insurance occupied an old Victorian-style home a block off of Main Street.

Luke Harrison, the proprietor and sole occupant of the big house, stood up from his desk and greeted me with a broad smile when I came through the door.

"Marley Dearcorn," he said, pumping my hand enthusiastically.

Luke wore a moustache that could be seen from space. His Wranglers looked a bit ridiculous tucked into his cowboy boots, and his belt buckle was the size and shape of a dinner plate.

"Have a seat. Let's talk about your insurance needs."

"I don't have any insurance needs, Luke," I began. "But it would be great if you could take a look at something for me and answer a couple of questions."

He looked disappointed but shrugged that off and offered a smile. "Whatcha got for me?"

I handed him the insurance policy that Leif had taken out on himself, naming Jarek as the beneficiary. Luke's eyes bulged when he saw the amount, and to his credit he didn't blurt out any inappropriate remarks as he skimmed the document.

"This is a standard term life insurance policy. I'm confused about why Leif didn't make you the beni on this? But, maybe he had another way of protecting you that I am not aware of."

"He did."

"Was this person someone he needed to offer financial protection for?" he asked.

"Yes, at least Leif wanted it that way."

Luke hummed to himself as he scanned the document. "Not from around here? This Jaroslaw fella? I recognize Legerski, of course, but not his first name. Jaroslaw sure is a mouthful."

"No, he's not from around here. I can get in touch with him though. But my question is about the policy itself. Are there any circumstances that would mean this wouldn't be paid? I mean, are there any stipulations about the policy being withheld for any reason?"

Luke rubbed a hand under his jaw while he considered the fine print. "There are only two."

"What's the first one?" I asked.

"In the event that the policyholder died after the ten-year contract period has expired and opted not to continue the coverage," Luke said. "But since that is not what happened, the policy is valid."

"And the other circumstance?" I asked.

"In the event of a suicide by the policyholder."

I was quiet for a moment while that information sank in.

The phone rang while I was mulling over the facts and Luke held up one hand. "Just a moment, Marley. I'll make this quick."

I leaned back in the chair to consider what he had said. The baseball card that Leif had left inside the safe deposit box was definitely a message, and I was starting to put it together now.

"Luke Harrison, Harrison Home and Health," he said. "Yes, Rebecca. What can I do for you today?"

Rebecca had to be Rebecca Winthrop, the unfortunate pediatrician with a sick mother still dying an inch at a time in the Parkman hospital.

Cecilia Winthrop had been a strong, vibrant woman in her time. She'd deteriorated so much over the last two years, and her recent stroke had incapacitated her. A woman like Cecilia would hate the thought of languishing in a hospital bed waiting for a slow death. It had to be such a helpless feeling.

Given the chance, most of us wouldn't choose to end their life in a vegetative state if they could help it. If Leif had been faced with such a dilemma, he probably would have found another way.

And after hearing what Luke had just said, it was obvious to me now what had really happened to my husband. As painful as it was to admit, I had finally uncovered the truth.

A man who was brave enough to take incredible risks on a battlefield and spent his life traveling the globe, and who thought that deep-sea spear fishing was a pleasant diversion, wasn't the type of man who shied away from danger. Throw into the mix the fact that Leif hated to be at the mercy of circumstance. Losing control had been his least favorite state of being.

Of all of Leif Gable's qualities, the desire to be in charge was the most painfully obvious.

But what if he was told that all of his autonomy was going to slowly slip away and he would die an inch at a time, like Cecilia Winthrop? What if a doctor gave him a diagnosis that was incurable and unbeatable?

What if he had been told that he suffered from ALS, also known as Lou Gehrig's disease?

Luke spoke intently into the receiver. "Rebecca, I've told you a hundred times, girl. You see a deer in your headlights, you smack 'em. Right? Don't swerve. 'Cause if you swerve and hit something else, now the accident is your fault and it don't have nothing to do with the damn deer. Hit the thing, and hit it hard."

I was only half-listening to Luke instruct Rebecca in the finer points of collision protocol.

A heavy sadness crept over me and sat on my heart like a black cloud. The only reason Leif would have carefully set that baseball card on top of the file folder was so that I would see it displayed in a prominent place. He had been trying to tell me something that he couldn't say directly. He had been trying to tell me that he had taken matters into his own hands.

"Becky, darlin'. This is the second deer you've run down in a year. Don't cha think it's about time we upped your comprehensive coverage?"

No wonder Finn had come back to Killdeer so quickly after Leif's death. He'd known in advance what was going to happen. The night Leif and I had been married, I'd seen the two men talking together and the conversation had been brief but very intense. Shortly after that conversation Finn had disappeared from town and hadn't reappeared until now. It seemed that, as incredible as it sounded, Finn had a sense beforehand of what was about to happen to my husband. He'd come back to Killdeer because he knew in advance that I was going to be a widow.

Luke droned on. "Fine, fine. But take it to Parkman this time. Mo's garage here in Killdeer is a bank-breaker. Alright? And ask him to check your high beams while he's at it."

It was pure speculation on my part, but something told me I was right. Leif had known he was going to die and had taken matters into his own hands while he still could. Before crashing his plane, Leif had taken steps to protect me, to protect his son and to settle all of his affairs.

Now that I really thought about it, I couldn't understand why I hadn't seen all of the warning signs before.

"It's okay, Rebecca. Listen, I've got to let you go now. But remember what I said, ya hear? You see a deer, you smack 'em hard."

He hung up the phone and I managed a weak smile.

Luke passed the insurance policy back to me. "Sorry I couldn't be of much more help. It looks like it's all in order, though. You got any more questions?"

"No, I think you told me everything I needed," I said. "Thanks, Luke."

I stood up to leave and shook his hand.

"You ever need to reevaluate your home owner's insurance policy, you stop on by," he told me.

"I will do just that," I said.

Before leaving I paused, thinking about something he had said to the pediatrician. "Hey, Luke. Why did you tell Rebecca to get her high beams checked out?"

"Her track record is way too shabby," he said. "Look, it's not right for me to talk about it like this, but the truth of it is that either Rebecca drives like a bat out of hell, or else her high beams are not working because she hits a deer every six months."

"That's a lot," I said.

"Too much. So that's what makes me think she's got a problem with her headlights."

"Nobody hits deer in the daytime?" I asked.

Luke shook his head. "Around here? Nope. They always clobber 'em at night. You would think that folks around Killdeer could recognize it when they see it."

"Recognize what?" I asked.

He tilted his head a bit to the side. "Eyeshine. If yer paying attention. How could you miss all that eyeshine out there?"

I stared at him as my mouth dropped open. "That's it, Luke."

"What's it?" he asked.

I backed towards the door in haste. "I gotta go, Luke. Thanks. You may have just answered another question for me."

The last thing I heard as I sprinted from his office was Luke calling after me.

"What question?"

CHAPTER 20

The Gas N Dash was hopping busy. It was close to midnight and I sat at the picnic-style bench doing what I could to stay awake.

I'd been waiting for the three vagabonds to come wandering in so that I could pick what little there was of their brains and try to get a better sense of Phoebe Robinson and what passed as her social life. That, and at exactly 3:00 I planned to drive up to Jim Creek Hill and see the place she had been killed, at about the same time that it had happened, so I could get a better picture in my head of what it might have looked like from the perspective of the man driving the truck. Until then, I had a couple of hours in which to attempt to stay awake and ferret out what I could about Phoebe's day-to-day existence.

Marianne Morgan was manning the counter and Dustin, Animal and Larry jockeyed for position, and attention. They buzzed around her like flies. Marianne bantered with the three misfits fearlessly, and it was obvious she was pretty comfortable with them. She'd probably known them all since her first day on the job and most likely they were quite familiar with each other by now.

I sipped a coffee and savored the almost burnt taste. It was the only thing keeping me from slipping into unconsciousness.

The three vampires eventually got bored with courting the pretty girl behind the counter and two of them peeled off to molest the slushy machine and hunt for a meal. They drifted back to the counter after foraging in the warmer and paid for their foot-long hot dogs, sharing spare change and generally jostling each other.

After they left the counter it didn't take them very long before they spotted me. All three of them looked right at me and had no idea who I was. The last time they had seen me up close I had been wearing a sleek red dress. It was obvious they didn't have any idea who I was, sitting in the booth in an old Carhartt jacket and jeans with a stocking cap pulled over my ears.

Animal and Larry were involved in some deep, philosophical conversation about religion, which was so convoluted it was making my head ache just listening to them, and Dustin was leaning on the counter trying his best to convince Marianne that he was the man of her dreams, when the coal miners came in.

Two of them, big burly men with arms like bull riders, shouldered their way through the vampires and selected bags of beef jerky and Hershey's bars for the ride home. They looked exhausted and had probably ended their shift at eleven.

After they checked out at the counter the coal miners staggered back outside and climbed into expensive trucks and drove off into the darkness.

I made my way to the counter and paid for the refill on my coffee.

"Thanks," I said, giving Marianne a slight smile.

She hadn't warmed up to me any more than the last time we'd spoken. She still looked at me as a hostile invader.

I couldn't blame her.

"What are you doing in here, anyway?" she asked.

"I came to talk to Animal and company," I said.

She screwed her face into a baffled expression. "What for? They're all nuts."

"Phoebe kept a pretty low profile," I said.

She shrugged violently. "So? What do you care?"

I rolled my neck around, trying to get it to crack. It was stiff from leaning on my palm for the last hour while I waited for the vampires to arrive.

"I care because nobody really seems to know what Phoebe was actually like. Did she have a boyfriend? Did she have any plans for the future?"

"She had a boyfriend, but he dumped her and moved to Colorado," Marianne said. "Got a job working in the oil fields."

"How long ago was that?"

"Six months or so. Maybe more. Chad. He was a jerk anyway," she said.

Marianne wasn't bothering to work, other than to ring up purchases. She hadn't lifted a broom or filled a cigarette dispenser since I'd been there.

"What about her plans? Did she want to go to school? Maybe she was looking for a new job?"

"She couldn't even think about school," Marianne told me bitterly. "Not with her scum mom milking her dry. Anyway, why is this stuff important?"

"Honestly? I don't even know," I admitted. "My gut tells me there is something that I'm not seeing here. Some reason she got killed that nobody has been able to pin down."

"But I thought Betty . . ." she trailed off.

"It's possible, but if you want to know the truth, I think they arrested the wrong person. I don't doubt for one second that Betty was using a skimmer and stealing credit card information, but I think killing someone is totally out of her depth."

"Yeah. Me too," she said.

I propped a hip against the counter and watched the three misfits while they took over my abandoned picnic table. "I guess I'll go talk to them."

"What do you think they can tell you that I can't?" Marianne asked.

That brought me up short. "Good question."

"Like, what do you want to know?"

"There are some things that don't seem to fit," I said.

She crossed her arms and jutted her chin out. "Try me."

It was worth a shot. "Okay. First off, I know she went up on Jim Creek Hill that night to look for quarters."

"Adam told me that's what the sheriff said. Hell, if I'd known about all that money just sitting up there in the grass I probably would have been right next to her looking for it."

"There wasn't any money up there," I said. "She was on a wild goose chase. So that's why I can't figure out why she didn't hear the car coming. Even if she had her back to the road and was bent over looking for quarters, why didn't she hear the car running down the reflector posts and try to get out of the way?"

"She wouldn't have heard it if her earbuds were in," Marianne said.

"She didn't have an iPod, did she?"

"God no. Too expensive. It was her crappy cell phone. It had music on it, 'cause the radio in her car never worked, but she listened to music all the time. She hardly took the things off. Adam even yelled at her a couple of times for listening to music when she was supposed to be working."

I hadn't seen a cell phone when I'd found her body. But it was possible it was thrown a great distance and I'd missed it.

"It would explain at least that much," I said. "But the rest of

214

it? I'm having a really hard time making sense out of something that looks so random but feels planned."

"Random?" Marianne asked incredulously. "Look around, would you? There ain't a damn thing random about this place."

"It seems random to me."

"Because you don't work here day after day," she said. "You could almost make it through an entire shift without even having to look at the clock once, and you'd still know what time it was."

"How?" I asked.

"By who's in here at any given moment."

I looked around the interior of the store, noticing that the vampires were the only occupants. "But it's just the three of them. How can you tell me what time it is by who's in the store?"

"The 11 shift just blew through here, that means it a quarter till midnight. They always come in at that exact same time, get their Hershey bars and head home. At a quarter to 3, Animal and Larry and Dustin go home. Every night."

"Why at a quarter to 3?"

"Because the Northern Lights strip club closes at a quarter till, and they go park behind the dancers' entrance and watch the girls walk to their cars in their underwear. It's creepy. But they are too damn cheap to pay for the entrance fee so they go get a free show after the club shuts down."

I was impressed with her knowledge. "And after that?"

"At 3:30 the Highway Patrol guy comes in, gets a bag of Doritos and washes the bugs off his windshield. If it's winter, and the bugs are all gone, he just gets Doritos."

"Why at 3:30?"

"Because he is off at 4 a.m. and he uses that last half hour before heading back to the station in Parkman to wind down and finish his paperwork in the parking lot."

"Is it always like that?" I asked. "Predictable, I mean?"

"All the time. These people are pathetic. They don't ever *do* anything. It's always the same drill, night after night. Week after week."

"The night Phoebe got killed, Adam said nobody came in here, of consequence, I mean, between the hours of 3 and 5 that morning."

"You think this is the only place with a regular schedule?" she asked. "A loser is a loser, no matter what he likes. I will guarantee that if the scumbag who killed Phoebe wasn't in here that night, he was not far from here doing what it is he has always done. I mean, what else is there to do out here at that time? And I know it couldn't have been one of the coal miners because they always come in at a quarter to midnight, way before Phoebe got killed. No, I think it was someone going home after his recommended daily allowance of T and A."

"The Northern Lights," I said. "Are you talking about the strip club?"

"You bet your sweet ass I am."

"Where is it, exactly?" I asked.

"You can't see it from the highway. You have to turn at the Taco Bell billboard just before mile marker 9."

I didn't have anything else to do before 3 a.m. and going to a strip club alone wasn't the worst idea I'd ever had, which showed the quality of my ideas.

"Thanks, Marianne. I appreciate your help."

She tossed a look over her shoulder into the parking lot. "You better go. The Fuzz is here."

I looked through the window and saw a brown sheriff's truck pull into the parking lot.

As I stepped outside I saw Finn easing the truck into a parking place. Much to his chagrin, he overshot the curb just a bit and had to put it in reverse to back the front tires off the lip of cement.

He climbed out and came towards me with his head bowed. "Not a word about my driving."

"Bad day?" I asked.

He rubbed his eyes with thumb and forefinger. "Yes. You wanted to see me?"

I glanced at my watch. "That was yesterday."

"You did not indicate it was urgent," he said. "You said at my earliest convenience. Well, this is my earliest convenience."

"How did you know where I was?" I asked.

"Did you have something you wanted to discuss?" he asked.

"Maybe it could keep till you've had some sleep."

"In which case we will not be able to communicate until Friday," he told me.

I fidgeted. "It's about Leif."

His irritation evaporated and he nodded towards his truck. "It's warm."

We climbed inside his truck and he started the engine and flipped on the heater.

After a moment he turned and faced me, giving his full attention.

I wasn't sure where to begin so I dove straight into the middle. "He had ALS."

Finn looked puzzled. "Had what?"

"It's also called Lou Gehrig's disease."

His eyes rested on his hands. "Yes. That scans."

"The night we got married he told you that he was sick, didn't he?" I asked.

"He said it was unlikely he would survive to the end of the year."

"Finn," I said reluctantly. "Did he ask you to come back to Killdeer?"

"No. That is something I did on my own. He asked me to stay away."

217

That wasn't what I expected to hear. "I don't understand."

"He knew there was little time left. He wanted the two of you to share an idyllic few months together. Part of that included my absence."

"He asked you to leave town?"

"Yes. I gave you the cell phone to contact me in case of an emergency. It seemed like a hiddie move to pull a runner on you."

"Hiddie?"

"Hideous," he said.

When he was unhappy or stressed, Finn's South African slang always made an appearance.

"When you phoned me mum, I got the message and came home."

"What did you just say?" I asked.

"When you called me mum? Tell me you know what that means."

"No, you said you came home. Is that how you see Killdeer?"

His eyes looked glassy. "Sure it is."

We sat in silence for a moment.

After his radio squawked a few times he listened intently and then shook his head. "Nothing to do with me. The HP just calling in a traffic stop."

"I thought he might have asked you to come back, after he . . ." I said quietly.

He shook that off. "Leif always thought you could take care of yourself."

"Usually that's the case."

Finn sighed heavy and long. "But sometimes it isn't."

That was the God's honest truth.

"About the plane crash," I said.

"I need you to not say anything about that. I'm a law officer now, remember? There is a protocol."

My eyes pooled with tears. "Alright, if you say so. I believe you, though. It was important for me to tell you that. It really was his choice. I wish he would have told me what was wrong, but I understand why he did things that way."

Finn relaxed against the seat and offered me an earnest smile. "Thank you. That means a great deal."

"I should let you get back to work."

"What are you doing out here in the middle of the night?" he asked.

"Just talking to Marianne about Phoebe."

He groaned. "We made an arrest. The case is closed."

"Just keep an open mind about the whole thing. Would you?"

He closed his eyes and reluctantly nodded. "Open mind. Check."

When he opened his eyes again I was stepping to the pavement. "Hey, thank you for leaving when Leif asked you to go. It must have been hard. Thanks for doing that for us."

"I left Killdeer for Leif," Finn said as he put his truck in gear. "I came back for you."

I closed his door and he drove away slowly, leaving me with a lot to think about.

But that could wait until later. Right now I was focused on other things. Like the possibility that I was one step closer to figuring out who really killed Phoebe Robinson.

I was convinced of one thing, after talking to Marianne in particular. He drove the road between Killdeer and Parkman regularly. I didn't think it was a stranger who had hit her. It was more likely that the killer was someone local.

The list of names was still inside my jacket pocket where I'd left it after Thomas had weeded out the least likely suspects. And he was right. I was looking for a man. One man in particular.

It wasn't the fact that Harvey Wilson had possession of a big chrome truck grille guard that made me think he was responsible, it was the fact that he hadn't wanted me to see it. He'd been upset at me for surprising him inside his steel building when I'd gone to pick up Lil Nipper, and the only reason I could think of that he would have a reaction so intense was because he hadn't wanted me snooping around his equipment.

Me of all people. If there was anyone in Killdeer who had a reputation for putting random information together and coming up with a motive, it was *That Dearcorn Girl.*

Harvey owned a big burgundy Ford Super Duty F-350 that he drove from time to time. Since his ranch was still fully operational, even though he leased the ground out, he still held onto all his equipment and could finance a nice pickup. He also owned a battered Chevy Silverado, but it was not a dually. And his "going into town" car was a bright blue 2001 Pontiac Aztek, possibly the ugliest vehicle ever built. Whenever I'd driven past Lil's over the last few days, I'd seen the Pontiac parked there, not the burgundy pickup. In fact, I hadn't noticed Harvey drive his dually at all lately.

And if I had seen it, chances were it would be missing its grille guard.

I had to be the last person in town Harvey would want noticing a chrome grille recently removed from a truck. No wonder he had snapped at me when I'd stepped inside his steel building.

But that was only one piece of the puzzle. I still had a little more verification to do.

If I could find someone at the Northern Lights strip club who knew Harvey Wilson, and who could tell me that the plump rancher had been there the Monday night that Phoebe had died, then and only then would I believe the case was truly closed.

CHAPTER 21

The music was so loud it hurt to even think.

I'd managed to find the Northern Lights dance club, half convinced that it would be like a Playboy mansion in miniature, and been horribly shocked when I'd walked inside.

The women's bathroom had no door, for starters. It had apparently been torn from its hinges a few months ago and hadn't been replaced. The floor was covered in sawdust and I didn't even want to think about what was down there. The bartender had a swastika tattoo in the middle of his forehead, not a look that I personally would have gone for, but hey.

And then there were the girls.

Five strippers worked at the Northern Lights. Two stringy blondes, an angry redhead and two tired-looking brunettes. I'd watched one performance and it had been the redhead up on the tiny stage dancing. Her theme song could be described as hostile. Something by a band called Nine Inch Nails, which told me a great deal about how she felt about her job.

A trio of professional looking businessmen sat at one of the round tables, hooting and jeering their coworker, who had just been victimized on stage by the redhead. She had handcuffed him to the stripper pole, taken off his belt and repeatedly lashed him with it, poured ice down the front of his pants, and if the act had taken place under any other circumstances, the rest of the performance could have been classified as assault in some states.

I thought about Harvey Wilson. I'd known him all my life. He didn't strike me as the type who would go in for humiliation and so I crossed the redhead off of my list of dancers to talk to about him.

Asking the bartender about Harvey was completely out of the question. I didn't even feel comfortable touching the glass of 7-Up he gave me. If Charles Manson and Cher had conceived a child it would have been this guy.

The other dancers drifted in and out of the bar area between their sets. At the moment, the two blondes sat beside customers in dark corners, trying to wheedle the men into buying them drinks.

Something told me the drinks with actual alcohol in them cost about ten bucks a pop. My soda had been six-fifty.

One of the blondes was perky, talked loud and batted her eyes a lot. She was big in every way. Big laugh, big breasts and big gestures. She looked like she could drink any guy under the table and still do a couple routines and not wobble once in her stilettoes.

I mentally crossed her off the list, too.

The other blonde was petite, quiet and less curvy. She whispered in the ear of the customer next to her, and looked down at her lap constantly. Demure was a good description for her personality. Not exactly what I expected from a stripper.

The man she was coercing at the moment looked like he was from the blue-collar side of the tracks. I stood up and headed for her, thinking that this was as good a time as any.

I stopped at the table where the demure blonde sat and smiled. "Hi. I'd like to talk to you if that's alright."

"Twenty-five bucks," she said, seeming instantly not as demure as I'd originally thought.

"I was just about to pay for a lap dance," the man said.

"I'll give you fifty," I told the woman.

"Follow me," she said, hopping to her feet instantly.

"I'll give you a hundred if you both give me a lap dance," Mr. Blue Collar said hopefully.

I ignored him and followed the blonde into a private area behind a cheesy red curtain. A wooden chair sat in the middle of the small room.

I'd left my stocking cap on. Wearing jeans and a canvas coat, without a hint of makeup, I must have given the impression I preferred women. That revelation hadn't seemed to bother the woman one bit. She held out her hand.

I opened my wallet and peeled off a fifty-dollar bill and handed it to her. "I don't want a lap dance."

She narrowed her eyes. "You a cop?"

"I just want to ask you about a customer that comes in here regularly."

She glared. "I don't talk about my guys."

I looked at her shoes. They were more like medieval torture devices. "Why don't you sit down?"

She looked suspicious for a moment so I gestured towards the chair. "Really. I only want to ask you about whether or not a guy named Harvey comes in here regularly."

After hesitating for a moment, she shrugged and dropped gratefully into the chair. "Whatever. It's your dollar."

Her walking-around clothes were more a suggestion of clothing. She wore a purple kimono-style robe that covered all the important bits, but exposed just enough to be interesting. A stylized dragon snaked across the back.

"Does that name mean anything to you? Harvey. Harvey

Wilson?" I asked.

"No. What does he look like?"

"A rancher," I said.

She laughed outright at that. "If you said he looked like an Amish dude I could probably tell you if he comes in here. But do you know how many ranchers we get?"

I shook my head.

"Dozens."

"Every week?" I asked.

"Try every day."

She leaned against the chair back and rubbed her neck.

"It's not easy work, is it?" I asked.

"It's a living."

If you could call it that. "He's about fifty-five. Sort of chubby. He wears a John Deere baseball cap all the time. Probably sleeps in it."

"Johnny D?" she piped up instantly. "Oh, sure. He's a Monday/ Wednesday guy."

"Monday and Wednesday?" I asked.

"Two for one drink and lap dance night," she said. "We call him Johnny D because of the hat. I tried to take it off him once and he didn't give me a tip."

"That sounds just like him. He's a regular?"

She stretched a leg and I heard her knees pop from the effort. "Jesus, you could set your watch by some of these guys."

She reminded me of Marianne in many ways. Living in the middle of nowhere Montana wasn't always easy. You took a job that you could get, as my father was fond of saying. I didn't judge anyone who was pulling in a paycheck, but a part of me felt incredibly sad for this woman. When she was a little girl she had probably not dreamed of growing up to be a stripper.

"Was he in here last Monday?" I asked.

She thought about it. "Well, my memory isn't all that good anymore. There's a fifty-fifty chance he was. Maybe another fifty will help me remember."

I pulled out my wallet. "Here."

She snatched the money and it vanished somewhere. "He was at the bar, in his usual spot last week. I remember because he got mad someone was sitting there and Will had to ask the guy to move over a stool."

"Harvey has his own stool? Yeah, it's definitely him. What time did he leave?" I asked.

"When we closed down at three. Like usual," she said.

"Has he come in since then?"

She scrunched up her face. "You know, come to think of it, I don't think he has. Oh, wait. I *did* see him, but he wasn't in the bar like normal."

"Where was he?"

"Out in the parking lot. Just sitting there in his car."

"What day was that?" I asked.

"I think it was Tuesday. Not his usual Monday night, but the night after. He didn't come inside."

I thought about that. "What was he doing?"

"Like I said. Just sitting there. I thought it was sort of weird, because those three losers were out there too. Well, gawd, they are there every damn night, but still. They weren't talking or anything, but he was parked sort of close by them."

"Would the three losers be the guys who hang out at the Gas N Dash every night?"

"I don't know where they go when they aren't here. The one with long hair who can't talk and his buddies? Johnny D was parked not too far away from them just sitting there."

The song playing over the speakers was coming to an end. I had no idea what to make of the fact that Harvey had come back to the Northern Lights the night after Phoebe had died, but I tucked that information away for later. The important thing was finding out that this was his regular nighttime destination.

"How long have you worked here?" I asked.

She got to her feet and gave me a brittle smile. "Time's up."

"Wait, I just have one more question. I don't suppose you remember what Johnny D was driving that night?"

"You think I sit out in the parking lot and write down their license plates?" she asked. "Seriously, lady. I do not care."

"But how did you know it was him sitting in the lot?" I asked quickly.

"Are you kidding? He was in some blue piece of crap. I didn't recognize it, but you can't miss his hat. I think he showers in it."

She breezed by and went back to the bar, leaving me standing in the little lap-dance room alone.

The floor was filthy and I was glad the lights were dim. What a nasty place to work. But I couldn't judge her. At least she was paying the bills.

I ducked under the curtain and went back to the bar. My 7-Up was gone, which didn't surprise me. Just on the odd chance that Harvey would be at his usual spot, I scanned the place, peering through the poorly lit bar area, but I didn't see the rancher anywhere.

I did see Thomas Dunne.

When I saw him he caught sight of me at the same moment and the look on his face was one of total shock.

He looked absolutely furious.

In six strides he stopped in front of me, nose to nose. "Ma'am, I do not think that this establishment is an appropriate place for an unattached woman to be seen."

226

He moved as if to grab my arm, but stopped himself and let out a long breath.

"Are you following me, Thomas?" I asked.

"I noticed your vehicle," he said smoothly. "Allow me to escort you out."

"Not a chance," I said.

His features twisted up like he was in physical pain. "I would be happy to walk you outside."

"I'm not in here because I want a two-for drink special," I told him. "The man I suspect is a frequent customer. I'm getting information."

"I assume you mean the gentleman by the name of Wilson."

My eyebrows shot up. "How in the world did you know that?"

"Process of elimination."

"What process?" I demanded.

"Four of the names on your list belong to individuals who were not in the vicinity the night in question. They were either out of town, at home in bed, or in the case of one of the men, incapable of being at the place where your girl was killed driving that make of vehicle."

"Incapable?" I asked.

"The truck belonging to that particular man was having it's clutch rebuilt at the time," he said.

"Thomas, what the hell have you been up to?" I asked.

"I took the liberty of sorting through the names. Of the seven left over from the initial eleven, four were easy to eliminate. That left three individuals who could be responsible," he went on. "Gossip tells me Mr. Wilson is the only one of the three who regularly travels the roads late at night. It was not a difficult leap."

"Why in the world did you feel like shoehorning yourself into this?" I asked.

"You seemed a bit preoccupied with discovering the man," he said.

"Not that I don't appreciate it, but you didn't need to go to so much trouble."

Thomas considered that. "I'm not entirely sure why I did, to be honest with you. It seemed like the right thing to do."

His tone was so cool I couldn't stop myself from asking the question that bubbled to the surface of my mind. "What are you really doing in Killdeer, Thomas?"

He closed himself off like flicking a switch. His face became carefully neutral. "Why, installing your sprinkler system, ma'am. But at this moment I'd prefer it if you would allow me to take you to your car."

"Right. You know what? You can walk me to my car after you start telling me the truth."

He stayed still and clamped his mouth shut.

I glared at him for a moment, waiting for him to volunteer something honest. He tried to smile but it didn't reach his eyes and I shook my head at him, disgusted.

"That's what I thought."

I walked past him towards the door and he caught my arm with two fingers.

"Marley, miss, please wait."

I whirled around. "Don't stand there with your holy sensibilities and tell me that I'm some sort of sinner because I'm standing in a strip club."

"I am a true Christian," he said quickly. His fingers still held my arm. "It is not my place to judge others. That belongs in the hands of the Lord."

"Then why are you here?" I jerked my arm out of his grasp.

"To make things right."

I stared at him. "I don't even know what that means."

"Is there a problem?"

A man the size of a house lumbered towards us and stood beside Thomas with a practiced smile.

He had hands that could crack open a skull like it was a hard-boiled egg. His head was shaved and I couldn't help but notice he had no neck. It was just muscle all the way up.

"No problem at all," Thomas said.

"I think the lady would prefer to be left alone," the bouncer said. He laid a massive paw on Thomas's shoulder when he said it.

"Now, friend," Thomas said dangerously. "This is a private conversation. I'd hate for your evening to be ruined. Kindly remove your hand, if you would."

I started to intervene but the bouncer cut me off.

"Maybe I should remove you from the building," the bouncer said.

Something in Thomas's eyes shifted. In the split second it happened I saw something in him that I hadn't seen before. He had changed before my eyes into a man who had absolutely no fear and I edged between them fast. Things were about to get very ugly.

"Wait. It's alright. He's a friend."

The bouncer looked back and forth between us for a moment, trying to judge the situation.

I deliberately took a big step back, forcing Thomas to move backward as well. With a little bit of space between him and the bouncer, Thomas seemed to calm slightly.

"I was just going," I said, more for the benefit of my gardener than the bouncer.

Before anything else nasty occurred, I marched for the front door and pushed through to the parking lot.

My heart was hammering in my chest like a running jackrabbit.

When I turned back, Thomas wasn't there. He'd obviously thought better of following me outside where he might have to explain himself.

I hurried to my SUV and climbed inside. The dashboard clock said it was 2:30, but as far as I was concerned it was close enough to 3 a.m. for my purposes. I drove to the bottom of Jim Creek Hill, still vibrating with adrenaline.

I pulled over into the ditch and cut the engine. For a long time I simply sat there, trying to make sense out of Thomas Dunne.

He wasn't telling me the truth. There was no question about that. And this recent stunt of getting involved with my unofficial search was a jaw-dropper. Sure, I'd asked him to look at a list of names, and go to the crime scene, but he could have said no. What in the hell could possibly motivate a man who hardly knew me at all to involve himself with my personal vendetta?

It was beyond me. I had to admit for the moment that any theory I could come up with was most likely going to be wrong, and for tonight, at least, there was no alternative but to forget about it and concentrate on the real reason I was sitting on the side of the road in the middle of the night.

I was at the bottom of Jim Creek Hill because I hoped to find something that I'd overlooked. The only problem with that? I had absolutely no idea what I was looking for.

CHAPTER 22

My left windshield wiper was missing. The metal arm screeched across the window, howling with irritation. I'd completely forgotten that Peanut had chewed it off and I hadn't replaced the thing. Thankfully it wasn't raining. A fine sheen of mist coated the windshield but it wasn't enough to prevent me from seeing, just enough to be annoying.

The moon had set hours ago. Even if it hadn't, I wouldn't have seen it through the misty cloud cover. I sat in the driver's seat staring ahead into total blackness.

Shivering.

Fed up.

What was this going to prove?

Luke Harrison's random comment about seeing the eyeshine from all the deer that wandered around the highway in the middle of the night was the real reason I was sitting out here freezing my butt off. That, and the fact that insurance salesmen tended to counsel their customers about what to do if they saw a deer lined up in their headlights.

Smack 'em. Smack 'em good.

It was a crazy thought, but what if Harvey Wilson had thought Phoebe was a deer and not a human being? Had he swerved hard and aimed right for her because he wanted the insurance money?

That made about as much sense as any of the other wild ideas I'd come up with.

The problem with Harvey was I couldn't think of a single reason why he would deliberately want to kill Phoebe Robinson.

I knew for a fact that Harvey never gassed up his vehicles anyplace other than the Stockyard, Killdeer's solitary fuel station, because he was too cheap to pay the extra two cents a gallon over at the Gas N Dash.

So Harvey and Phoebe would not have had that much contact with each other. Other than to see each other on the street from time to time.

I rubbed my forehead, feeling a headache creeping on.

This was ridiculous.

I started the engine. I kept the headlights off and flipped on the heater, warming up the interior and keeping my eyes on the road ahead like it would tell me what I wanted to know if I squinted just right.

This had to be the way it looked to Harvey as he had driven home that night.

The fog, according to the Parkman weather website, hadn't started to form on the outskirts of the valley until sunrise on the 16th. The night before it had been cloudy and damp, with a very slight drizzle but not a hard rain. Practically twin conditions of this night's.

My cold fingers found the headlight knob and I switched them on. Beams of light danced off the dry ditch grass, casting long shadows. The highway snaking up Jim Creek Hill rose in an ever steeper slope until just before the top, curved slightly, then plunged away down the other side.

What was different about this stretch of road? Was it special in some way that I wasn't seeing?

I kept my headlights on and climbed out again. Standing in the middle of the road, I shoved my hands inside my jacket pockets and stared at the pavement. My shadow cast a long dark stain on the asphalt, but the light was enough to see by.

It was an old highway with the usual dips and ruts, but not any obscenely huge potholes. Harvey wouldn't have swerved to miss a pothole or a deep crack in the highway because there simply weren't any big enough to do damage. The only truly rough patches were on the shoulder. And I couldn't understand why someone would deliberately wreck an entire line of reflector posts just to avoid a little bump.

"Okay, so he didn't swerve to miss a pothole," I said to myself.

My boots made soft thumps on the cold asphalt as I walked uphill a few yards. A flash of eyeshine caught my attention and I stopped in the middle of the road.

A deer, no, two of them, froze only a couple dozen yards away when they saw me and I could see their ears flicker back and forth with uncertainty. They sniffed the air, and when I didn't move they tentatively nosed across the highway like two kids sneaking out of the house, trotted a few steps and disappeared down the slope.

For someone coming over the top of the hill from the other side, those two animals would be invisible until the driver was directly on top of them. It was a hazardous place for wildlife; there was no doubt about it.

Why were they crossing at this spot?

"The deer ladder," I said, answering my own question.

I climbed in the driver's seat and pulled onto the highway. Creeping along at less than ten miles an hour, I kept my eyes on the side of the road until I was close to the first reflector post that Harvey had knocked down. My foot hit the brakes.

The deer ladder that allowed wildlife to traverse the barbed wire running beside the highway did its job, but probably a little too well.

The goal, most likely, had been to choose a place well traveled by animals that tended to get snagged by the barbed-wire fence, and give them an easier way to make it to the other side without getting caught up. Since the deer ladder had been installed, there had been fewer animals caught in the wire. But there had probably been a significant increase in the number of deer hit by cars at this exact spot. The highway department had obviously picked this place carefully during daylight hours, but hadn't really taken into consideration the conditions at night.

I flipped on my high beams and studied the side of the road. There was something different about this steep ascent going up to the top of the hill. But what?

Shifting into reverse I backed my SUV down the middle of the highway until I was back in the bowl at the bottom of the hill.

I saw the difference almost at once.

The reflector posts along the side of the highway were the double-decker variety. Since snow tended to drift at the bottom of the hill, the highway department had put in a post stacked on top of a post so the road plow crews could see them, even when the snow was very deep.

I threw the SUV into drive and hit the gas. When I got to the first downed reflector post, in spite of it being bent in half, I could see that the post had only one round reflector on the tip, and not two.

It was only about three hundred feet from the top of the hill. And what was at the top of the hill?

The deer ladder.

My instinct had been right after all. Squinting at the road just right, I'd found the missing piece to my puzzle.

The highway department had started out with good intentions, but installing that deer ladder at the top of the hill instead of finding a different location for it had led to the death of Phoebe Robinson.

Harvey Wilson drove back to Killdeer every Tuesday and Thursday at three in the morning after leaving the strip club. Every week. Week after week. He spent so much time at the Northern Lights he even had his own nickname. And every Tuesday and Thursday night he ran the gauntlet of shimmering eyes between the club and home.

Like all Montanans, I'd learned from the age of sixteen that whenever you drove at night you constantly checked the side of the road for eyeshine. When the headlights of your car glanced off the eyes of a deer, or any creature of the night for that matter, their big eyes reflected back at you out of the darkness like tiny lighthouses. The funny thing was, the round eyes of a deer looked an awful lot like the round tip of the reflector posts. At highway speeds and after a beer or two, it might be difficult to tell them apart.

I threw the SUV in reverse and backed up again until I was beside the double-stacked posts. It would be easy to tell them from an animal, because of the two reflectors. But as the posts progressed up the hill they only had one reflector and looked almost like the eyes of a whitetail hovering beside the shoulder.

"Son of a bitch," I whispered. "He wasn't aiming for Phoebe. He was knocking over the posts."

Harvey, in typical rancher fashion, had gotten angry and decided to make it easier for him to tell the shining orbs apart. He couldn't do anything about all the animals wandering down from the deer ladder, but he could sure as hell do something about the reflector posts.

I searched my memory. The clothes that Phoebe had been wearing the morning I'd found her body were old, worn and tattered. They were also colorless. If she were hunched over, no flashlight, using her little crappy cell phone as her only source of illumination, she would have been practically invisible.

Harvey hadn't even known she was there until he hit her.

A wave of utter sadness settled over me. If her mother hadn't bled Phoebe dry for rent and groceries, the girl wouldn't have been desperate enough to walk the side of a dark highway hoping to scrounge up a few quarters for gas money.

If she wouldn't have been digging in the dirt, trying to catch a break for once in her life, she would still be alive.

Who had ever looked out for Phoebe? No one. And in an instant she was gone. Almost like she had never even existed in the first place.

I cried all the way home, thinking about it. Thinking about the waste of a human life. If only she had managed to get a boost somehow. She could have been so much more.

My bed felt cold as I climbed in and pulled up the covers. My throat was raw from tears and anger.

Phoebe's death had dredged up all the pain from Leif's plane crash, and all the old buried feelings I still carried around from the loss of my mother when I was just a kid.

It wasn't that I expected life to be fair. But why did it have to be so damn *cruel* sometimes?

CHAPTER 23

"What year is your outfit, again?" asked the floor clerk.

"A 2011," I said.

He scanned a sheet of numbers in his hand. "What model?"

"It's a BMW," I said. "The X6."

He glanced at me out of the corner of his eye. "You ever think of selling it, you call me, right?"

"Sure, Roland. What wiper blade do I need?"

His finger fell on a number and he mouthed it to himself. He went back to the rows of wipers and pulled one off the shelf.

"You want some help putting it on?" he asked.

Roland's sharp green eyes twinkled. I could see he was having visions of getting his hands on my SUV.

"No thanks, I can manage."

"Just in the nick," he said, giving me the wiper blade. "It's gonna piss down cats and Saint Bernards in a bit."

"Will it snow?" I asked.

"On the verge. Could turn into freezing rain by tonight."

I thanked him and paid for the wiper blade and on a whim bought a pair of mittens. They were green knit, and decorated with snowflakes.

Winter was on its way to Montana and you could never have too many gloves lying around.

It was close to 4:30. I'd done absolutely nothing all day. Back at the house, Thomas had worked diligently in the yard and he was very nearly done with the project.

I wondered what excuse he would come up with to justify hanging around Killdeer after the sprinkler system was installed. It seemed unlikely to me that he would leave until his self-appointed tasked of helping me nail Harvey Wilson to the wall was complete. After all, he'd come this far.

As I left the store, the late afternoon sky seemed heavy. Low clouds churned overhead. The breeze blew cold. Everything looked gray and I felt lonely. Irene and my father wouldn't be back home for three more days and I hadn't been to work since Leif . . .

A catch tickled my throat and I managed to suppress it. I didn't want to be standing in the parking lot of the Big R hardware store and have all my neighbors see me sobbing while I tried to replace a wiper blade.

One bright spot, if it could be called that, was the arrival tomorrow of Scott with the urn, and the intention of spreading Leif's ashes at last. The kid and I had started out on the wrong foot the first time we'd met. But after he spent some time with me he figured out I hadn't married his father because I was looking for someone to take care of me, and I'd really done it for love. We had actually developed a fast friendship after that.

That Leif had deliberately crashed his plane was something I didn't think Scott needed to know. In fact I'd made up my mind that the truth about how he had died would never become public. I believed in my heart it was something Leif wouldn't want to be remembered for.

My fingers tingled from the cold as I struggled with the wiper blade. It refused to go on and I cursed it under my breath.

Leif's airplane had been insured for close to half a million dollars. It must have been the accountant in him, but my husband had armed himself to the teeth with insurance policies and financial Plan B's to the point of redundancy.

I had no idea what I would do with the money from the Baron. The airplane insurance money, according to Mr. Toomey, would probably come out to be around four hundred thousand dollars. I wasn't sure that money would ever be put to good use because I didn't exactly want anything to do with it. First of all, I struggled with the morality of the issue. It had been an accident according to the NTSB investigation, but I knew better, and because of what I knew the money wasn't exactly legitimate.

If Phoebe had been alive I would have gladly given her the money for college and a dorm room. At least it would be used for something good that way.

But she wasn't alive. She'd been wiped off the face of the earth in a single moment.

Had Louise Robinson sobered up long enough to understand what dire straits she was in now? Probably not. One of the unfair consequences of drinking was that alcoholics tended to drown everyone on the boat, not just themselves, when their ship finally went down. She had done nothing to help her daughter get ahead in the world. Now Louise was on her own, and who knew what would become of her?

I ground my teeth together as my chilly fingers struggled with the plastic snaps. Finally the wiper blade clicked into place.

As Roland had said, just in the nick. I pulled open my door and climbed in, the heavy air sighed deeply, and small raindrops pattered to the ground.

My hands felt heavy as they rested on the steering wheel. There was a problem I had to sort out but my brain felt sluggish. I was confident I'd finally unraveled the mystery of how Phoebe had been killed, but since it was technically an accident and Harvey hadn't deliberately murdered her, I had no idea how to compel the man to come forward and take responsibility for what he had done. Maybe I couldn't. Maybe this was going to be one of those battles I couldn't win in the end. Maybe it didn't matter anymore.

Except to Betty, that is.

A rap on the window at my elbow made me jump. I hit the button and lowered it.

"Roland, what's up?" I asked.

The floor clerk handed me a slip of paper. "You forgot your receipt."

I took it from him but instead of leaving he leaned both arms inside the window.

"Nice. Leather? And heated seats, right?"

"The SUV? Yes, it's got heated seats."

He lingered with his arms propped on the door. It was obvious that he just wanted a close look at the BMW.

"Hey, did your hired guy get all his sprinkler equipment sorted out?" he asked.

"Thomas? As far as I know," I said.

"When he first came in here a few days back? Hell, it's like the guy didn't know *what* he needed."

This made me pause. "You were working that day?"

"Yup. Nice fella. But he asked me more questions than a professional should, in my opinion. Sounded to me like you folks hired some fly-by-night."

"What sort of questions?"

"Well first off he comes in and says that Leif Gable hired him. Which made me sort of look at him crossways on account of Leif getting killed and all. Sorry, Marley. Then he goes on to say he needs to get supplies for the job."

"Did you have what he needed?" I asked.

"He didn't tell me what he needed. Said he wasn't sure where to start with a job that big."

"He didn't say what the job was?"

"Nope. So I says to him, what? Did you get a contract to put in the sprinkler system that Leif was always talking about?"

"Let me guess," I said quietly. "He said yes."

"And he says that maybe he ought to think about renting a trencher, but he wasn't sure. And then he wants to know if Nathan was around so's he could maybe help him lift it out of the truck later."

"He asked about my father?"

"I told him he was on his own and it was his own damn problem 'cause you didn't have anyone to call to help you out on account of your dad going out of town on vacation."

"Did you, now?"

"And the fool didn't even know where your place was, so I had to tell him how to get there. Seems to me like Leif was just doing this bum a favor," Roland said.

"Sounds like you were very helpful," I said bitterly. If Thomas had been a stalker, Roland would have been his dream come true. Nobody in this town thought twice about little things like personal privacy or confidentiality.

"As much as I could be. Well, he was awful nice about it and you should have seen the gals behind the register bending over backwards to help him out. Poor southern-fried simpleton who needed looking after, was sorta what I made of him. The gals helped him with names of folks he might call if he needed someone to lift out that trencher."

"Uh-huh."

"Course, I told him right away that he wouldn't be able to use a cell phone here in the valley, cause with all the hills and such we can't get a signal anyplace. Said if he needed to call someone to help him lift the trencher he could probably use the phone here at the Big R. Come to think on it, he said he didn't even own a cell phone."

My growing anger evaporated and I stared at Roland. It hit me like a sledgehammer between the eyes. "He didn't have a cell phone?"

"Said they was a waste of money."

I threw my SUV into gear. "Sorry, Roland. I need to go."

He gave my BMW one last long look as I sped away.

I ignored the stop sign and screeched onto Main Street. A block later I braked hard and stopped in front of the sheriff's station. Leaving the motor running, I ran up the front steps two at a time and pushed through the glass doors.

Loy was tipping powdered creamer into a Styrofoam coffee cup when the front door sailed out of my hand with a bang.

Creamer and coffee spilled across the counter.

"Dammit. You scared the living hell out of me, Marley."

"Loy, did you find her cell phone?" I came to a stop at his shoulder.

Valerie, Loy's dispatcher, raised both eyebrows and slowly spun her chair around so her back was to us. She found something on her desk that needed immediate attention.

The sheriff glared. "My office."

He did what he could to mop up the coffee, grabbed the cup and spun around. I followed on his heels and when we were inside his tiny office he closed the door behind us.

He set his coffee on the desk and slowly eased himself into his chair, looking like he was forcing himself to slow down. He took a breath and stared at me hard. "I'm only going to say this once. This is an active investigation. We have made an arrest. I cannot, nor will I, comment. On anything. Got it?"

"Did you find Phoebe's cell phone? She had it with her when she died. I would stake my life on it."

He grimaced. "Hun, I wish you wouldn't say things like that."

"He took it with him afterwards, didn't he?" I asked.

"Who took what from where, when?" he asked.

"Harvey Wilson. He took it with him and that's why you didn't find her cell phone."

Loy's eyes flashed like he'd just sat on a scorpion. "Where did you come up with that name?"

My cheeks warmed. "It's a long story. Loy, are you listening to me?"

"I'm listening. I just don't particularly like what I'm hearing."

"Harvey Wilson killed Phoebe. But it was an accident. Betty didn't do it. She couldn't have. She drives a beat-up Chevy Malibu."

The sheriff held up both hands. "Whoa, whoa there, Annie Oakley."

"Harvey took the chrome grille guard off his Ford Super Duty right after he ran her over because it probably had damage. But he's so damn cheap he couldn't part with it, so he hid it inside his steel building."

Loy slammed a fist on his desk. "That's enough. You need to explain to me what you were doing snooping around his property."

I leaned on his desk with both hands and annunciated each word precisely. "Loy. Did you find her cell phone?"

He shook his head, an expression of rapid frustration spreading across his features like a fast-moving infection. "No. And nobody else has that information. I would really like to know how you came by it."

"She didn't have a flashlight. I didn't see one when I first found her body. It was the middle of the night and pitch black. She had to be using something to look around on the ground for the quarters. And she was listening to her music. That's why she didn't try to get out of the way when Harvey started knocking over reflector posts. She didn't hear him coming."

"Assuming you are correct," he said with a tight jaw, "why would he hit her, get out, and not try to help her or even bother to report the accident? And then why would he take her phone and nothing else?"

"It was an accident, but it wasn't," I said.

"God almighty," Loy grumbled.

"He was knocking down the reflector posts because he was sick and tired of hitting the deer."

Loy blinked at me like he had something sharp in his eye. "Did you fall down and hit your head?"

"The posts, Loy. They look like eyeshine. Harvey drives back twice a week from the Northern Lights and when he gets to the bottom of Jim Creek Hill he always knows there's going to be deer waiting for him at the top. That's where the deer ladder is, remember?"

He swiveled in his chair. "Alright. I'll grant you that. But why take her phone?"

"What if he wanted to check it to make sure she wasn't talking to someone when he ran her over? Harvey doesn't know anything about cell phones. He wouldn't be able to glance at it and tell what it was being used for. He had to take it with him so he could study it at home."

"And then?"

"Then he ditched it. She wasn't talking to anyone, she was listening to music. That meant there wasn't going to be a witness to worry about. So he probably smashed it into a million pieces, dropped it into a coffee can filled up with motor oil, took it out into one of his pastures and buried it."

"Girl, for once I would like to look inside your head and figure out what sort of hamster wheel powers your imagination."

"It's probably buried somewhere out on his property, Loy."

The sheriff studied me hard. "This information stays in this office. Got it?"

I frowned and nodded. "Of course."

He made an unhappy face. "Her phone still rings. It's not smashed. We are guessing it's outside of the valley someplace because it gets enough of a signal to ring, and you know how it is down here in Killdeer. Wherever it is, it's still in one piece. But we haven't located it yet."

My head buzzed with questions. What could he have done with it? "It doesn't have one of those GPS finders, does it?"

"It's just an old cell phone, nothing more. It doesn't have GPS capability and that could be why the battery has lasted this long. But it can't hold out much longer. We might never find it."

"Harvey knows where it is. He took it, then he got rid of it," I said.

Loy groaned. "Hun, remember what I said about your imagination?"

"It was an accident. But he killed her. He ran her down, and drove away when he saw what he'd done. Aren't you going to do something?"

"We did do something. We made an arrest," he said.

"You and I both know Betty wasn't driving a dually pickup truck that night."

The sheriff stood up and held out a finger. "You listen to me. We have been following up several leads. An arrest is sometimes a strategic play to make someone else feel overly confident. I have told you and told you, Marley. We are not the Keystone Cops here. We actually solve crimes from time to time and I sure as hell would appreciate it if you could back off and let us do our job."

"But Loy—"

"I know you have had a rough patch lately, and that's why I'm giving you gigantic leeway. But right now you need to get out of my office and not talk to anyone about this. We're done."

His face was rigid with anger. In the past I'd pushed Loy too far, and even though I knew everything I'd just told him was true, it seemed unlikely he was going to pursue any of it.

"You are making a huge mistake," I said.

Before he could reply I stomped outside and the moment my feet hit the stairs a deluge of rain poured from the sky.

By the time I'd managed to get my door open and climb inside I was drenched.

"He's going to get away with it," I said to myself. "The lying bastard is going to get away with it."

That was something I couldn't stand.

I rolled all the facts around in my brain like marbles. There had to be something I'd missed. But what?

Why hadn't Harvey smashed the phone? What had he done with it?

Then I remembered what the blonde stripper had told me the night I'd gone into the Northern Lights. She had seen Harvey there, not on his usual night, sitting in the parking lot.

Just sitting in the parking lot, doing nothing.

That had been Tuesday. The day after Phoebe was killed.

Why would he be there that night? He hadn't just been sitting there for no reason. He was up to something. But what?

Then I realized what I'd been missing. He was waiting for his chance to get rid of the cell phone.

The blonde had said you could set your watch by the habits of her customers. They always did the same thing, night after night. Routines were established and people were almost always predictable. What was the one thing Harvey could always count on when it came to the Northern Lights? He could count on the fact that the three vampires would be parked by the back door at a quarter till three. Like they always were, night after night.

Harvey knew they would be there. What better way to get yourself off the hook than put someone else on it?

My palms slammed against the steering wheel. "Not if I can help it."

Everything clicked into place and I suddenly knew what I had to do. Harvey was setting up three innocent men to take the fall for him. Nobody else was going to stop him.

It was up to me.

It was like my hands moved without any direction from me at all. I watched like a spectator as I put the SUV into gear and drove down the street to Lil's café.

At least a dozen cars I recognized filled the lot and Lil's was packed with the usual dinner crowd. Finn's brown sheriff's truck was parked there, as was Thomas's screaming yellow Barracuda. But I wasn't looking for them. I was looking for the ugly blue Pontiac Aztek that Harvey had been driving since the accident.

I saw it at once, taking up a handicapped space.

Rain gushed down on me as I walked across the lot, one foot in front of the other, like I was going to war.

The greeting bell tinkled above me when I walked through the door, and Judy Isley looked up from behind the counter and gave me a bright smile.

"Hey-ya Marley. Need a menu?"

I didn't say a word. My face felt numb.

Judy stared at me, her expression shifting from happy to confused. "You alright?"

The noise in the café dimmed and I focused on my mission.

Finn was seated at the counter and when he looked up his coffee cup halted midway to his lips. Suddenly he was watching me with a worried look.

Someone in a booth to my left turned towards me and started to rise, but then stopped and sat back down again.

I noticed the person who had turned towards me and realized it was Thomas. He looked equally concerned but he didn't speak, simply studied me carefully.

I must have looked like a crazy person, standing there, dripping on the floor, with an exression of savage determination.

Harvey Wilson sat at the end of the counter in his usual spot, toothpick firmly clenched between his teeth. He eyed me suspiciously.

I let my gaze wander the café, looking at no one in particular and everyone in general.

"I know who you are," I said, casting my gaze around the entire room.

"Marley, what are you going on about?" Judy asked. She tried to laugh but when she took in my expression her mouth closed slowly.

The café fell into total silence. No one moved.

"I know who you are," I said again.

Everyone in the diner stared at me.

"And I know what you did with the cell phone."

Finn's eyes bulged and he half rose from his stool.

"Ma'am," Thomas whispered plaintively. "Please don't."

"You have until dawn to turn yourself in," I said. "And if you don't I will take you down."

Thomas's face fell. He closed his eyes and shook his head back and forth.

Finn's eyes shot sparks as he stared at me.

I didn't bother to see what Harvey Wilson was doing, because I already knew. If I was right, the plump rancher would be pale as milk. I turned on my heel and strode outside.

I walked through the rain, oblivious to the chill. Adrenaline surged through my body.

When I reached my SUV a hand touched my shoulder.

I glanced behind me and saw Thomas standing there, the rain coming down in cascades over both of us.

"Please, ma'am. Please go back in there and explain it was just a prank, or that you were only trying to get a rise out of folks. Could you please do that?"

"Thomas," I said. "Haven't you ever read the instructions on a stick of dynamite before?"

He heaved a deep sigh. "Yes, ma'am. I have."

"Then you know what they say."

Thomas looked mournful. "Yes, ma'am, I do."

I climbed inside my vehicle and slammed the door, and there was absolutely no chance I was going back inside Lil's.

The warning label on dynamite was printed carefully in easy-to-read letters. It said, in bold type, *Do Not Return After Lighting Fuse.*

I'd just lit a stick of dynamite after all, and I knew how to follow instructions.

CHAPTER 24

Marianne Morgan stood behind the counter at the Gas N Dash watching me. She knew something was up, but she couldn't figure out what it was and she leaned against the counter with both arms folded unhappily. Every few minutes she glanced outside, expectant.

I'd been relieved to see her working the graveyard shift. Having Marianne here was absolutely essential.

It was a quarter to midnight and I'd been sitting at the picnic bench inside the store since 10:30, waiting.

I knew if Larry, Dustin and Animal followed their usual routine, I wouldn't be waiting much longer.

The air was cool and damp but we'd managed to evade snow for one more day, and the roads had mostly dried from the afternoon rains.

I hadn't bothered to tell Loy where I was. After my stunt at Lil's, I doubted very much I needed to. Everyone in Killdeer would be talking about what I'd said inside the café. After getting what I needed from Marianne and the vampires, Phoebe's cell phone would be making its appearance any moment. Then I could call Loy and he could arrest Harvey.

Either that, or Harvey Wilson had already gone to the station in Killdeer and turned himself in. If that was the case this errand wasn't necessary. But I simply couldn't picture Harvey suddenly developing a conscience. No, I was definitely doing the right thing. Any man selfish enough to simply drive away after running someone over would need to be dragged kicking and screaming to justice.

The overhead doorbell sounded and the three vampires shuffled inside right on schedule, shivering from the chill air and engaging in their usual banter.

They took a moment to harass Marianne, but when she gave them one- or two-word responses through tight lips they sensed she wasn't in the mood and drifted to the hot dog warmer.

"Hello, boys," I said.

Larry threw a glace over one shoulder.

Animal stopped, turned around and stared at me. "We don't like her, right?"

I blinked at him with surprise. He'd actually said something coherent. Of course, it was derogatory, but it was a start.

"Right," said Dustin. "We don't like her."

I got to my feet slowly, like I was trying to sneak up on a trio of startled rabbits. "This time I'm here to do you three a really big favor."

"You want to invest in our home brew beer business?" Larry asked.

"I came to warn you."

Dustin was reaching inside the warmer, but stopped with the tongs halfway to a Polish sausage. "Warn us?"

"Somebody is trying to set you up," I told them.

Larry's eyes darted around the store. "I knew it. This place is bugged, isn't it?"

I rolled my eyes. "Can we go outside into the parking lot for a second? It's about Phoebe, not your former careers with the CIA."

Dustin and Larry exchanged a look. Animal swayed back and forth behind them, a worried look creasing his forehead.

"What's out in the parking lot?" Larry asked.

"Your truck. More important, though, something that's in the back I think you need to know about."

The three vampires hesitated, unsure and undecided.

"Fine," I said. "I'll do it without your help. But when the sheriff comes looking for you wanting to know how Phoebe Robinson's cell phone got into the bed of your pickup, don't say I didn't warn you."

"The hell you say," Larry muttered. He slammed his soda cup down on the counter and started for the door.

Animal and Dustin leapt to follow, and the three of them spilled into the parking lot before I could even make it to the door.

"What's going on?" Marianne asked.

Her face was a mix of anger and confusion.

"Call Phoebe's number," I said.

"You think her phone is in their truck?" she asked. "I don't get it."

"Just call it. I'll explain in a minute."

I dashed outside and saw Larry lowering the tailgate of his battered pickup. The bed was littered with debris. Soda cans, a square of old beige carpet, an empty box, partially squashed, that had once held a humidifier, a bicycle tire and various other odds and ends were strewn there.

"If someone planted a bug on me," Larry said, "I'd know it."

I studied the truck bed and the mountains of garbage inside it. "Sure you would."

I looked through the door at Marianne and gave her a thumbs-up. Frowning, she picked up the phone underneath the counter and dialed a number.

The four of us held our breath.

For a moment nothing happened at all. Then Animal hopped sideways and pointed. "I hear it!"

Larry heaved himself into the back and started sifting through the mess. "I don't see it, man. Are you sure?"

I strained my ears and held up my hand. "Quiet!"

Everyone froze.

I heard a faint ring.

"It's inside the cab," I said.

Dustin beat me to the door and ripped it open. A mechanical chirp filled the air and he looked at me, horrified. "Oh Jesus, oh Jesus. It's in there Larry. Dude it's totally in the truck."

"Hey, get it out of there, Dustin!" Larry squalled desperately. "She's trying to say we did it!"

I held up both hands. "No, that's not what I'm doing at all. Someone else put it there. I know you didn't have a thing to do with Phoebe's death."

Larry stumbled away from the truck and waved his hands frantically. "I don't care. I don't want it anywhere near me."

"Hold up, Larry," I said. "Leave it alone. It's better if you don't handle it. I'll go back inside and call the sheriff and he can come out here to pick it up."

"Damn, I can't figure how it's in there," Larry said, shaking his arms with nervous energy.

"Last week, did you get out of your truck over at the Northern Lights?" I asked.

The three misfits stole looks at their shoes.

Dustin mumbled. "Maybe."

"It wouldn't have to have been for very long. A couple seconds might have been long enough," I said.

"We sometimes go dumpster diving," Larry admitted.

"At the strip club?" I asked.

Dustin shrugged. "Sometimes they sweep the sawdust off the floor, bag it and throw it out with the trash. Guys'll drop dollar bills when they're really drunk and those get thrown out too. We found a twenty one night."

"Hey, one man's trash," Larry started to say defensively.

"Okay, okay," I said. "Lock up your truck and wait here until Loy can get over from Killdeer."

I went back inside the store and Marianne was crying, something I didn't expect to see.

"They didn't kill her, right? 'Cause if they did I swear to God I'll—"

"Someone else is trying to make it look like they did. I doubt seriously Larry's truck can even make it up to highway speeds without falling apart. It's not the vehicle that killed her."

"You know who it was, don't you?" she wiped her eyes.

I felt my shoulders slump. "Yes, I do. Can you call Loy? He needs to come and pick up that phone before he sends the wrong person to jail."

She snatched the telephone from under the counter and started dialing.

"You have the sheriff's number memorized?" I asked.

"I work graveyards," she said. "And it's not Loy's number. It's the cell for the HP who comes in every night."

She fidgeted while the phone rang. "Levi? Hey, it's Marianne over at the Gas N Dash. Sorry to bother you but could you radio over to Killdeer and get Sheriff Shucraft to come over here? Yeah, it's important. He's been looking for a cell phone? You know, from when Phoebe got killed?"

The highway patrolman spoke a few words.

Marianne glanced toward me. "No, I didn't. Tell him that, would you? I don't want mixed up in this."

She listened for a moment and hung up the phone. "He's going to radio over there now. It usually only takes Loy about fifteen minutes to get here when he's in a hurry. And I think he'll be in a hurry this time."

I felt vindicated, exhausted, and my anger was like a hot air balloon that had just crash-landed. It was finally over and I was completely spent.

"Thanks for your help," I told her. "Tell Loy he can reach me at home if he needs a statement."

"You're leaving?" she asked. "You're the one who figured this out. You can't just take off."

I managed to give her a tired smile. "Honestly, now that it's over I don't think I can force myself to stay here for one more minute."

I trudged to the parking lot. The relief and satisfaction of being right about what Harvey had done weren't enough to stave off the feelings of exhaustion and bitterness. It was time for me to go home.

Larry was doing what he could to lock his truck. Every time he tried to close the door the lock would pop up again. He had plenty of help from the other two and I left them to it.

Loy would be able to sort it all out, of that I was certain. The hidden grille in Harvey's steel building with the telltale damage it likely had from the reflector posts would be a good start. And I was almost certain I'd seen a security camera overlooking the parking lot over at the Northern Lights. Surely it had managed to get at least one shot of Harvey's ugly Aztek parked beside Larry's truck.

The crotchety old rancher would have been better off destroying Phoebe's phone. But he'd kept it, hidden it under Larry's seat, and probably planned to get a tip to Loy so the three vampires would suddenly find themselves at the top of the suspect list. The moment

Sheriff Shucraft had told me Phoebe's phone was still working I'd figured it out. Harvey Wilson had outsmarted himself.

I pulled out of the Gas N Dash and drove slowly down the highway. As I passed the Taco Bell billboard where the turnoff to the strip club carved a path toward paradise, a pair of blindingly bright headlights ahead of me winked in the darkness and I glanced away, irritated.

"Jerk."

As I passed the car I flipped my high beams on and kept my attention focused on the road ahead. This time of night there would be a lot of deer activity between Parkman and home. I needed to keep my eyes on the pavement in front of me.

I eased the wheel around the first wide turn leading toward Jim Creek Hill and passed the speed limit sign. The limit was 55 but I drove 50 so I would have more time to react if something shot across the road in front of me.

My jaw popped as I yawned. I had to blink my eyes hard to get them to focus on the road. Until now I hadn't realized how exhausted I'd felt.

My foot pressed down on the gas pedal and my speed inched up to 55. With any luck Loy would pass me on the way home and I would be able to sleep easy tonight, knowing he was on the case.

As I made the second wide turn heading for the hill something flickered in the rearview mirror and I tried to focus on what I'd just seen.

It happened so fast there wasn't time to react. The back end of my SUV lifted from the ground and my entire body heaved up off the seat from the impact.

My hands slipped as the steering wheel spun out of control and the nose of my SUV drifted sideways with a sickening screech. The tires wouldn't grip. I was in a skid. My foot searched for the brake frantically while I tried to hold the wheel steady.

Instinct told me to slam the brake as hard as I could, but at the last moment I straightened the tires and hit the gas instead.

The rear tires gripped and the wild skid turned into a violent acceleration. The SUV shot forward and the back end recovered.

My teeth ached from the impact. I shot a glance to my mirror but couldn't see anything. Someone had just rammed me from behind. But his headlights were off and all I could see were two pinpricks of light from the running lamps.

The pinpricks were getting bigger.

He was coming at me for another go.

I pressed the gas to the floor and my SUV inched away from the tiny lights. My BMW slowly pulled ahead.

The bottom of Jim Creek Hill came into sight and when I started to climb up I was doing ninety.

The running lights hadn't veered off. They trailed after me like a demented bloodhound.

The SUV's suspension bucked when the wheels hit a dip and I fought to keep from skidding. I crested Jim Creek Hill and roared down the other side, gaining speed. But so were the running lights behind me.

The pinpricks came closer as gravity helped them along. Just as they lurched towards my back bumper for another hit, the tiny lights seemed to float sideways in slow motion. Headlights from a third car lit up the darkness and I watched in my mirror as the running lights peeled from the road, lifted into the air and careened wildly. A flash of tumbling metal faded into the darkness behind me. Nobody was trying to ram my back bumper at the moment, but my foot refused to let up from the gas pedal.

There was still another set of headlights behind me and I was determined whoever it was would have to blow their engine to catch me. I slammed down the gas.

A flash caught my eye and a screaming yellow streak appeared next to me. Thomas's Barracuda effortlessly pulled up alongside my SUV and I saw him wave me to the side.

Instantly I backed off the accelerator and the engine noise dropped from a squeal to a normal hum once again.

By the time I'd pulled off the road Thomas had passed me, turned around and was heading back.

He stopped in the glow of my headlights and parked beside me. I stepped out, my hands shaking, and the ground felt incredibly reassuring under my feet.

I walked to his door, and for someone who had just PIT maneuvered another vehicle into a violent crash, he looked incredibly calm.

"Are you alright, ma'am?"

My trembling had reached all the way down to my feet. "I think so."

"It's probably safe now. I flipped him a ways back."

"Who?" I asked.

"Mr. Wilson, of course."

"Were you following Harvey?" I asked.

He shot me a surprised look. "Course not. I was following you."

I didn't know what to say.

He nodded back down the road towards the wreck behind us. "Shall we go take a look'n see if he pulled through?" he asked.

"You think he's dead?"

"Can't imagine he survived. I believe the car rolled six times."

Before I could stop him, Thomas put the Barracuda in gear and drove by me. I stood there for a moment, trying to get my breath back.

Finally, I steadied my breathing and reluctantly followed him in my SUV back down the road.

We'd been traveling so fast when Harvey's car started to roll we had to backtrack quite some distance.

I stopped when my headlights lit up the wreck. Pieces of metal lay on the road. Plastic bits were scattered around the white lines like confetti.

Thomas had parked sideways behind Harvey's car and he was climbing out, his lean frame moving across the dry ditch grass smoothly.

I stood next to my SUV, but couldn't bring myself to get any closer.

"You dead in there, Mr. Wilson?" Thomas called out.

There was no movement from within the hunk of twisted metal that I could see. My gardener crouched down and peered inside the passenger-side window, which was now facing the road. The car had come to a rest upside-down.

"Do you see anything?" I asked.

He stood up. "Not sure. Could be he's still alive. Perhaps we should call an ambulance."

I marveled at how calm he seemed.

My teeth were chattering from the adrenaline.

A sound wailed from the top of the hill and flashing blue lights sped for us.

Finn practically threw himself from his sheriff truck when he screeched to a stop behind my vehicle. He sprinted for us, his face a mask of shock.

"There's never a cop around when you need one," I said.

Finn put both hands on my shoulders. "Are you injured?"

"No, but I think Harvey Wilson may be dead. He tried to run me off the road."

He drew his gun and motioned to Thomas. "Step away from there, please."

260

Thomas bent down and peered inside the wreck. "Hold up there deputy. Something's moving around. Might be he's coming to."

I looked towards the passenger window on Harvey's car and a spark of light winked in the darkness. The sound was so startling I felt all the nerves in my body jump.

The crack of gunfire ripped the still night air.

I watched as Thomas stood up with a look of utter shock on his face, step back twice and fall to the ground.

It took my brain a moment to understand what I'd just seen. Thomas hadn't fallen over from being startled. He'd been shot.

The sounds of gunfire beside me nearly made my heart stop. I managed to cover my ears and step aside.

Finn was in front of me, pistol in hand, spraying the Aztek with bullets. He moved as he shot. His feet carried him sideways smoothly and his aim was deadly. Sparks flew from the cab of the car as Finn peppered it with relentless precision.

Before I knew what I was doing my knees hit the pavement next to Thomas. His hands gripped the right side of his chest and a horrible wheezing sound erupted from his lips.

"Finn I need you!" I said, moving Thomas's hands aside so I could get a look at the damage.

"Finn!"

"Move." He was on the ground beside me shoving me out of the way.

Finn had a lot more medical training than I did and I shuffled out of his path quickly.

He leaned down and used his flashlight to see the wound. His face hardened when he examined Thomas.

"Marley, get on my radio and call for an ambulance."

"How bad?" I asked.

Finn shot to his feet and grabbed my arm, heaving me away

from Thomas. His voice was low. "He's got a sucking chest wound. If we don't get an ambulance here in about ten minutes he's going to die."

"They won't make it in time," I said. "The ambulance takes twenty minutes to make it here from Parkman."

Finn grimaced. "That's our only option."

"You could drive him," I said desperately.

"My truck is not nearly fast enough."

My eye fell on the yellow Barracuda, idling on the side of the road, the door hanging ajar. "Help me get him in there."

"You cannot move him, not with that much damage to his lung."

"Nine minutes," I said.

To his credit, Finn didn't argue. He hurried to Thomas and helped me lift him inside the car.

We managed to get Thomas into the back and laid him out carefully. He groaned in pain, blood spilling from his chest.

Finn leaned down and studied the gearshift on the car. "Where is first on this thing?"

"What?"

He looked at me, a mixture of helplessness and panic in his wide eyes. "I can't drive a stick."

I stared at him. "Get out of the way."

I climbed in and pulled the seat up. Everything Thomas had taught me rolled through my head like a movie and I slammed the door.

Finn was already backing towards his truck. "I'll tell them you are coming. Drive!"

There wasn't time to buckle my seat belt. I shifted into gear and the Barracuda roared. The tires bit into the asphalt and we shot forward like we'd been fired from a cannon.

Thomas coughed from the backseat. The sound was sickening.

My throat was tight but I managed to get words out. "We're going to the hospital, Thomas. Stay still."

My feet worked the pedals like they had on the Killdeer airport runway and if I thought my heart had been racing before, it was nearly bursting now.

I didn't waste time looking down at the speedometer so I had no idea how fast we were moving. I did know I'd never driven this speed in my life, and I said a silent plea under my breath that nothing got in the way.

The headlights could barely keep up. The only reason we didn't fly off the road and crash into the ditch was my experience. I'd driven this highway a thousand times and knew every turn and every bump. Even at the speed we were moving I knew what to do next. Each corner and pothole of this road was seared into my brain like a tattoo.

"Sarah," Thomas said. "Sarah."

His breathing wheezed horribly and I had to force myself to keep looking ahead.

The last thing I wanted to see was a pair of headlights coming straight for us, but suddenly there they were. Not just headlights, but flashing ones at that.

The Parkman highway patrolman crested the rise directly in my path and I had to take my foot off the accelerator, brake once and turn slightly to miss him.

The car groaned as the wheels fought for purchase and we almost slid off the shoulder, but the big tires grabbed at last and we lunged forward again.

The HP turned behind us. I could see the glint from his headlights dance across the road. He drove an intercept cruiser but I doubted even he could come close to catching us.

The outskirts of Parkman looked deserted and I was so grateful

I nearly sobbed. To even out the corners and save time I drove straight down the middle of the road.

We blew by the Gas N Dash and the bright lights from the station were only a fuzzy flash.

In a matter of moments we screamed through the center of town. Parkman's Main Street had six lighted intersections and I blew through all of them in less than thirty seconds.

A flashing light to my left distracted me and I realized the Parkman HP cruiser was trailing us close.

Did he know I was not trying to evade him?

I'd figure that out if he started shooting.

The first hard right turn was just ahead and I braked so fast I was afraid Thomas would fall to the floor. The wheel shook as I spun us around and started up the hill toward the hospital.

The next hard right turn loomed ahead. I tapped the brake and eased in the clutch but the heavy front end refused to cooperate and the back tires skidded out of control. The Barracuda spun sideways and I sucked in air through my teeth.

My hands fought for control of the wheel. "No no no!"

The back end started to skid and I almost slammed on the brakes purely by reflex, but managed to stop myself.

I forced my foot to hit the gas and put the Barracuda into a controlled spin that whipped us around in a full circle. I managed to straighten the wheel and left half the tires on the asphalt behind us. Suddenly we were back in control and roaring up the hill.

We blasted up the street and I could see the bright lights of the emergency room ahead.

A series of painted arrows helpfully indicated the entrance and parking area and I drove right over the top of them. The main doors sat underneath a protective arch that kept the rain off of the ambulance crews, and instead of easing into the unloading area I jerked the wheel and drove straight up on the sidewalk.

The tires screamed and the car practically floated sideways as I slammed the brakes and threw open my door.

"Gunshot!" I yelled.

Two stunned nurses stood by the main door smoking.

They gaped at me.

I shouted at them. "Move!"

They threw their cigarette butts and ran towards the car frantically. I was so frazzled it wasn't even clear to me if they were men or women.

At that moment the Parkman HP rolled up behind my car and screeched to a halt.

I half expected him to pull out his pistol and start shooting. At that moment I didn't even care if he did.

When he came towards me his face was moist with a sheen of sweat. "Did we make it?"

I sank to my knees where I stood. "I don't know. I think so."

The nurses were frantically unloading Thomas onto a stretcher. He was limp, but still appeared to be breathing.

The HP crouched down and put a hand on my arm. "Do you have any idea how fast you were going?"

I grabbed his arm and looked directly into his eyes. "No. And don't you *ever* goddamned tell me either."

CHAPTER 25

Leif's son Scott and I stood on the tarmac at Killdeer airport, a faint breeze swirling bits of cottonwood fluff and fall grass in circles at our feet. The sun was rising, bathing everything with pale silver fingers of light in a cloudless sky.

"Are you sure about this?" I asked.

Scott smiled reassuringly. "It's what he would have wanted."

The kid was probably right. Leif had always been on the unconventional side. Still, it seemed a bit dramatic to me.

"Here you go," Scott said.

I took the steel urn holding Leif's ashes and wished I'd bothered to take some Dramamine.

My eyes fell on the old airplane that was fueled up and ready to go, and I swallowed. It was an old modified biplane that had been converted into a crop duster. It looked about twice as old as me.

The crop duster pilot, a wild-eyed former navy man with several dogfights under his belt, clapped a hand on my shoulder and grinned at me like a fool. "Ready?"

I felt my stomach clench. "Okay."

Since Killdeer wasn't known for its rolling wheat fields but was known for its sharp cliffs and high power lines, the only crop duster

267

crazy enough to service the area was Smokey Collins. Nobody knew his real first name. I imagined we'd all read about it in the paper someday after he killed himself crashing into power lines or nose-diving into a mountain.

I just hoped that today wasn't that day.

Mr. Toomey stood in the shade of the hangar, watching us with a solemn look. He had driven me here, and along the way he'd given me all the information his research had uncovered concerning Thomas Dunne.

As I'd suspected, Mr. Toomey had managed to find out a great many things about Thomas that were unnerving. I'd already assumed most of it, but hearing the words was still a shock.

Thomas Dunne had been in and out of prison several times over the course of his life. He had driven a getaway car twice for bank robbers, once for a duo who had robbed a payroll truck, and occasionally he helped move persons of interest in criminal investigations from one side of the country to the other, in a hurry.

His real name was Keith Granger. Thomas was one of his many aliases. The name Eugene Reisner was the alias he used for the registration on his car, but Granger was his family name. It just so happened that it was an old family name from Montana.

His life hadn't started out on the wrong side of the law. Thomas/Keith had graduated from high school in Billings and had gone on to engineering college, making high marks. His bright future had jackknifed in late July of 1985 when he had been a nineteen-year-old kid driving home to Billings, Montana, after a party at a friend's house in Parkman. He'd been drinking, was convinced of his ability to handle the drive home in spite of that fact, and had broadsided a little Toyota Corolla driven by a twenty-nine-year-old wife and mother, named Sarah.

Sarah Dearcorn.

My mother.

He'd killed her almost instantly.

The pilot was checking the fuel by shaking the plane wing with both hands and listening. "Sounds like we got plenty of gas."

"Ahh," I managed to say.

"Now remember, when we are at the top of the loop, that's when you let 'er go," Smokey said.

"Right," I said. "Top of the loop."

This was crazy.

I glanced over at Mr. Toomey and gave him a worried smile. He shook his head once with disapproval.

From his perspective my life was filled with unnecessary risks. He'd mentioned this fact to me again on the drive to the Killdeer airport, in between telling me the history of my gardener.

Thomas had spent eight years in prison for killing my mother. After he was released, he'd become a professional criminal and moved to the south. Ironically it had been my mother's death that prompted him to become such an accomplished driver. He had apparently made up his mind that he would never get into another wreck as long as he lived.

"You might feel like your stomach is going to fall out when we are up there," Smokey said. "Just hold yer breath and you'll be fine."

He ambled towards the biplane and waved me towards the seat. I had to force my feet to obey.

Thomas had married, become a father, and divorced over the course of a decade. Then he'd done what he could to live a normal life by working demolition at a coal mine in Kentucky. Mr. Toomey surmised that even after all these years he still kept up with the news from home, and that theory was supported by the fact that the Parkman newspaper had been delivered to his address in Kentucky for many years.

He'd seen the headlines in the Parkman paper with my photograph on the front page after Phoebe's death. He'd read the quote attributed to me that whoever had killed my friend would pay for it. Maybe he had returned to Killdeer out of some twisted sense of guilt, and a vague hope of making amends. But my guess was that he had come back because he believed he could find some kind of redemption by doing what he could to protect me from harm. Anyone stupid enough to threaten a heartless killer in the newspaper was someone who definitely needed looking after. Apparently Thomas had returned and appointed himself my personal watchdog for the duration of the investigation to make up for killing my mother. As if anything he ever did could make up for that.

Smokey motioned me forward again.

Scott rushed forward and gave me a fierce hug. "Thanks for doing this. You know how I feel about flying."

"The same way I will feel after this is over?" I asked.

He smiled. "Don't forget to buckle your belt."

"Not a chance."

I juggled Leif's urn while Smokey helped me get settled in. He would pilot the biplane from the backseat, and I would try not to throw up in the front.

My palms were already sweating.

Thomas was on his way back to Kentucky now with his ex-wife. He'd nearly died in the emergency room, but the doctor working the graveyard shift had pumped him full of donated blood and operated for four hours to mend the wound. He would never run a marathon again, but he was alive.

The doctor had told me after he was finished operating that if I hadn't gotten Thomas to them as fast as I did, he wouldn't have survived.

I'd saved the life of the man who had killed my mother. That knowledge was surreal to me. But even if I had known who Thomas really was at the time, I would have tried just as hard to get him to the hospital. He'd saved my life, after all. There was no question Harvey Wilson had been on an uncontrollable rampage that night, and if Thomas hadn't intervened I would have probably met the same fate as Phoebe Robinson.

The harness around my shoulders felt a little bit on the loose side, but the biplane's big engine was already coughing to life so it was too late now to complain about it.

Mr. Toomey had spoken to Thomas in the hospital before he'd been released. My attorney had delivered the message to him that it would be better for everyone concerned if he never came back to Killdeer again. Not because I wished him any harm, necessarily. I simply couldn't bear the reminder of what he had done in his youth.

I didn't know how I felt about Thomas. It was a mixture of gratitude that he had risked his life to save me, plus a horrible anger and sadness at what he had done when he was a teenager.

Something told me it would take years to sort out my emotions.

My stomach lurched as Smokey throttled down the runway. He paused long enough to radio any incoming air traffic, glanced a little too fleetingly at the wind sock, and rambled into position for takeoff.

Harvey Wilson had survived the rollover, but not Finn's bullets. Loy was irritated because his new deputy was now on mandatory administrative leave pending an investigation. But considering Harvey had almost killed someone, the investigation would be short. Harvey had shot Thomas in the chest from only a few yards away, and he'd still had several shells left in the pistol when Finn had opened fire. If Finn hadn't reacted as quickly as he did, there might have been more than one fatality that night.

Loy expected his deputy to be cleared for active duty again in a few weeks, at which time he would be attending the law enforcement academy. So, it appeared that Angus Finn would be hanging around Killdeer for a while.

My father and Irene were scheduled to land at the airport in Billings that afternoon. I planned to pick them up—if I survived this, that is.

We lifted off the ground and I felt the familiar momentary thrill of weightlessness as we swooped over the airport.

Scott waved at us and we banked hard and spiraled into a steep climb.

I gripped Leif's urn so tightly my fingers were white.

He'd loved flying more than anything. It was his one true passion, and the air seemed like the perfect resting place for my husband's ashes.

Leif had called it The High Lonely. He'd told me once that being in the air alone was his religion. When he was flying he knew his place in the world, and it made him feel at peace.

I'd taken the insurance money that I'd received from the policy on Leif's airplane, and with Mr. Toomey's help, had used it to establish the Phoebe Robinson Community College Scholarship Fund. Each year a young woman from the valley would be chosen to receive a full-ride scholarship to the community college in Parkman. There was no shortage of poor girls living around Killdeer who needed an opportunity. I couldn't save them all, but at least I could give a few of them a fighting chance.

Marianne Morgan was to be the first recipient of the scholarship. I'd mailed her a letter the day before, telling her of her award.

"Hold on, darlin'!" Smokey shouted. "Here we go!"

The biplane arched sideways and I gasped as we started our high loop.

As the blood rushed to my head I heard Smokey shout behind me and the plane seemed to slow to a crawl.

I pulled the top from the urn and held it high over my head, holding on to the lip with my fingers so it wouldn't plummet to the ground.

Leif's ashes cascaded from the urn into the morning sky like stardust, blowing through the air behind the biplane and sailing into the breeze, forming swirls from the wake of the propeller.

It took only a few seconds to completely empty the urn and Smokey whooped like a madman in his seat behind me as he forced the nose of the plane forward to regain airspeed and complete the loop. The G force grabbed hold once again and I felt smashed into the seat. The urn lay empty in my lap and I replaced the lid, worrying that my tears were splashing Smokey.

It was heartbreaking and exhilarating. Scott was right. Leif would have loved this.

Smokey banked and the biplane swooped over Killdeer Valley with the left wingtip drawing lines through the pale vapor. The air was icy cold but I didn't feel it. My whole soul was warm with knowing my husband was exactly where he always wanted to be.

Up in The High Lonely, with never a need to land again.

JESSICA McCLELLAND is a fourth generation Wyoming native raised on a cattle farm twenty-five miles from the Montana border. She is a librarian, avid archer and has explored the Australian outback around Brisbane, performed with the New York Philharmonic orchestra in a guest chorale production, and spent a decade hunting dinosaurs in the Jurassic formations of Johnson county, Wyoming. She is the author of the Marley Dearcorn novels, and a graduate of the University of Wyoming. She and her husband divide their time between Colorado and Wyoming.

.

CPSIA information can be obtained at www.ICGtesting.com
Printed in the USA
BVOW05s0733280415

397935BV00004B/282/P

9 780990 498636